STORY BY
BRIAN SMITH

ART BY
ALFA ROBBI

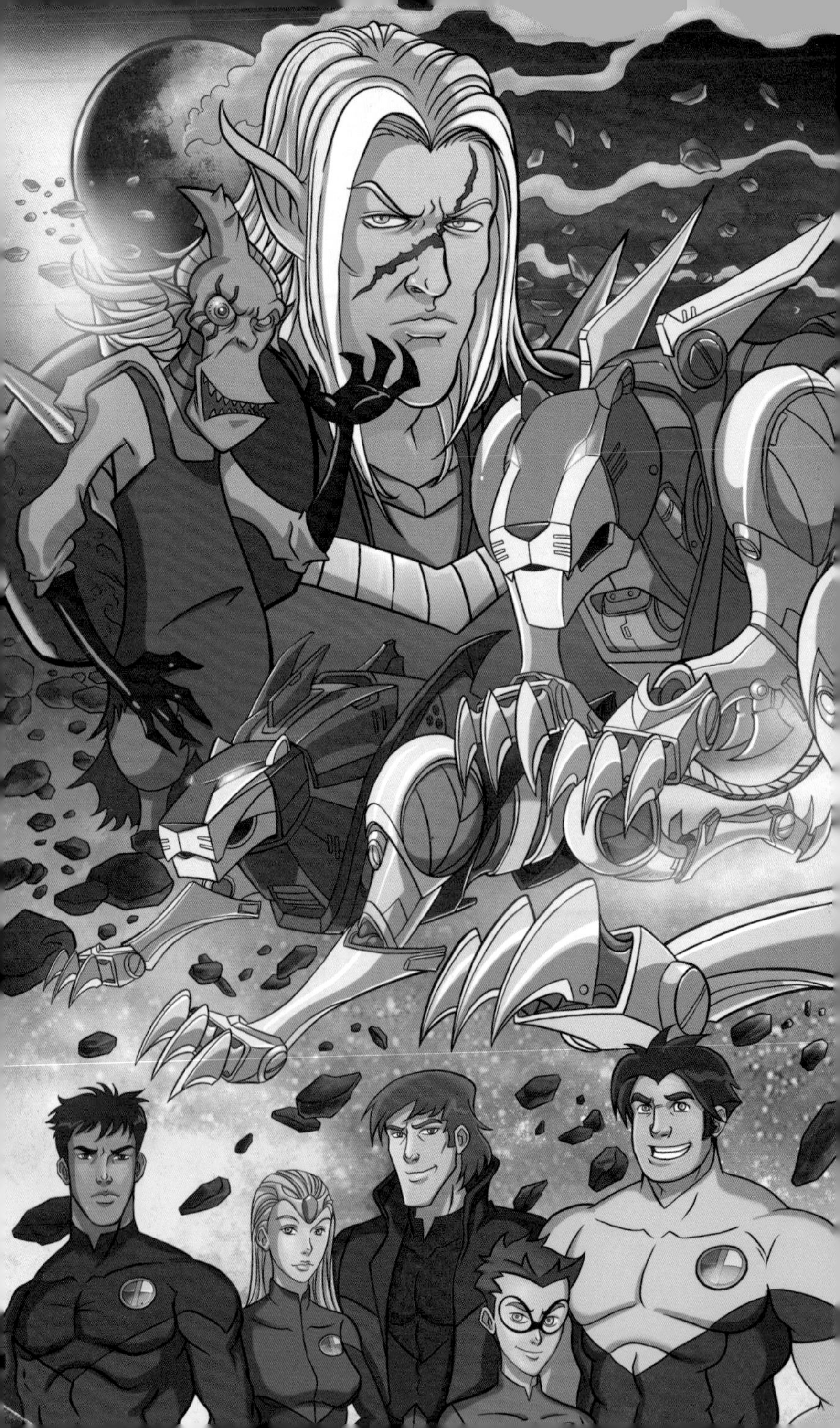

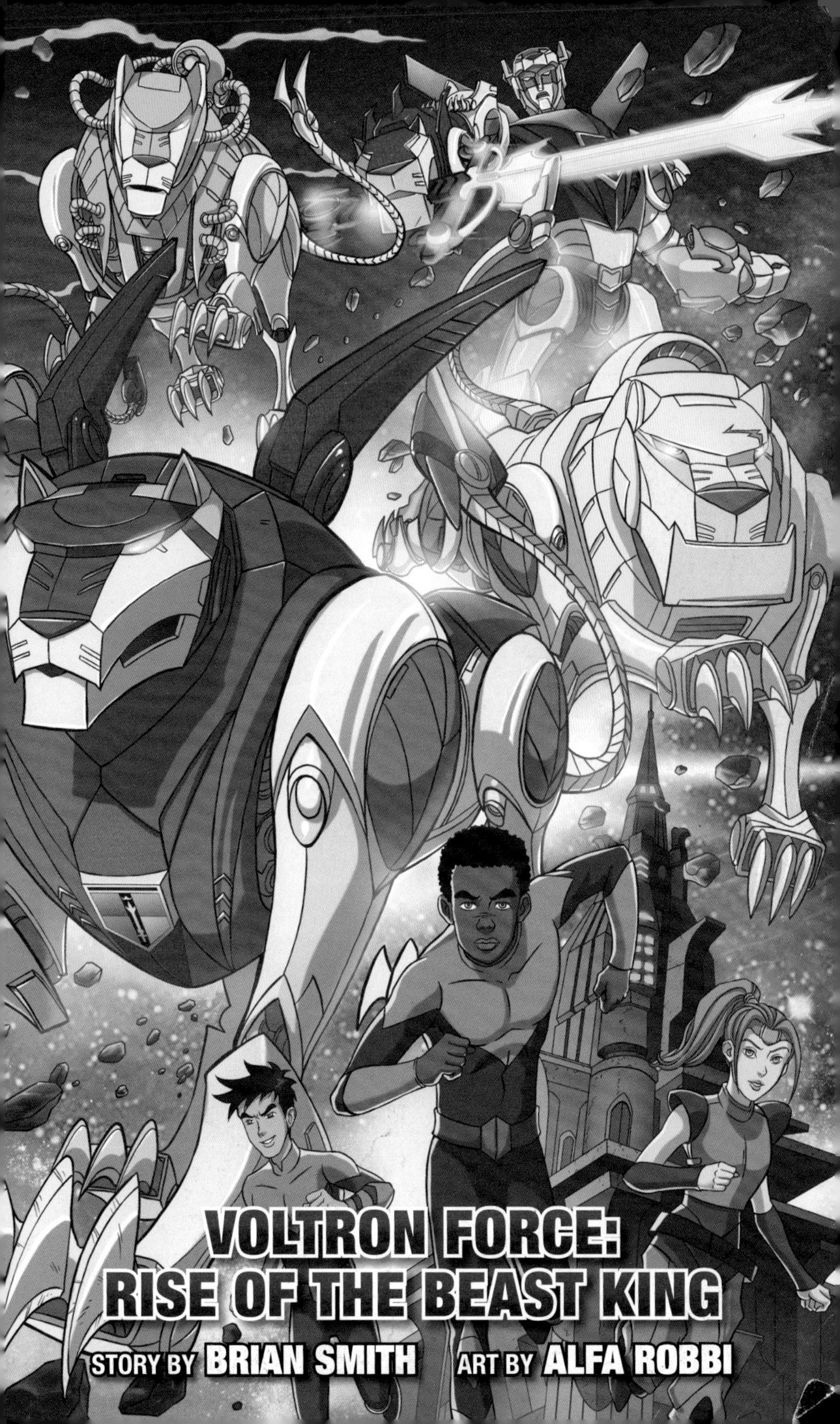

VOLTRON FORCE: RISE OF THE BEAST KING

STORY BY **BRIAN SMITH** ART BY **ALFA ROBBI**

VOLTRON FORCE
RISE OF THE BEAST KING

Voltron Force vol. 4: Rise of the Beast King
Story by Brian Smith
Art by Alfa Robbi
Colors by Burhan Arif
Letters by Deron Bennett

Cover Art/Alfa Robbi
Graphics and Cover Design/Sam Elzway
Editor/Traci N. Todd

Voltron Force ™ & © World Events Productions.
Under license to Classic Media.

Printed in China

Published by VIZ Media, LLC
P.O. Box 77010
San Francisco, CA 94107

10 9 8 7 6 5 4 3 2 1
First printing, October 2012

www.vizkids.com

www.viz.com

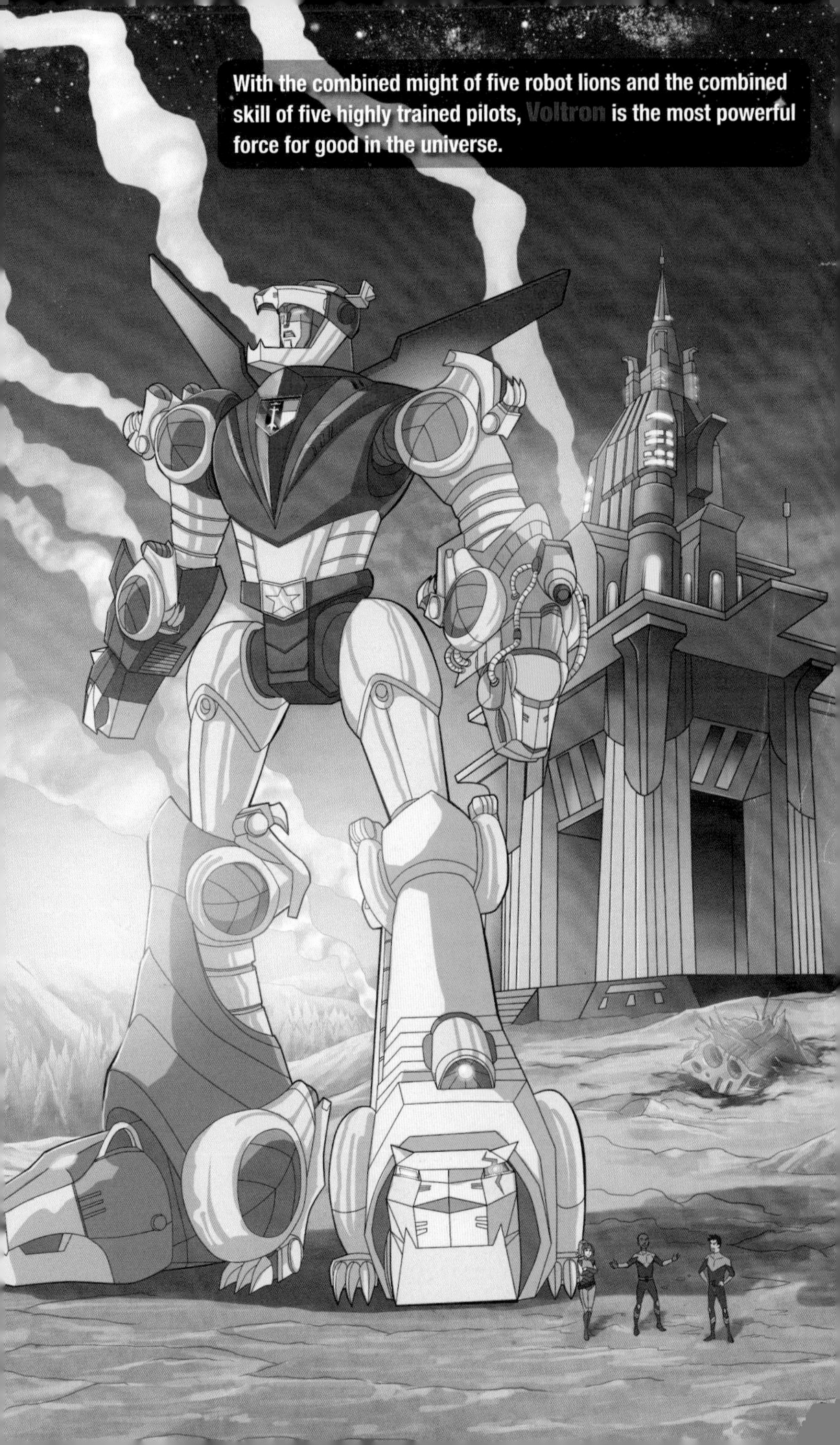
With the combined might of five robot lions and the combined skill of five highly trained pilots, Voltron is the most powerful force for good in the universe.

VOLTRON FORCE PILOTS AND CADETS

Keith is the Voltron Force commander. He pilots Black Lion.

Lance pilots Red Lion. He's quick with the one-liners and willing to bend the rules.

Hunk works with Pidge to update and repair the lions. Hunk is the Yellow Lion pilot.

Pidge is the resident tech genius. Pidge pilots Green Lion.

Allura is the princess of Arus, the planet that is home to the Voltron lions. Allura pilots Blue Lion.

Larmina is Allura's niece. She wants to be where the action is—and that's anywhere she can show off her martial arts training.

Daniel grew up dreaming of piloting Black Lion and is impulsive and fearless.

Vince possesses the same ancient, mysterious power locked inside Voltron.

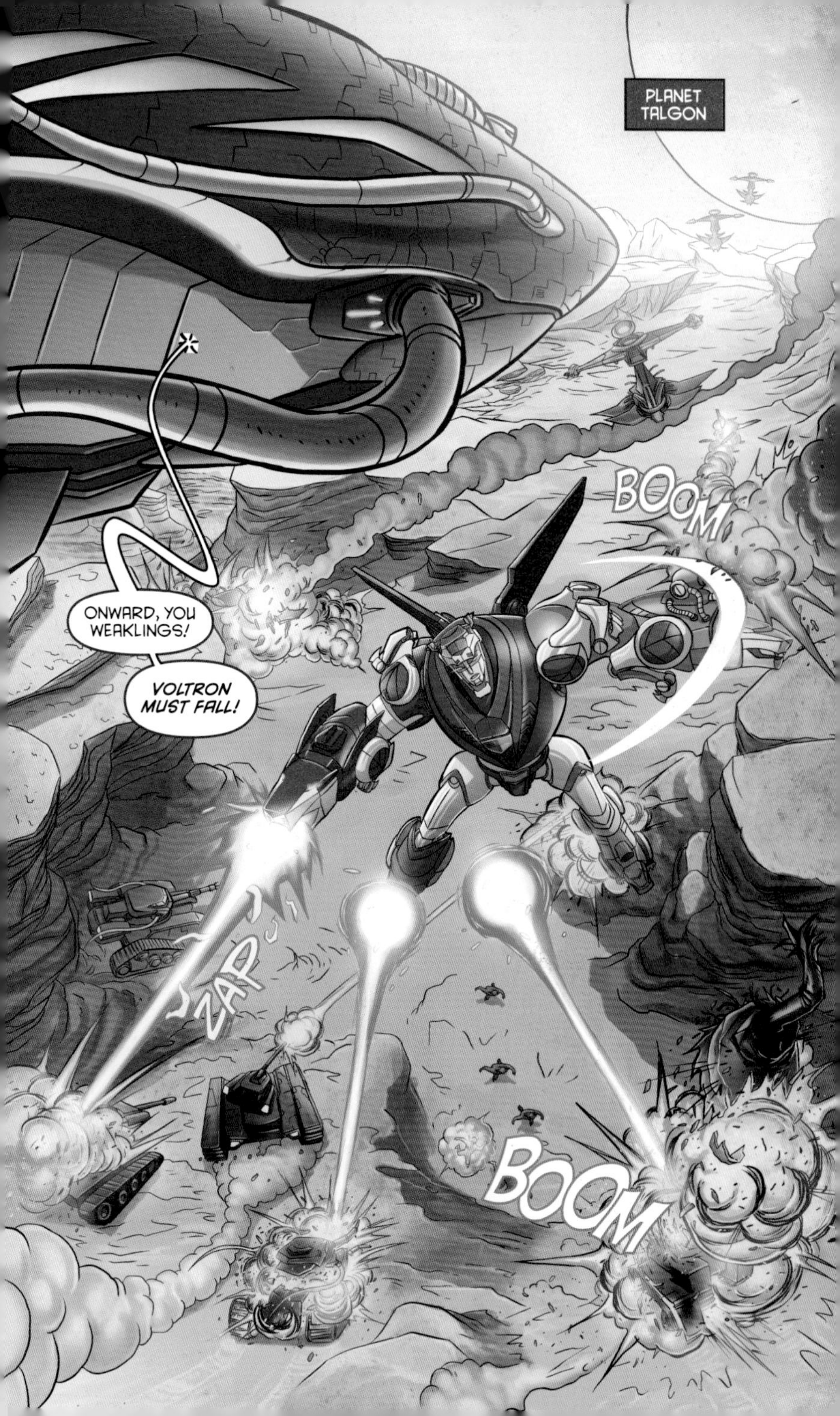
PLANET TALGON
ONWARD, YOU WEAKLINGS!
VOLTRON MUST FALL!
BOOM
ZAP
BOOM

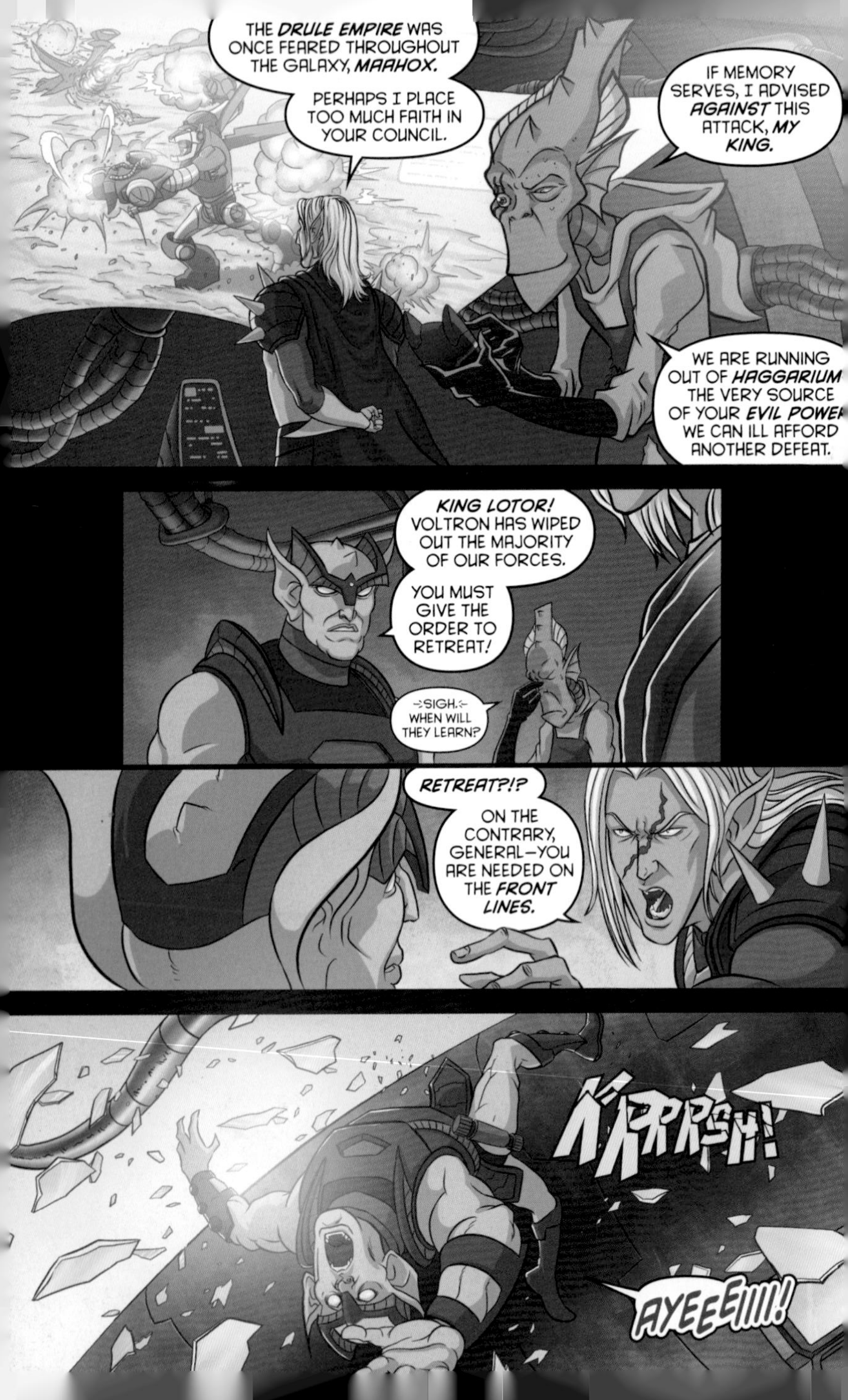
THE DRULE EMPIRE WAS ONCE FEARED THROUGHOUT THE GALAXY, MAAHOX.
PERHAPS I PLACE TOO MUCH FAITH IN YOUR COUNCIL.
IF MEMORY SERVES, I ADVISED AGAINST THIS ATTACK, MY KING.
WE ARE RUNNING OUT OF HAGGARIUM THE VERY SOURCE OF YOUR EVIL POWE WE CAN ILL AFFORD ANOTHER DEFEAT.
KING LOTOR! VOLTRON HAS WIPED OUT THE MAJORITY OF OUR FORCES.
YOU MUST GIVE THE ORDER TO RETREAT!
SIGH. WHEN WILL THEY LEARN?
RETREAT?!?
ON THE CONTRARY, GENERAL—YOU ARE NEEDED ON THE FRONT LINES.
KRRRSH!
AYEEEIIIII!

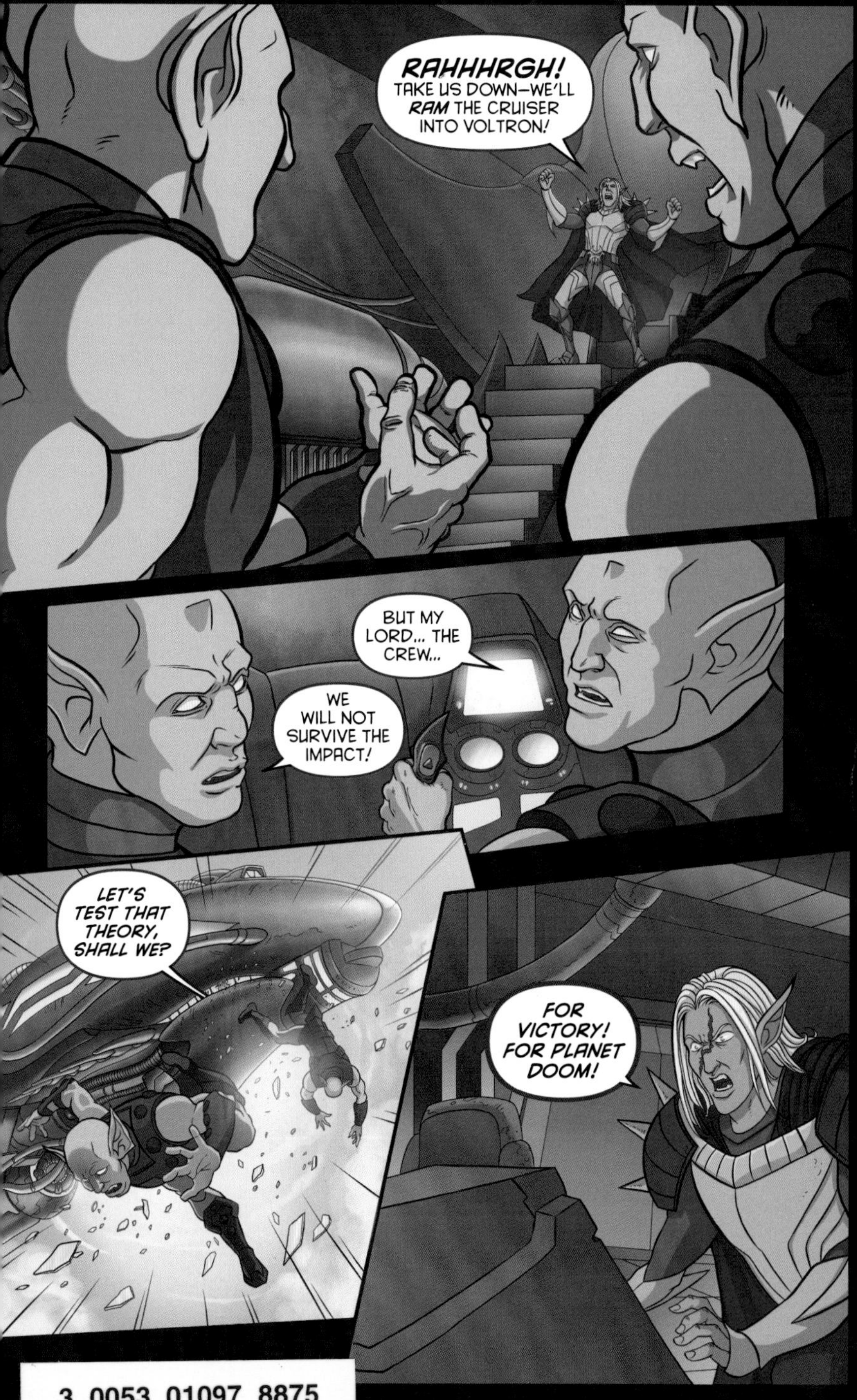
RAHHHRGH! TAKE US DOWN—WE'LL RAM THE CRUISER INTO VOLTRON!
BUT MY LORD... THE CREW...
WE WILL NOT SURVIVE THE IMPACT!
LET'S TEST THAT THEORY, SHALL WE?
FOR VICTORY! FOR PLANET DOOM!

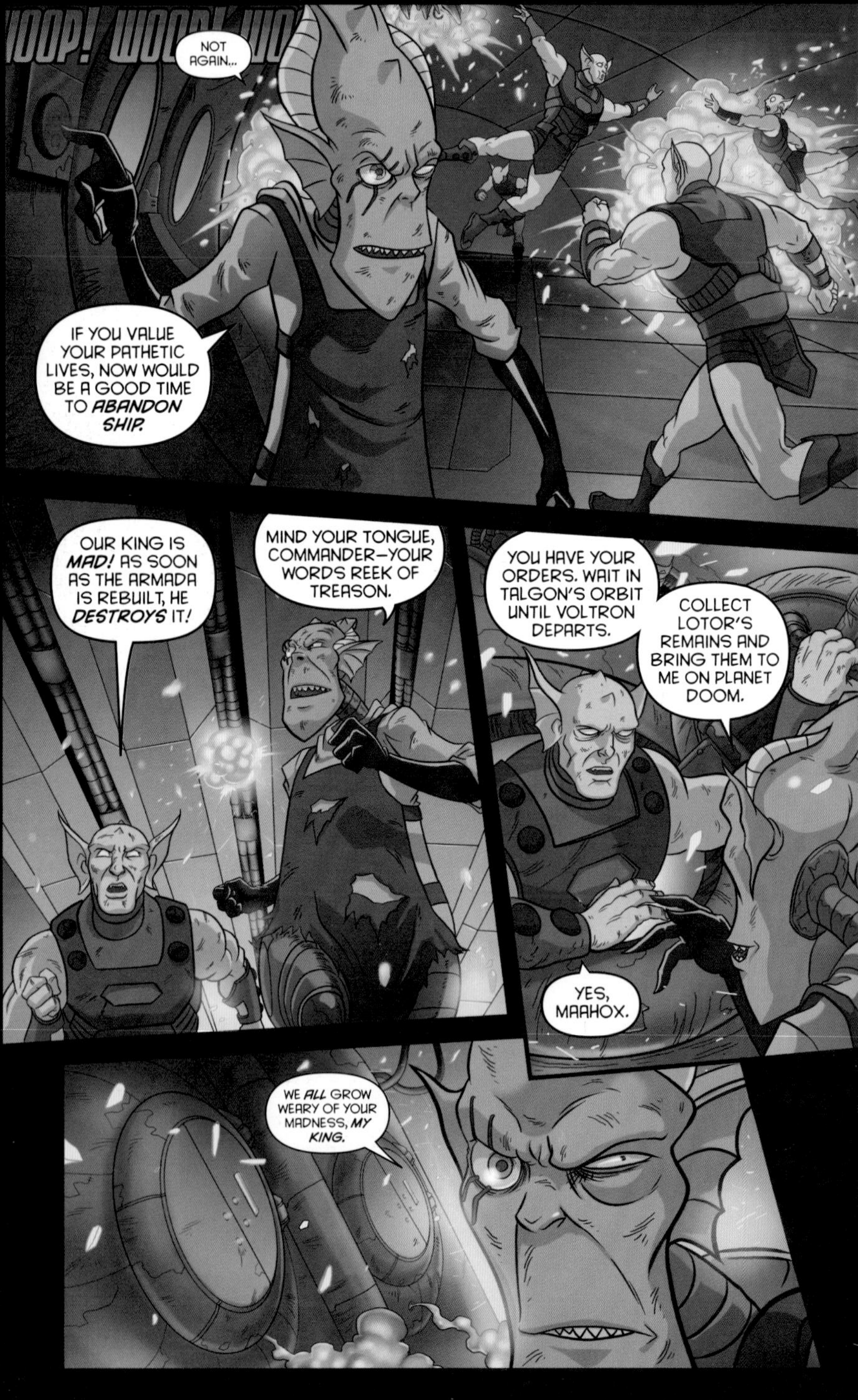
WOOP! WOOP! WO
NOT AGAIN...
IF YOU VALUE YOUR PATHETIC LIVES, NOW WOULD BE A GOOD TIME TO ABANDON SHIP.
OUR KING IS MAD! AS SOON AS THE ARMADA IS REBUILT, HE DESTROYS IT!
MIND YOUR TONGUE, COMMANDER—YOUR WORDS REEK OF TREASON.
YOU HAVE YOUR ORDERS. WAIT IN TALGON'S ORBIT UNTIL VOLTRON DEPARTS.
COLLECT LOTOR'S REMAINS AND BRING THEM TO ME ON PLANET DOOM.
YES, MAAHOX.
WE ALL GROW WEARY OF YOUR MADNESS, MY KING.

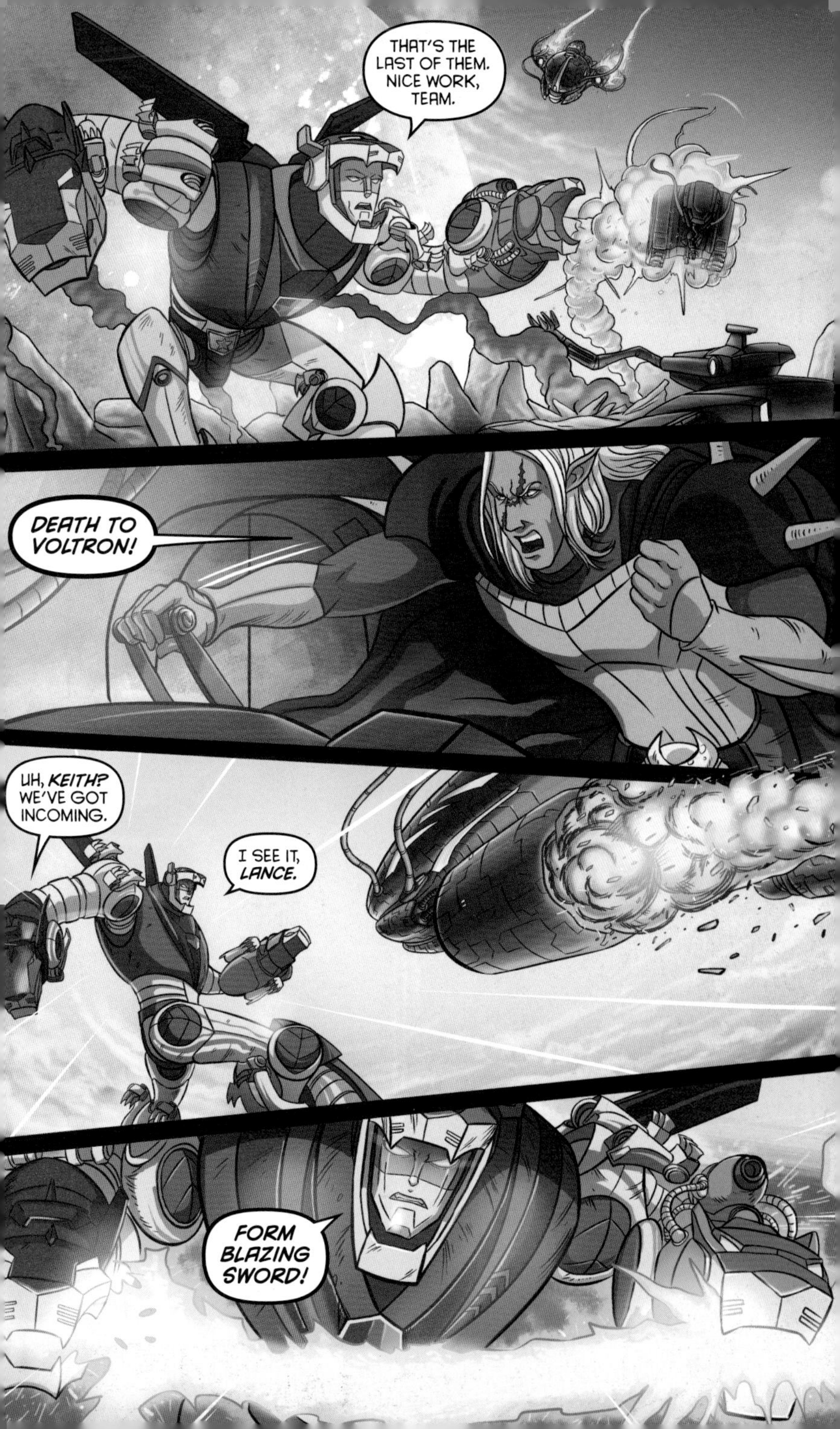
THAT'S THE LAST OF THEM. NICE WORK, TEAM.
DEATH TO VOLTRON!
UH, KEITH? WE'VE GOT INCOMING.
I SEE IT, LANCE.
FORM BLAZING SWORD!

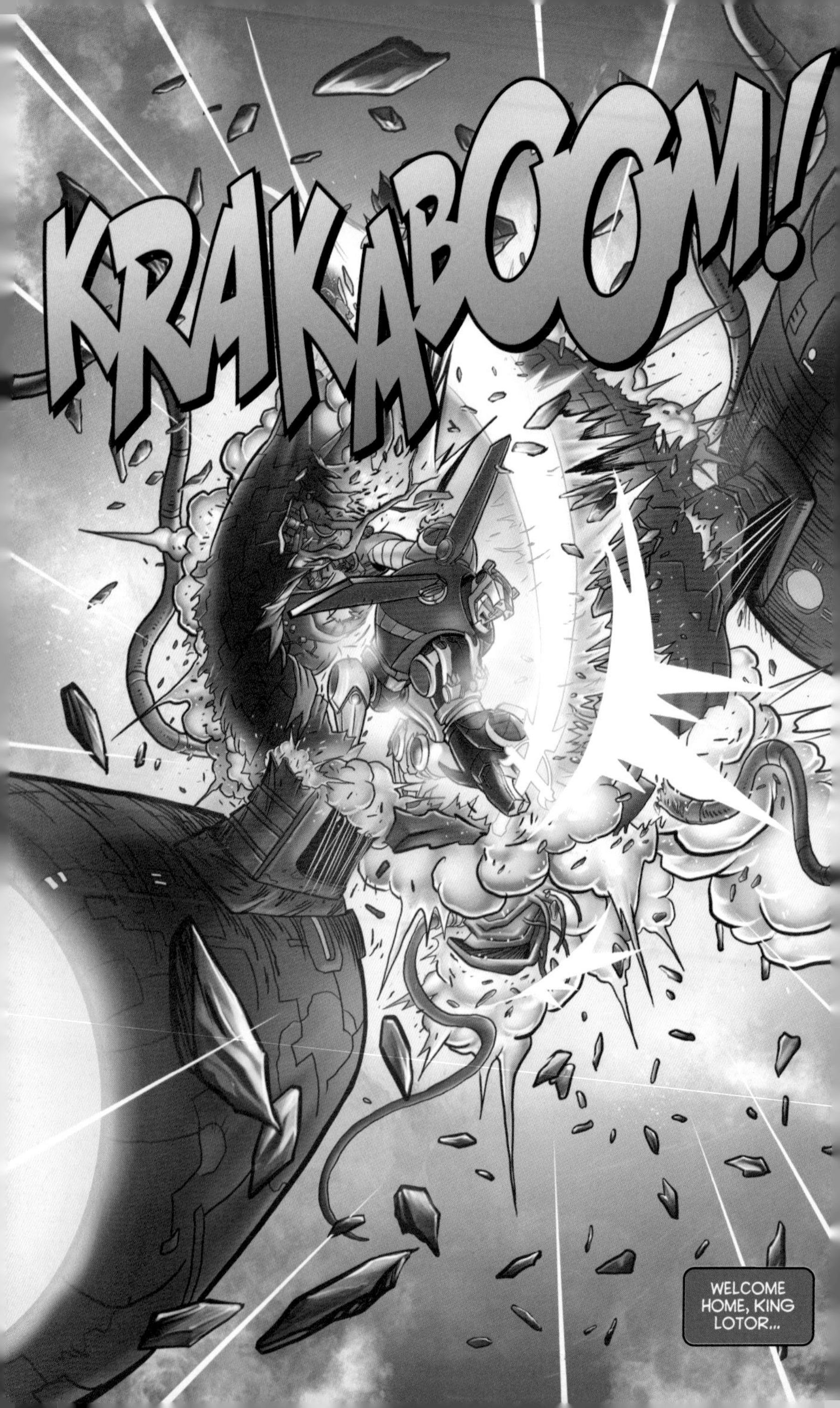
KRAKABOOM!
WELCOME HOME, KING LOTOR...

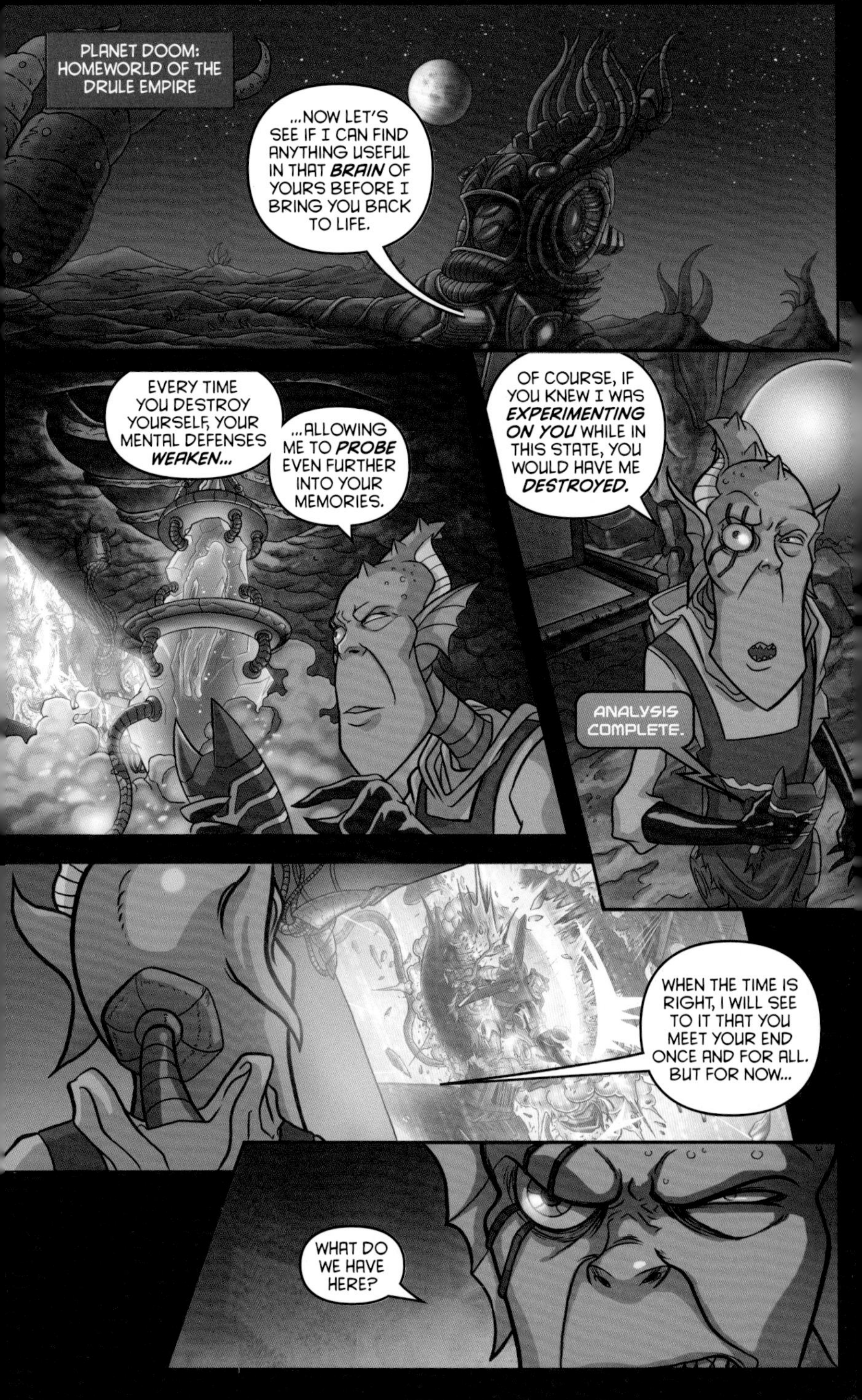
PLANET DOOM: HOMEWORLD OF THE DRULE EMPIRE
...NOW LET'S SEE IF I CAN FIND ANYTHING USEFUL IN THAT *BRAIN* OF YOURS BEFORE I BRING YOU BACK TO LIFE.
EVERY TIME YOU DESTROY YOURSELF, YOUR MENTAL DEFENSES *WEAKEN...*
...ALLOWING ME TO *PROBE* EVEN FURTHER INTO YOUR MEMORIES.
OF COURSE, IF YOU KNEW I WAS *EXPERIMENTING ON YOU* WHILE IN THIS STATE, YOU WOULD HAVE ME *DESTROYED.*
ANALYSIS COMPLETE.
WHEN THE TIME IS RIGHT, I WILL SEE TO IT THAT YOU MEET YOUR END ONCE AND FOR ALL. BUT FOR NOW...
WHAT DO WE HAVE HERE?

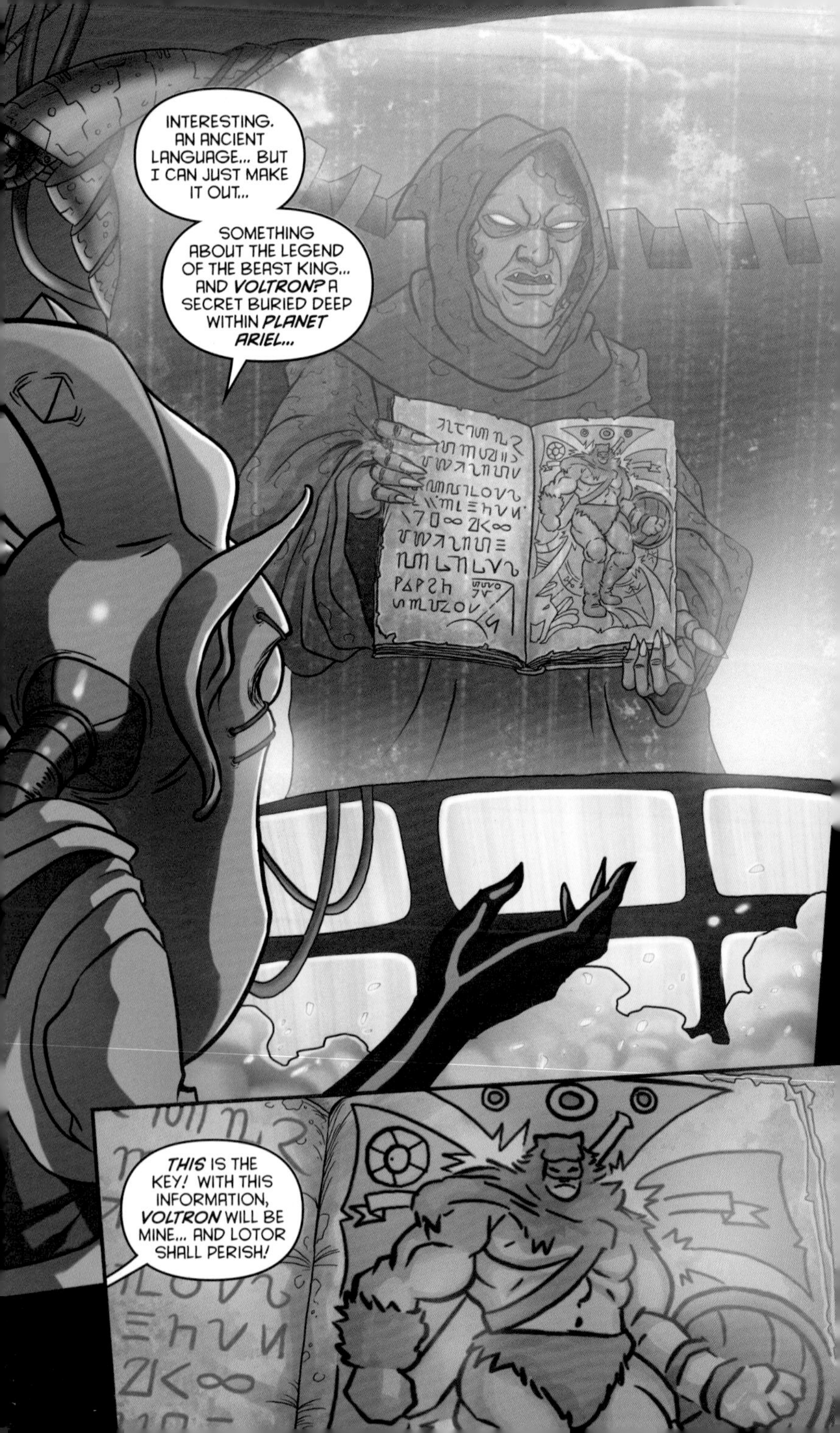
INTERESTING. AN ANCIENT LANGUAGE... BUT I CAN JUST MAKE IT OUT...
SOMETHING ABOUT THE LEGEND OF THE BEAST KING... AND *VOLTRON?* A SECRET BURIED DEEP WITHIN *PLANET ARIEL...*
THIS IS THE KEY! WITH THIS INFORMATION, *VOLTRON* WILL BE MINE... AND LOTOR SHALL PERISH!

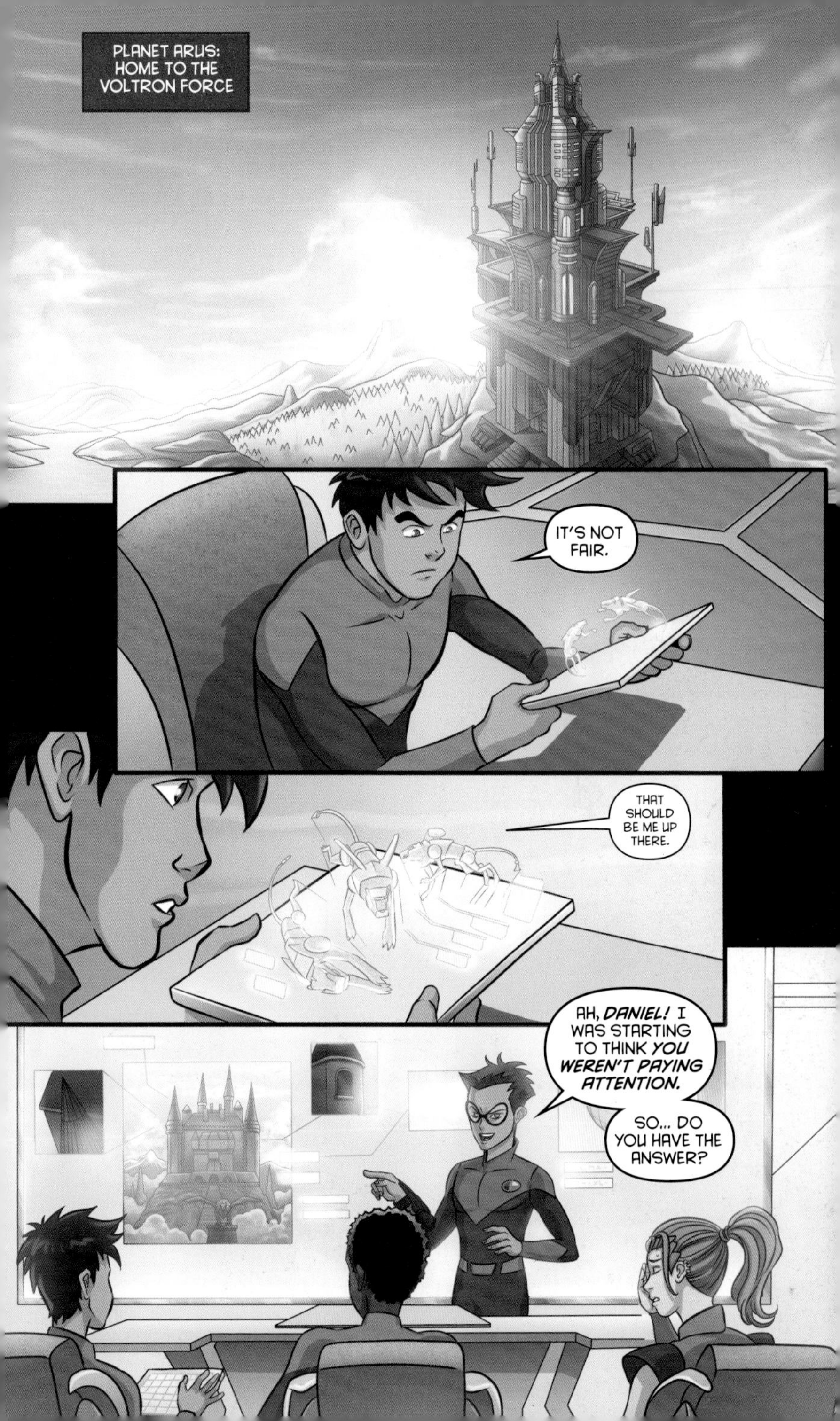
PLANET ARUS:
HOME TO THE
VOLTRON FORCE
IT'S NOT FAIR.
THAT SHOULD BE ME UP THERE.
AH, *DANIEL!* I WAS STARTING TO THINK *YOU WEREN'T PAYING ATTENTION.*
SO... DO YOU HAVE THE ANSWER?

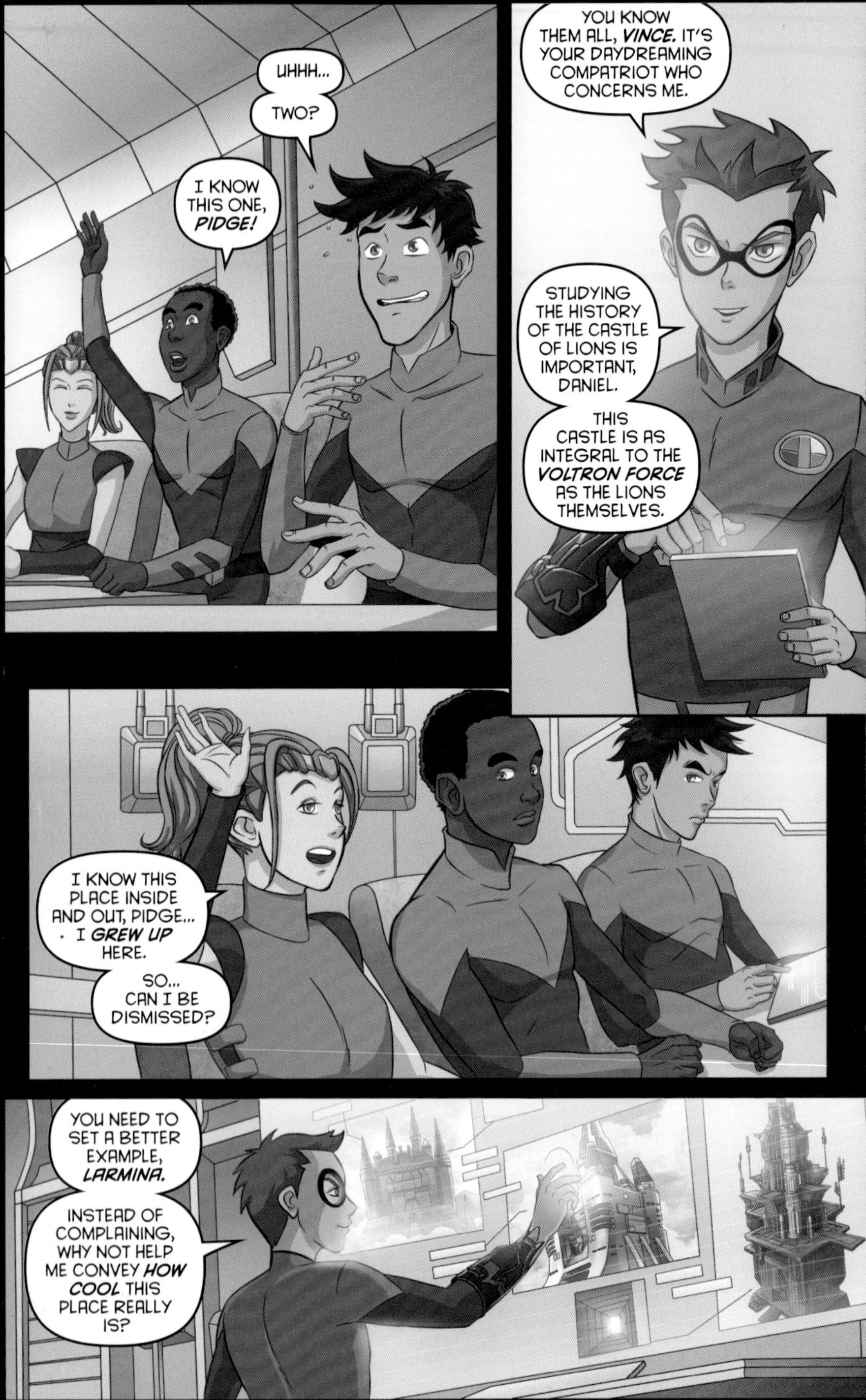
UHHH...
TWO?
I KNOW THIS ONE, PIDGE!
YOU KNOW THEM ALL, VINCE. IT'S YOUR DAYDREAMING COMPATRIOT WHO CONCERNS ME.
STUDYING THE HISTORY OF THE CASTLE OF LIONS IS IMPORTANT, DANIEL.
THIS CASTLE IS AS INTEGRAL TO THE VOLTRON FORCE AS THE LIONS THEMSELVES.
I KNOW THIS PLACE INSIDE AND OUT, PIDGE... I GREW UP HERE.
SO... CAN I BE DISMISSED?
YOU NEED TO SET A BETTER EXAMPLE, LARMINA.
INSTEAD OF COMPLAINING, WHY NOT HELP ME CONVEY HOW COOL THIS PLACE REALLY IS?

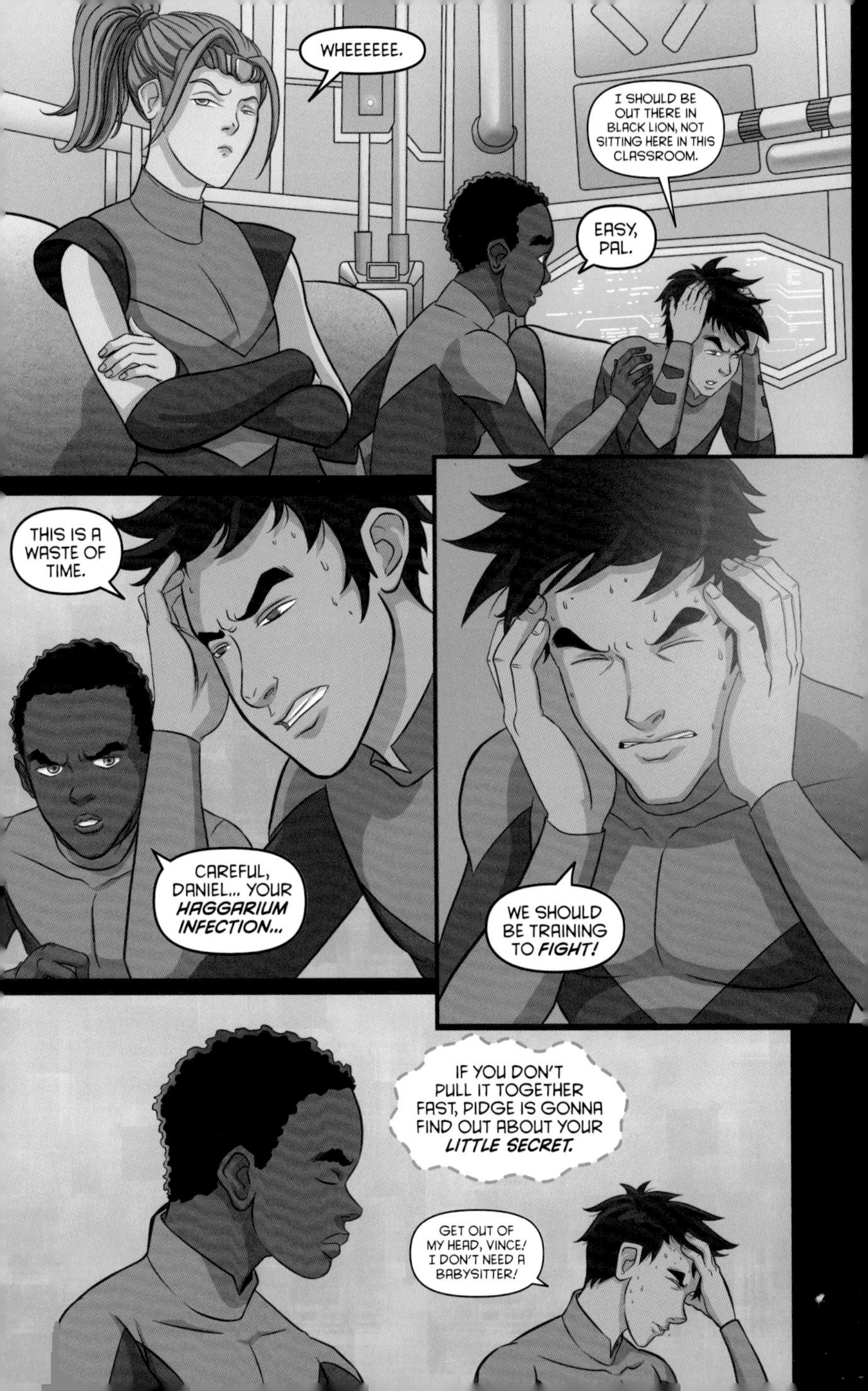
WHEEEEEE.
I SHOULD BE OUT THERE IN BLACK LION, NOT SITTING HERE IN THIS CLASSROOM.
EASY, PAL.
THIS IS A WASTE OF TIME.
CAREFUL, DANIEL... YOUR *HAGGARIUM INFECTION...*
WE SHOULD BE TRAINING TO *FIGHT!*
IF YOU DON'T PULL IT TOGETHER FAST, PIDGE IS GONNA FIND OUT ABOUT YOUR *LITTLE SECRET.*
GET OUT OF MY HEAD, VINCE! I DON'T NEED A BABYSITTER!

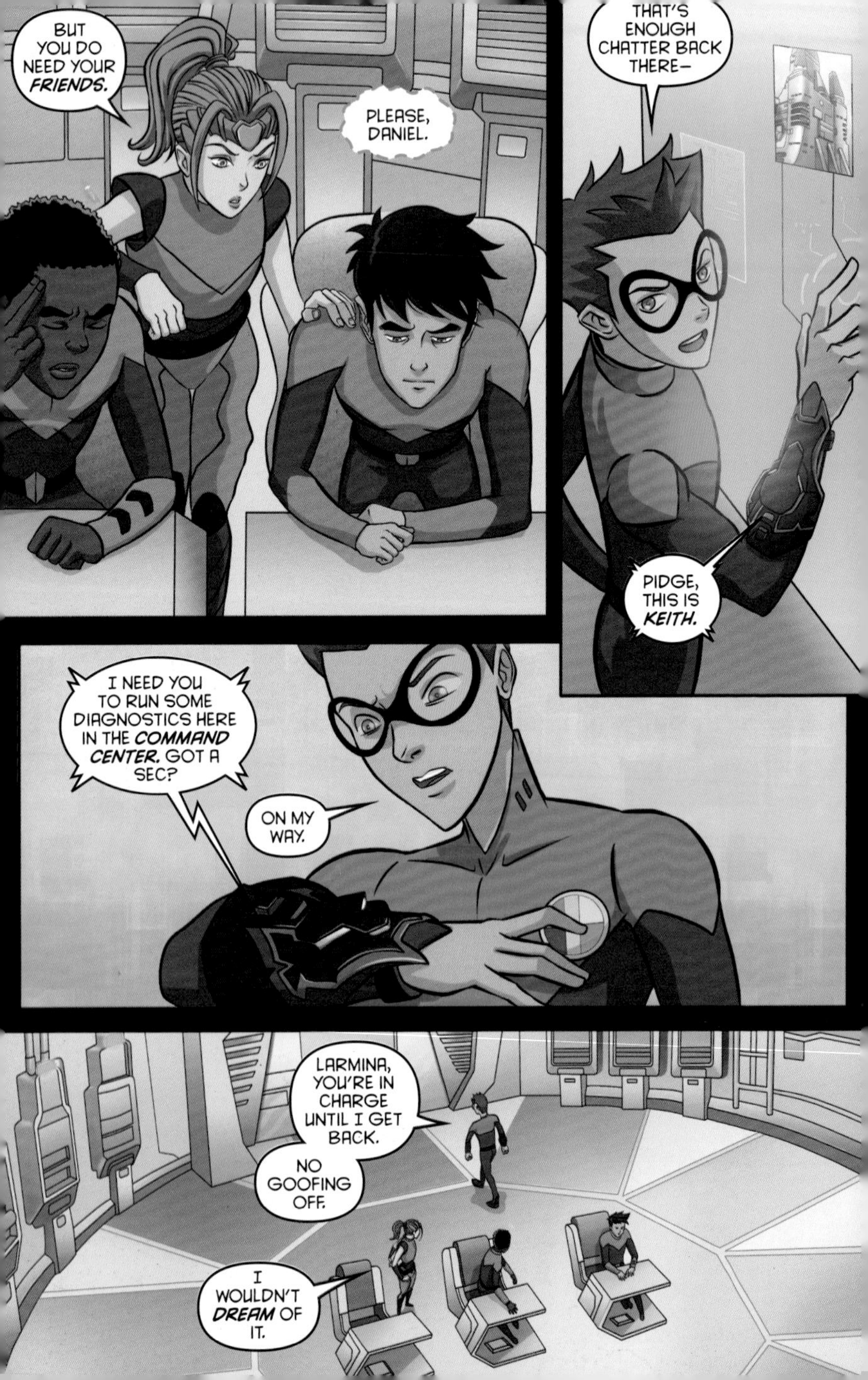
BUT YOU DO NEED YOUR FRIENDS.
PLEASE, DANIEL.
THAT'S ENOUGH CHATTER BACK THERE—
PIDGE, THIS IS KEITH.
I NEED YOU TO RUN SOME DIAGNOSTICS HERE IN THE COMMAND CENTER. GOT A SEC?
ON MY WAY.
LARMINA, YOU'RE IN CHARGE UNTIL I GET BACK.
NO GOOFING OFF.
I WOULDN'T DREAM OF IT.

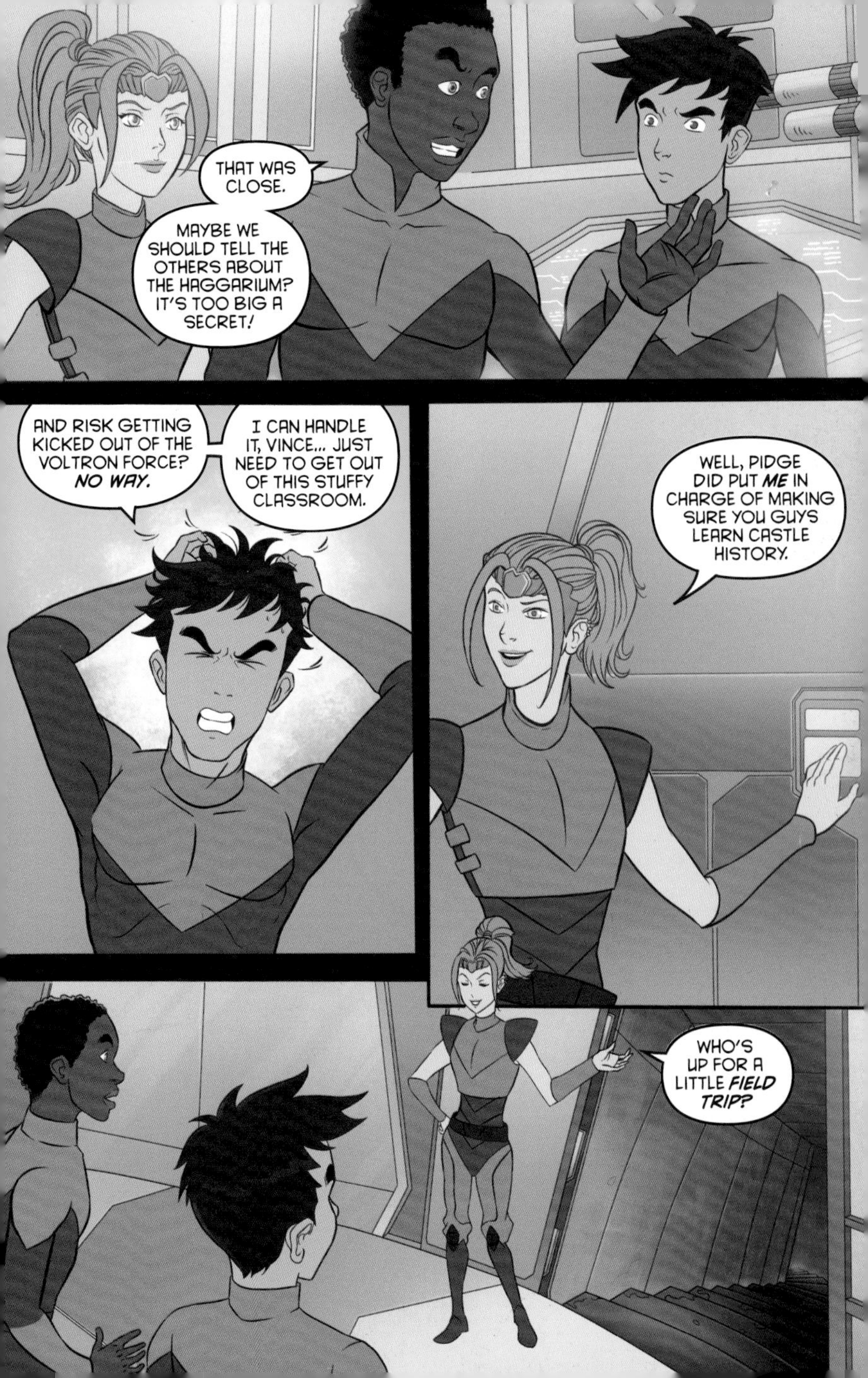
THAT WAS CLOSE.
MAYBE WE SHOULD TELL THE OTHERS ABOUT THE HAGGARIUM? IT'S TOO BIG A SECRET!
AND RISK GETTING KICKED OUT OF THE VOLTRON FORCE? NO WAY.
I CAN HANDLE IT, VINCE... JUST NEED TO GET OUT OF THIS STUFFY CLASSROOM.
WELL, PIDGE DID PUT ME IN CHARGE OF MAKING SURE YOU GUYS LEARN CASTLE HISTORY.
WHO'S UP FOR A LITTLE FIELD TRIP?

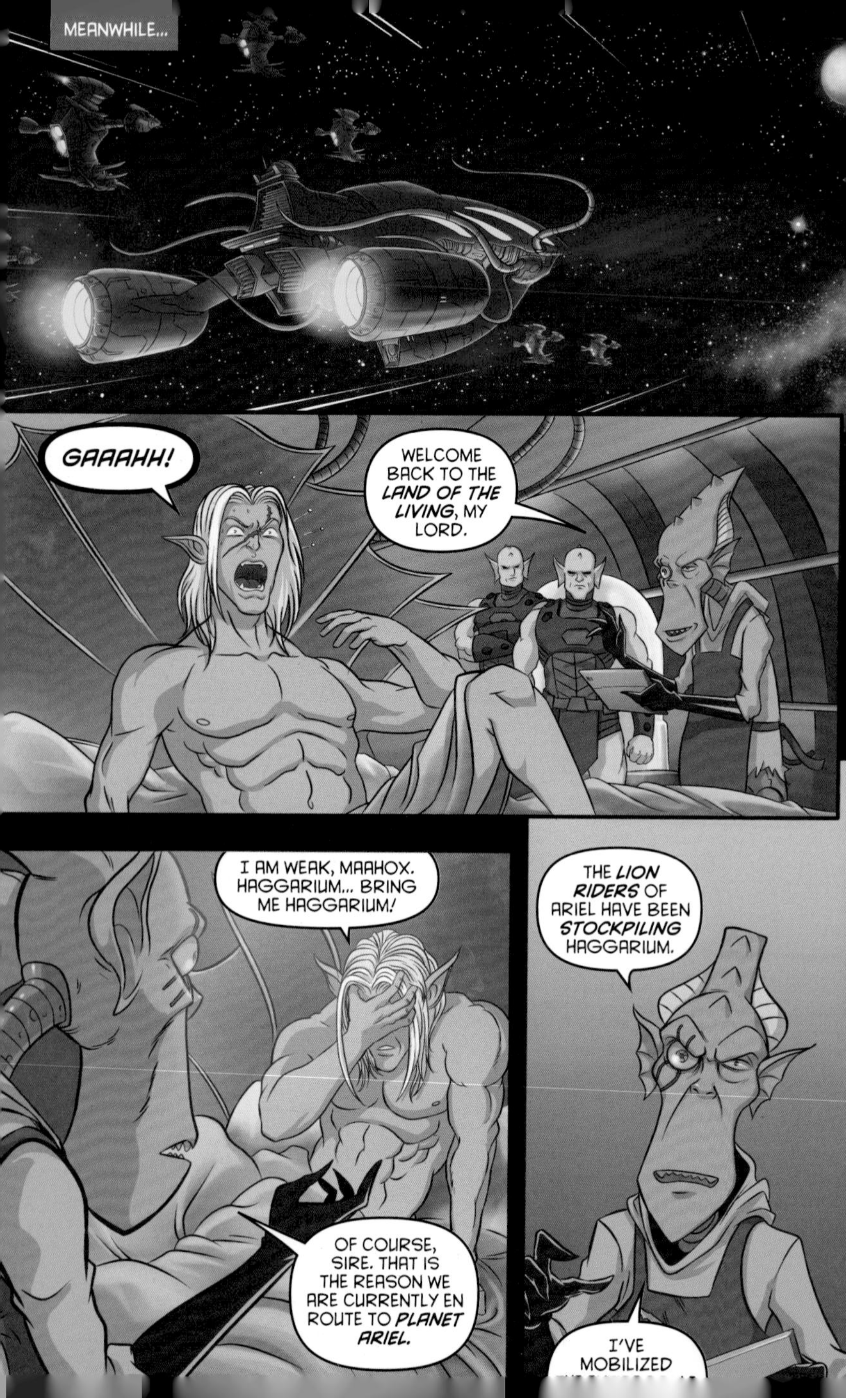
MEANWHILE...
GAAAHH!
WELCOME BACK TO THE LAND OF THE LIVING, MY LORD.
I AM WEAK, MAAHOX. HAGGARIUM... BRING ME HAGGARIUM!
OF COURSE, SIRE. THAT IS THE REASON WE ARE CURRENTLY EN ROUTE TO PLANET ARIEL.
THE LION RIDERS OF ARIEL HAVE BEEN STOCKPILING HAGGARIUM.
I'VE MOBILIZED

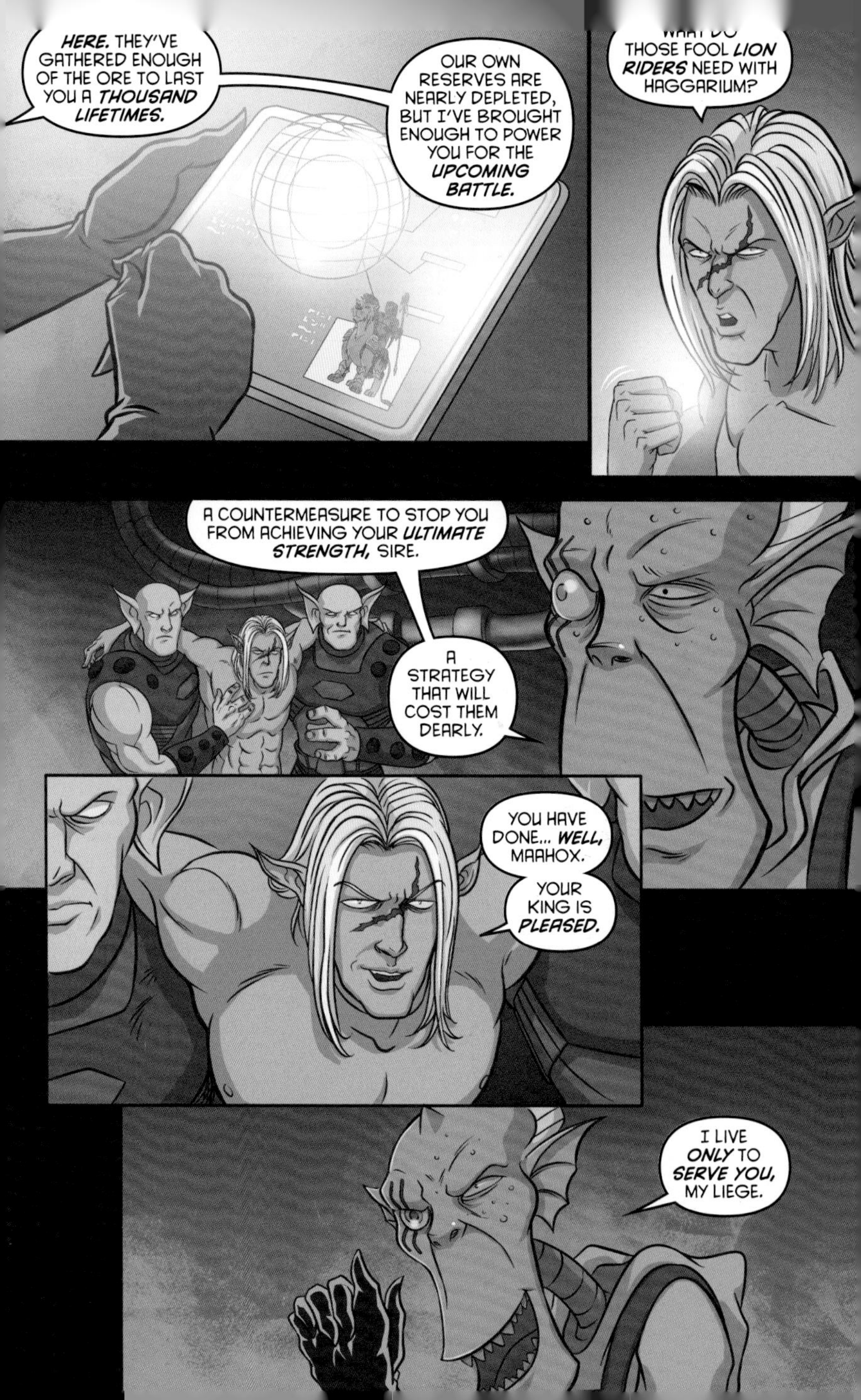
HERE. THEY'VE GATHERED ENOUGH OF THE ORE TO LAST YOU A THOUSAND LIFETIMES.
OUR OWN RESERVES ARE NEARLY DEPLETED, BUT I'VE BROUGHT ENOUGH TO POWER YOU FOR THE UPCOMING BATTLE.
THOSE FOOL LION RIDERS NEED WITH HAGGARIUM?
A COUNTERMEASURE TO STOP YOU FROM ACHIEVING YOUR ULTIMATE STRENGTH, SIRE.
A STRATEGY THAT WILL COST THEM DEARLY.
YOU HAVE DONE... WELL, MAAHOX.
YOUR KING IS PLEASED.
I LIVE ONLY TO SERVE YOU, MY LIEGE.

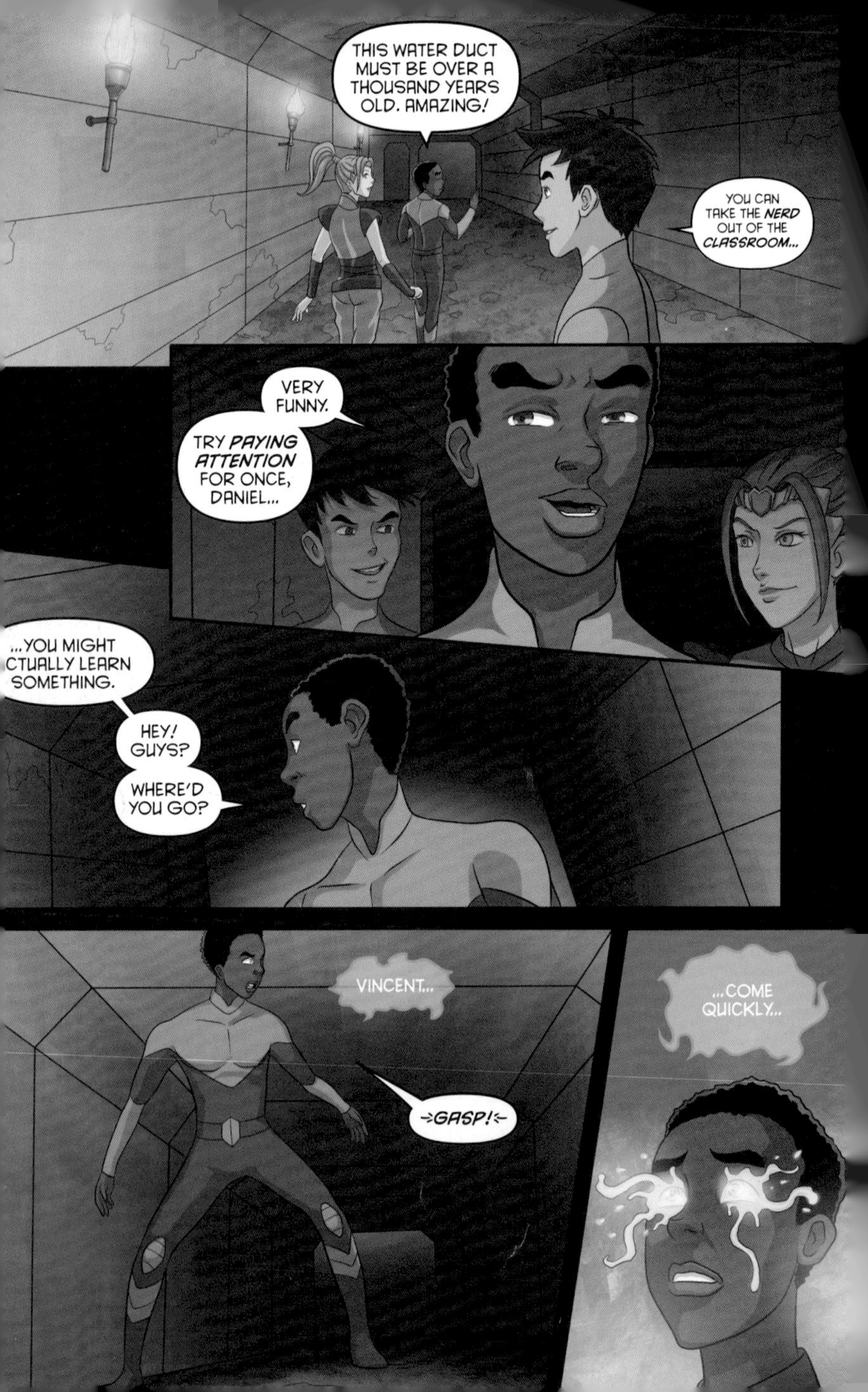
THIS WATER DUCT MUST BE OVER A THOUSAND YEARS OLD. AMAZING!
YOU CAN TAKE THE NERD OUT OF THE CLASSROOM...
VERY FUNNY.
TRY PAYING ATTENTION FOR ONCE, DANIEL...
...YOU MIGHT CTUALLY LEARN SOMETHING.
HEY! GUYS?
WHERE'D YOU GO?
VINCENT...
...COME QUICKLY...
GASP!

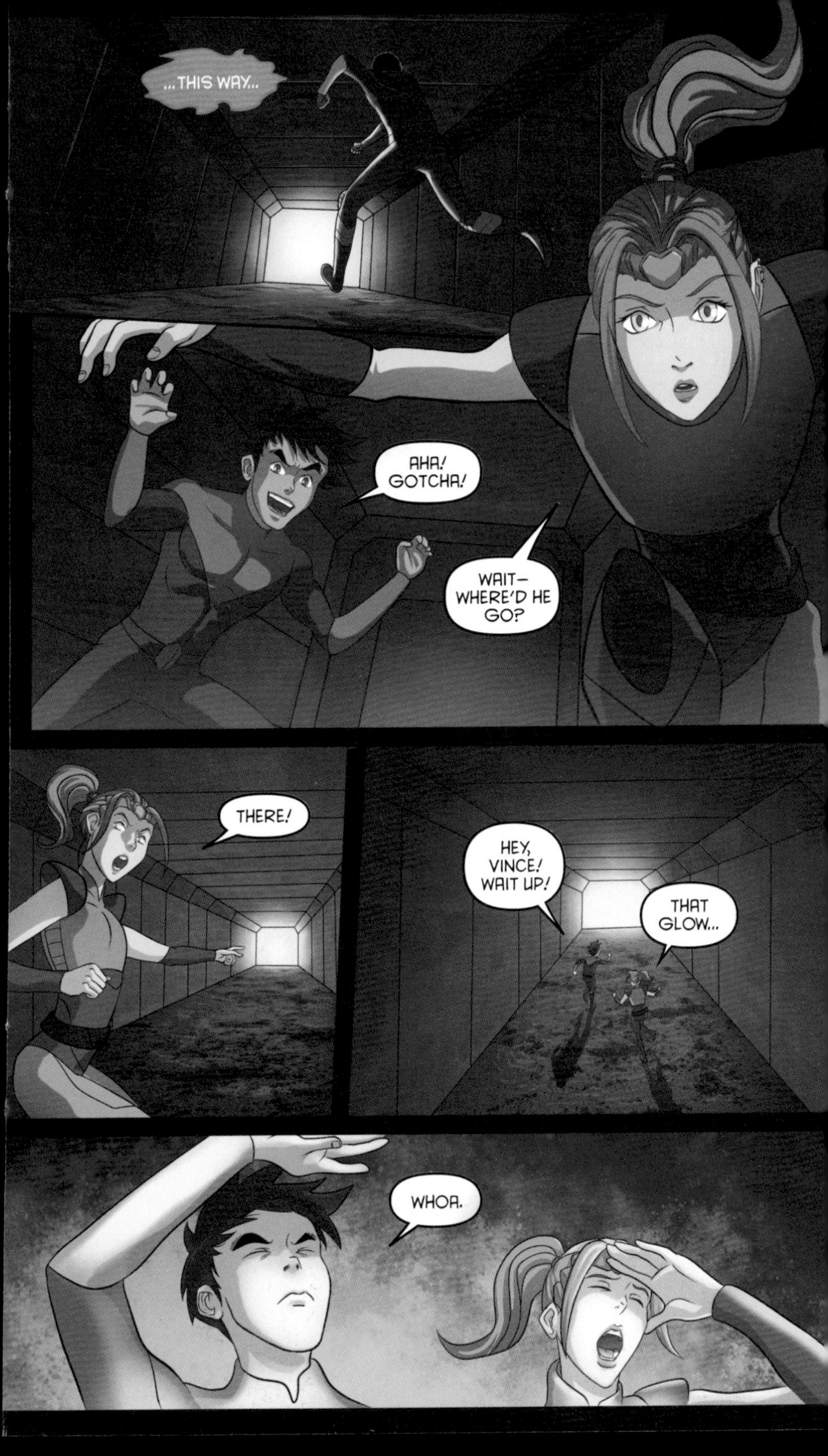
...THIS WAY...
AHA! GOTCHA!
WAIT— WHERE'D HE GO?
THERE!
HEY, VINCE! WAIT UP!
THAT GLOW...
WHOA.

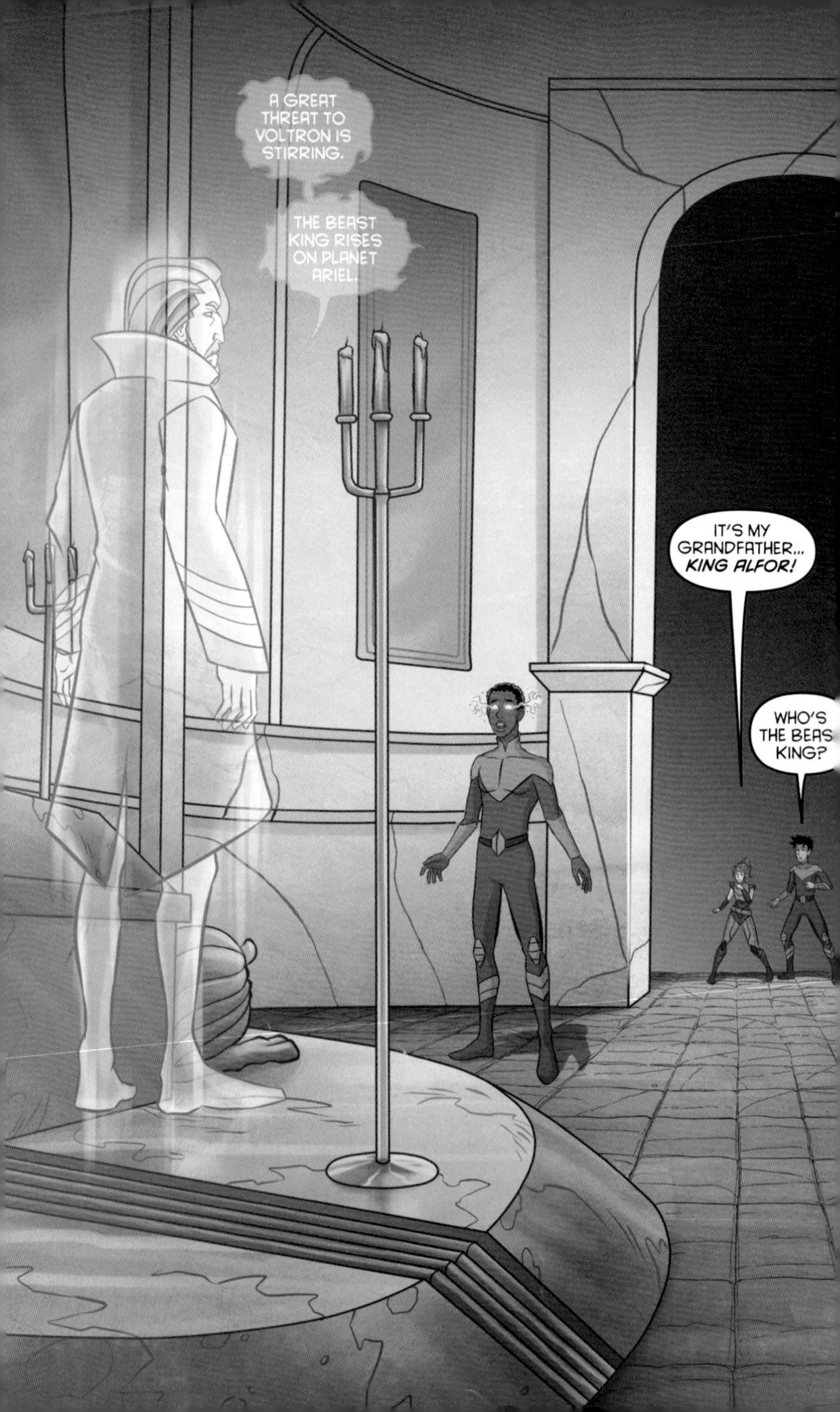
A GREAT THREAT TO VOLTRON IS STIRRING.
THE BEAST KING RISES ON PLANET ARIEL.
IT'S MY GRANDFATHER... *KING ALFOR!*
WHO'S THE BEAS KING?

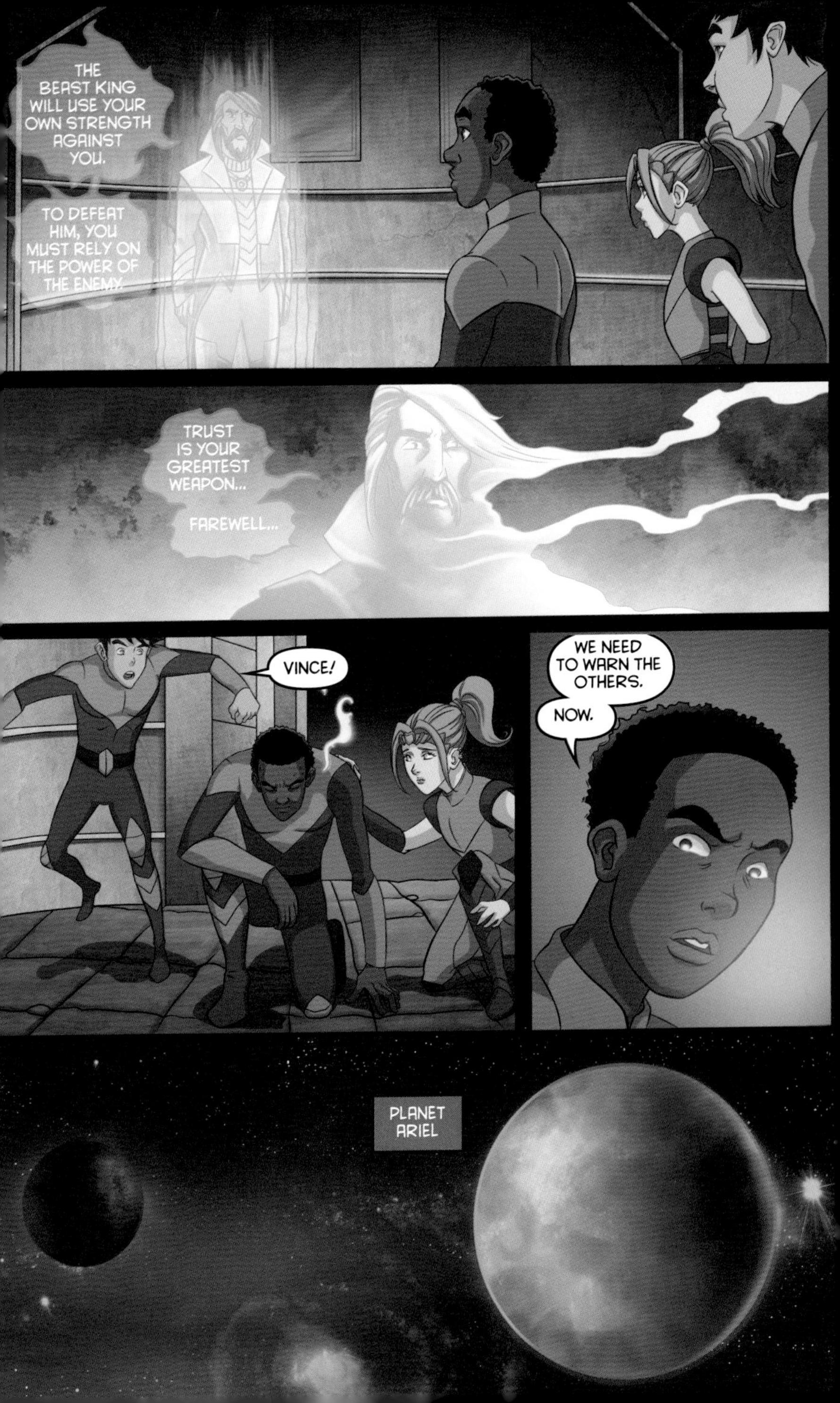
THE BEAST KING WILL USE YOUR OWN STRENGTH AGAINST YOU.
TO DEFEAT HIM, YOU MUST RELY ON THE POWER OF THE ENEMY.
TRUST IS YOUR GREATEST WEAPON...
FAREWELL...
VINCE!
WE NEED TO WARN THE OTHERS.
NOW.
PLANET ARIEL

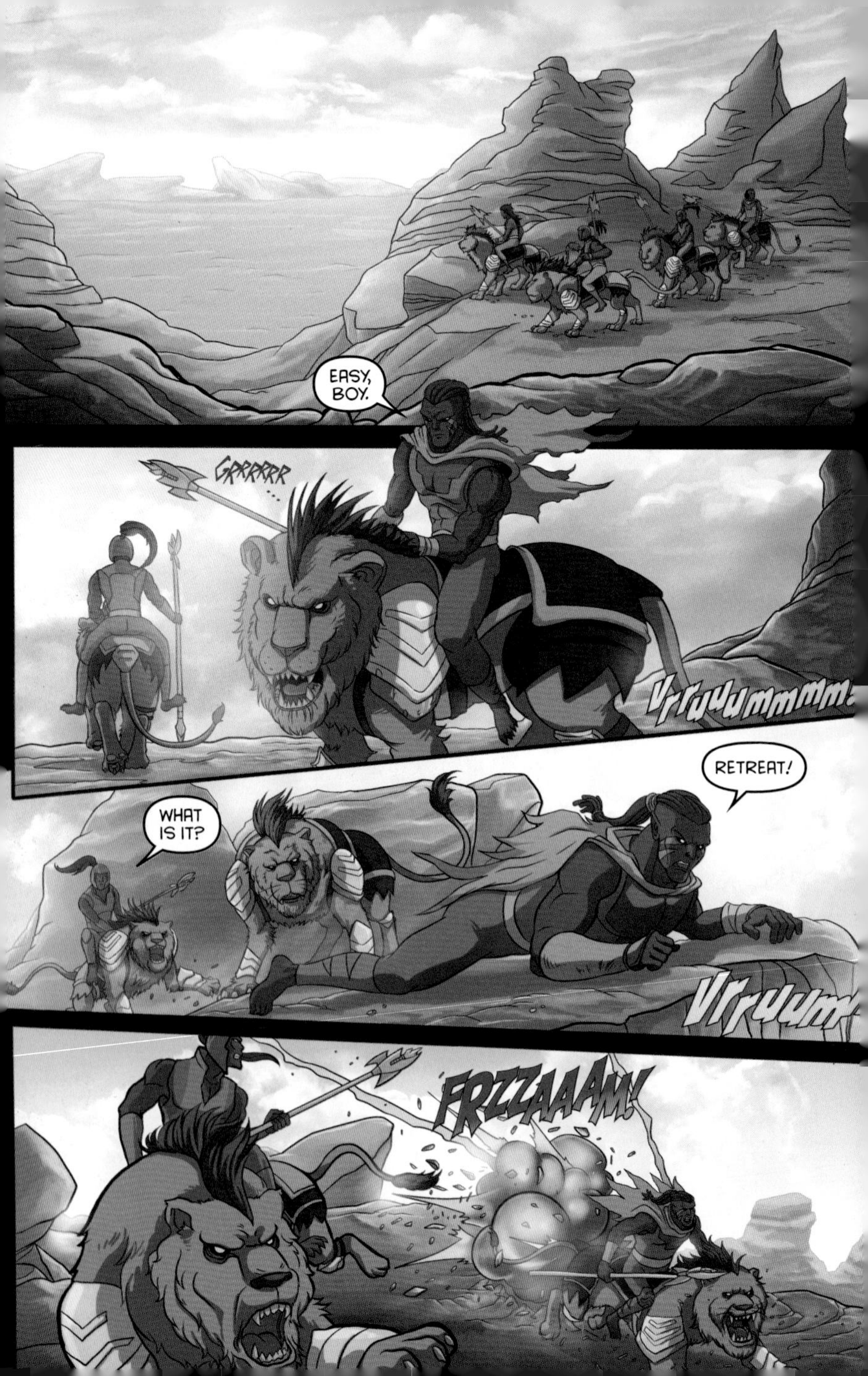

EASY, BOY.
GRRRRRR...
Vrruuummmm
WHAT IS IT?
RETREAT!
Vrruum
FRZZAAAM!

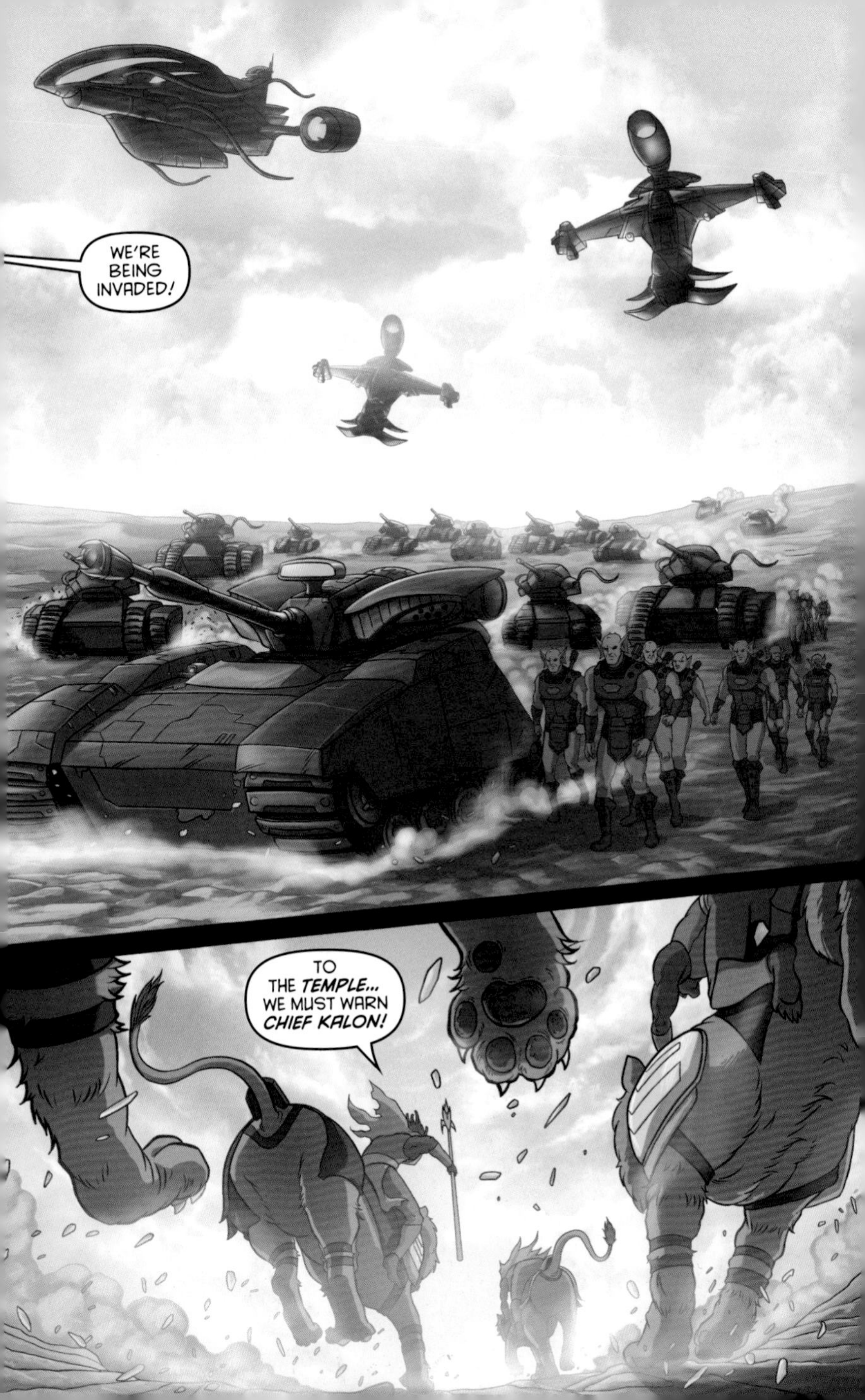
WE'RE BEING INVADED!
TO THE *TEMPLE*... WE MUST WARN *CHIEF KALON!*

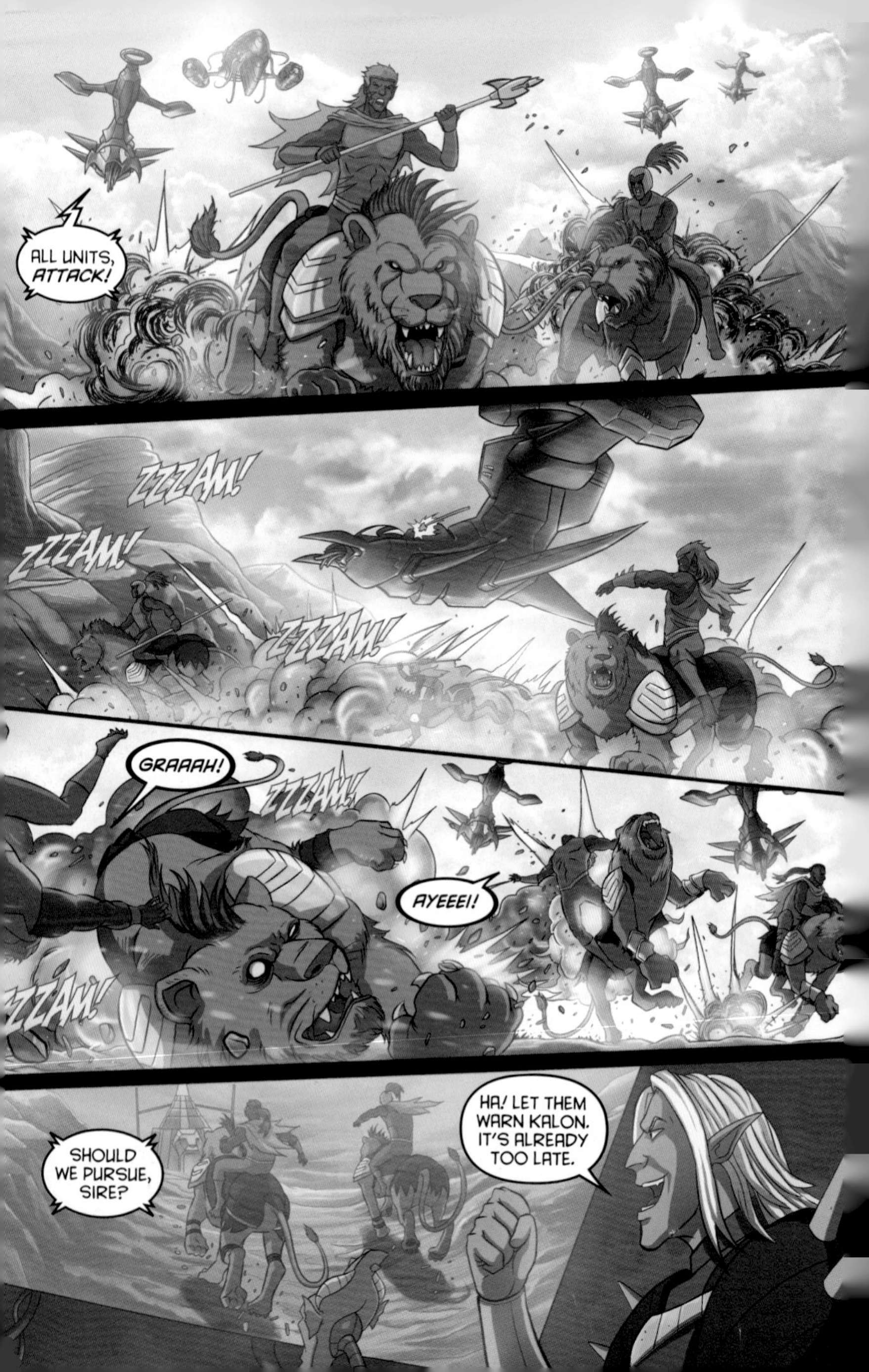
ALL UNITS, ATTACK!
ZZZAM!
ZZZAM!
ZZZAM!
GRAAAH!
ZZZAM!
AYEEE!!
ZZAM!
SHOULD WE PURSUE, SIRE?
HA! LET THEM WARN KALON. IT'S ALREADY TOO LATE.

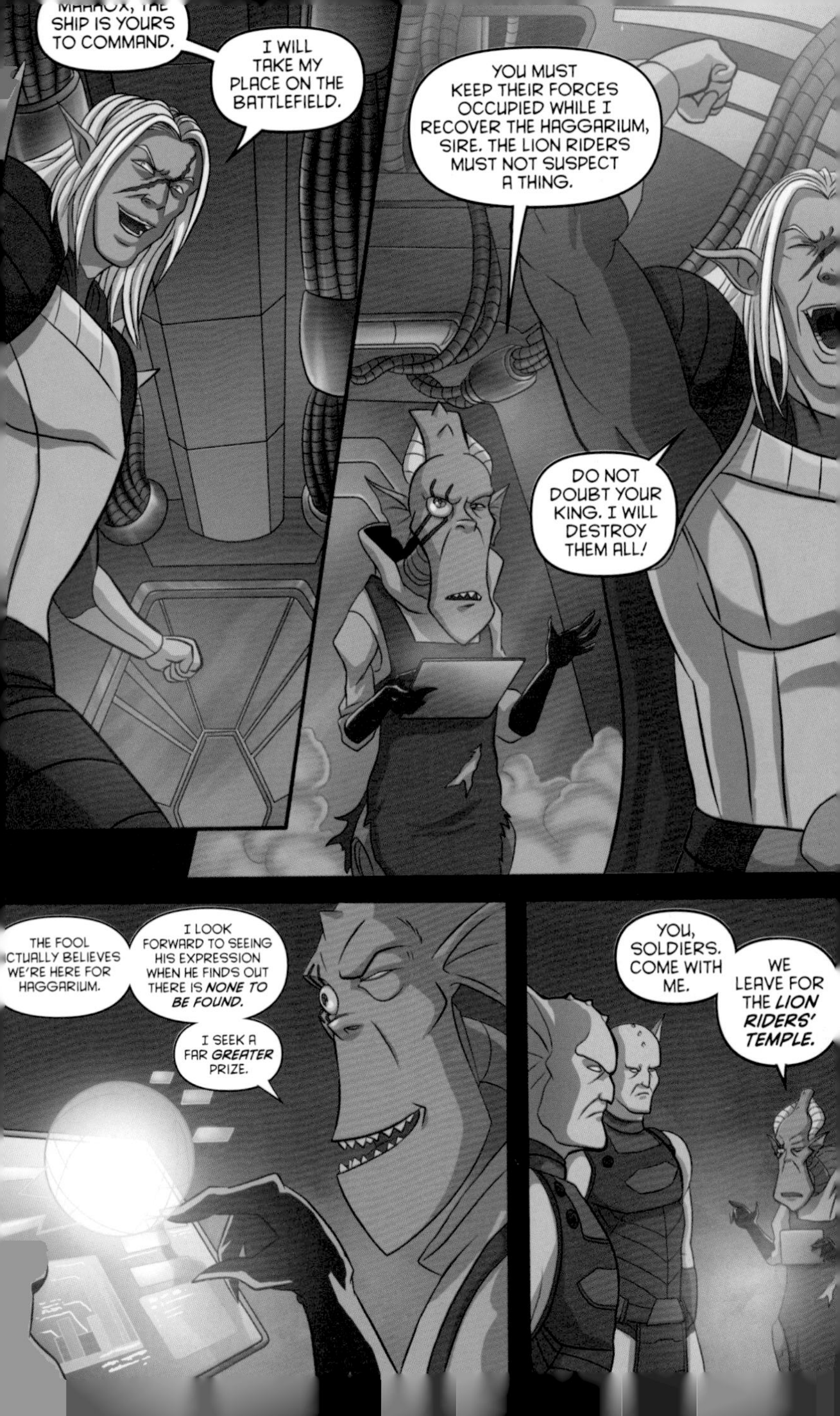
SHIP IS YOURS TO COMMAND.
I WILL TAKE MY PLACE ON THE BATTLEFIELD.
YOU MUST KEEP THEIR FORCES OCCUPIED WHILE I RECOVER THE HAGGARIUM, SIRE. THE LION RIDERS MUST NOT SUSPECT A THING.
DO NOT DOUBT YOUR KING. I WILL DESTROY THEM ALL!
THE FOOL CTUALLY BELIEVES WE'RE HERE FOR HAGGARIUM.
I LOOK FORWARD TO SEEING HIS EXPRESSION WHEN HE FINDS OUT THERE IS *NONE TO BE FOUND.*
I SEEK A FAR *GREATER* PRIZE.
YOU, SOLDIERS. COME WITH ME.
WE LEAVE FOR THE *LION RIDERS'* *TEMPLE.*

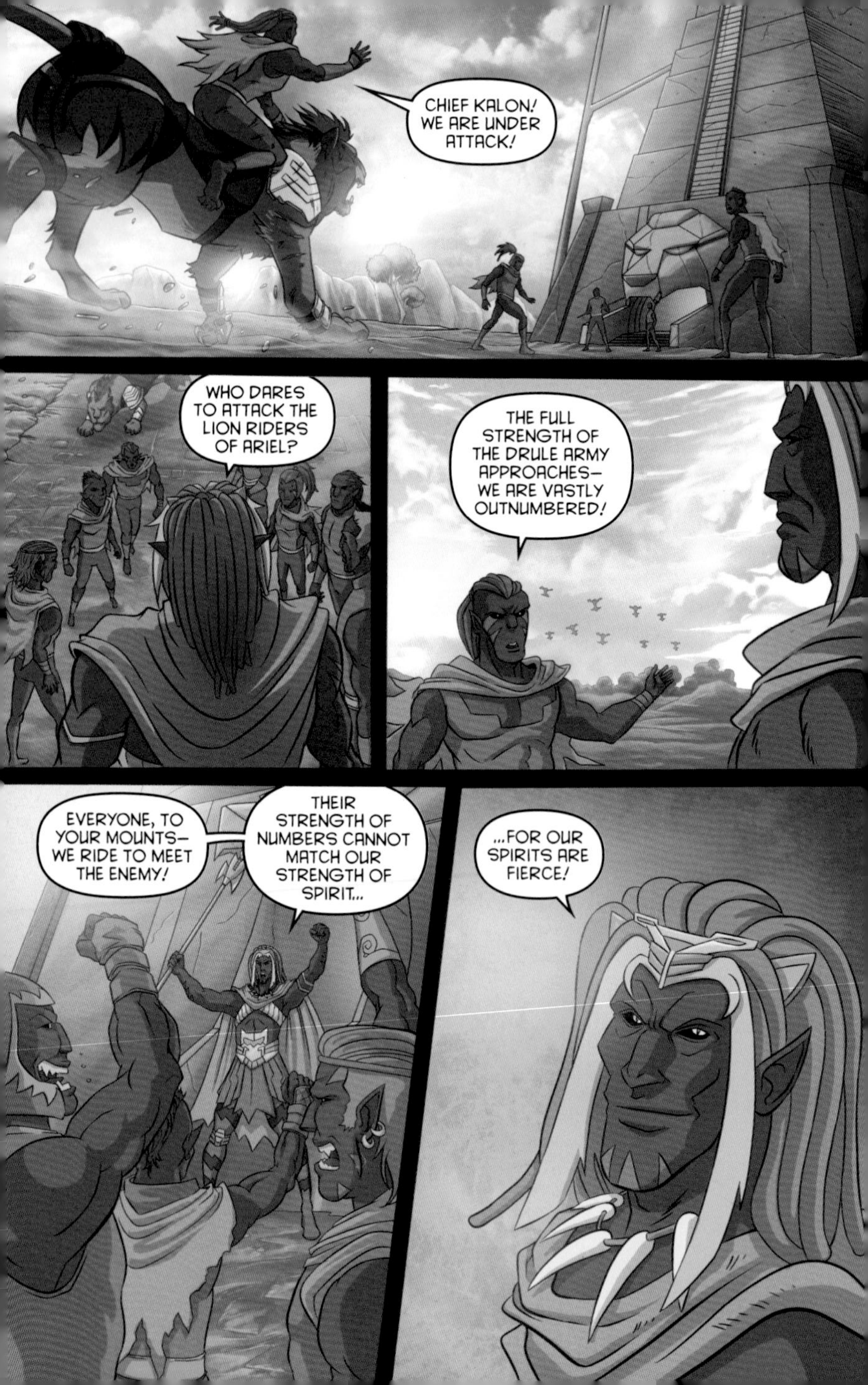
CHIEF KALON! WE ARE UNDER ATTACK!
WHO DARES TO ATTACK THE LION RIDERS OF ARIEL?
THE FULL STRENGTH OF THE DRULE ARMY APPROACHES— WE ARE VASTLY OUTNUMBERED!
EVERYONE, TO YOUR MOUNTS— WE RIDE TO MEET THE ENEMY!
THEIR STRENGTH OF NUMBERS CANNOT MATCH OUR STRENGTH OF SPIRIT...
...FOR OUR SPIRITS ARE FIERCE!

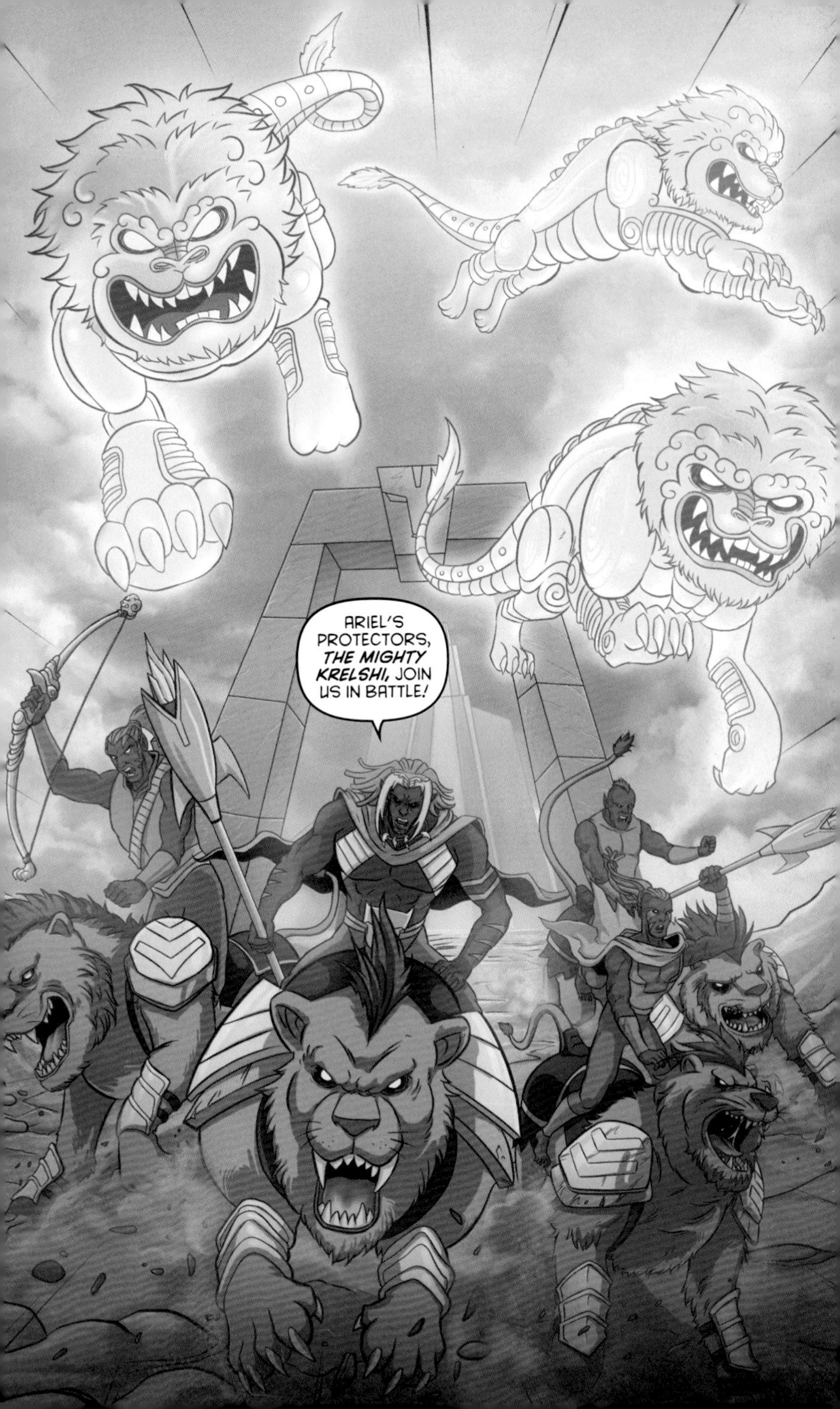
ARIEL'S PROTECTORS, THE MIGHTY KRELSHI, JOIN US IN BATTLE!

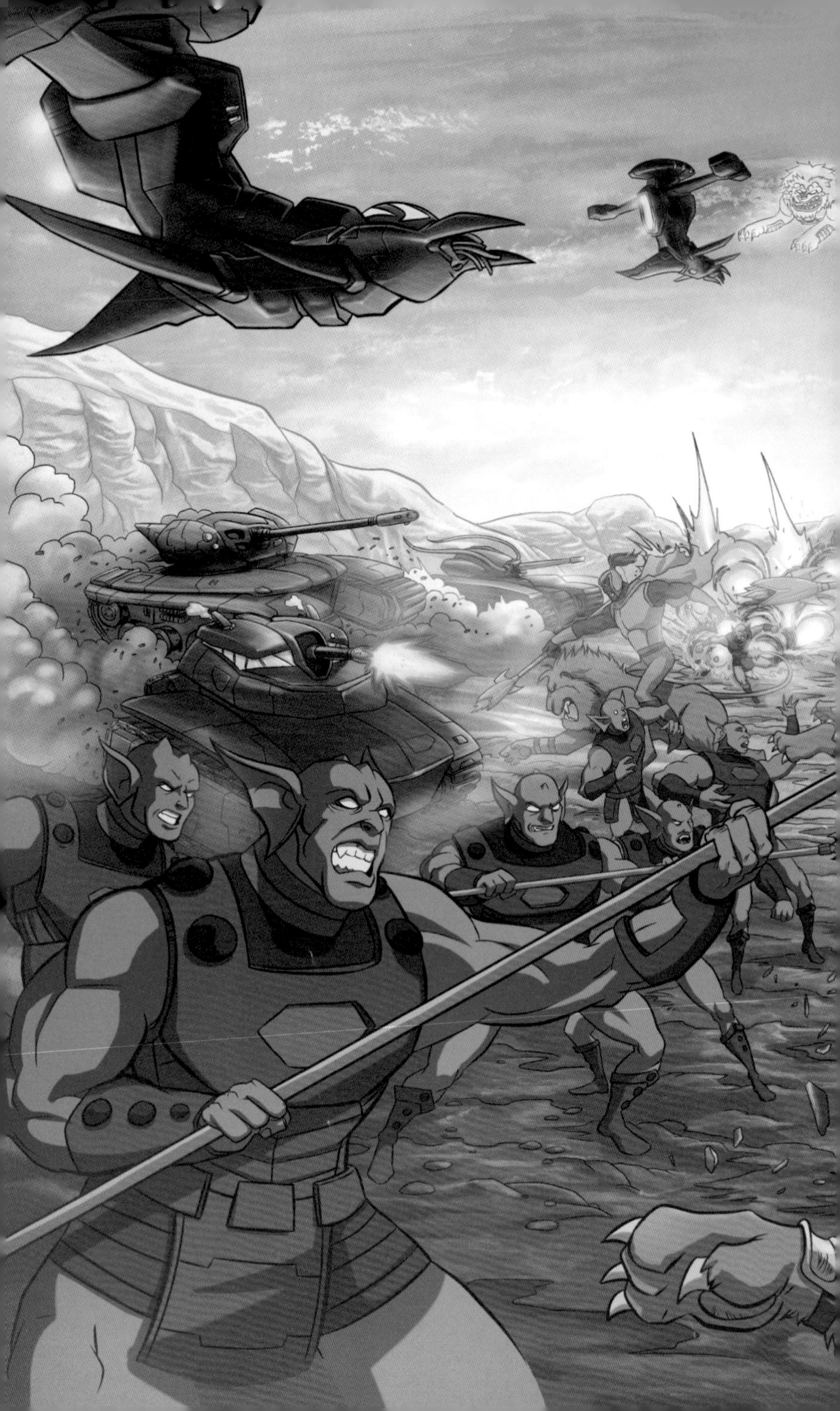

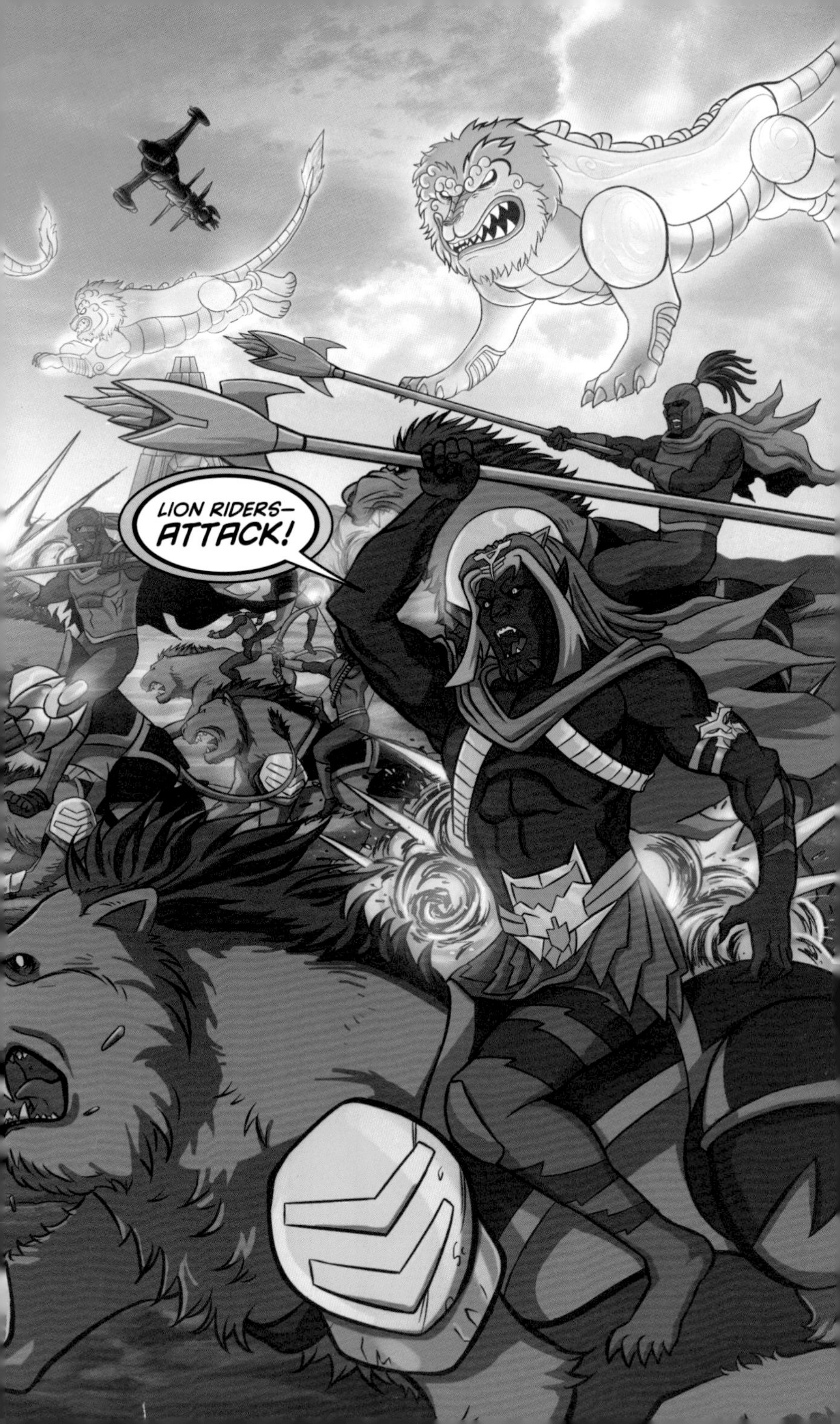
LION RIDERS—
ATTACK!

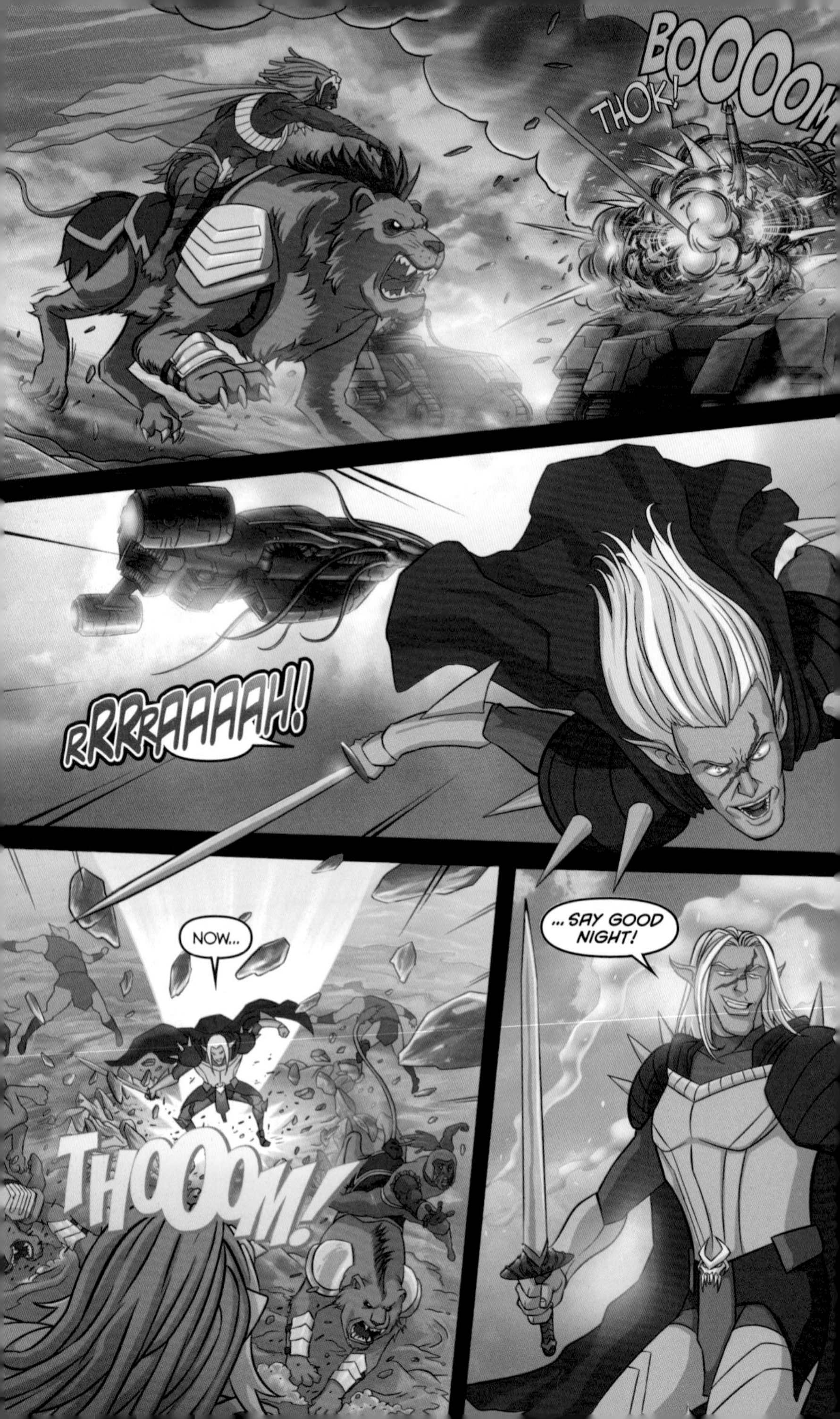
BOOOOOM!
THOK!
RRRRAAAAAH!
NOW...
THOOOM!
...SAY GOOD NIGHT!

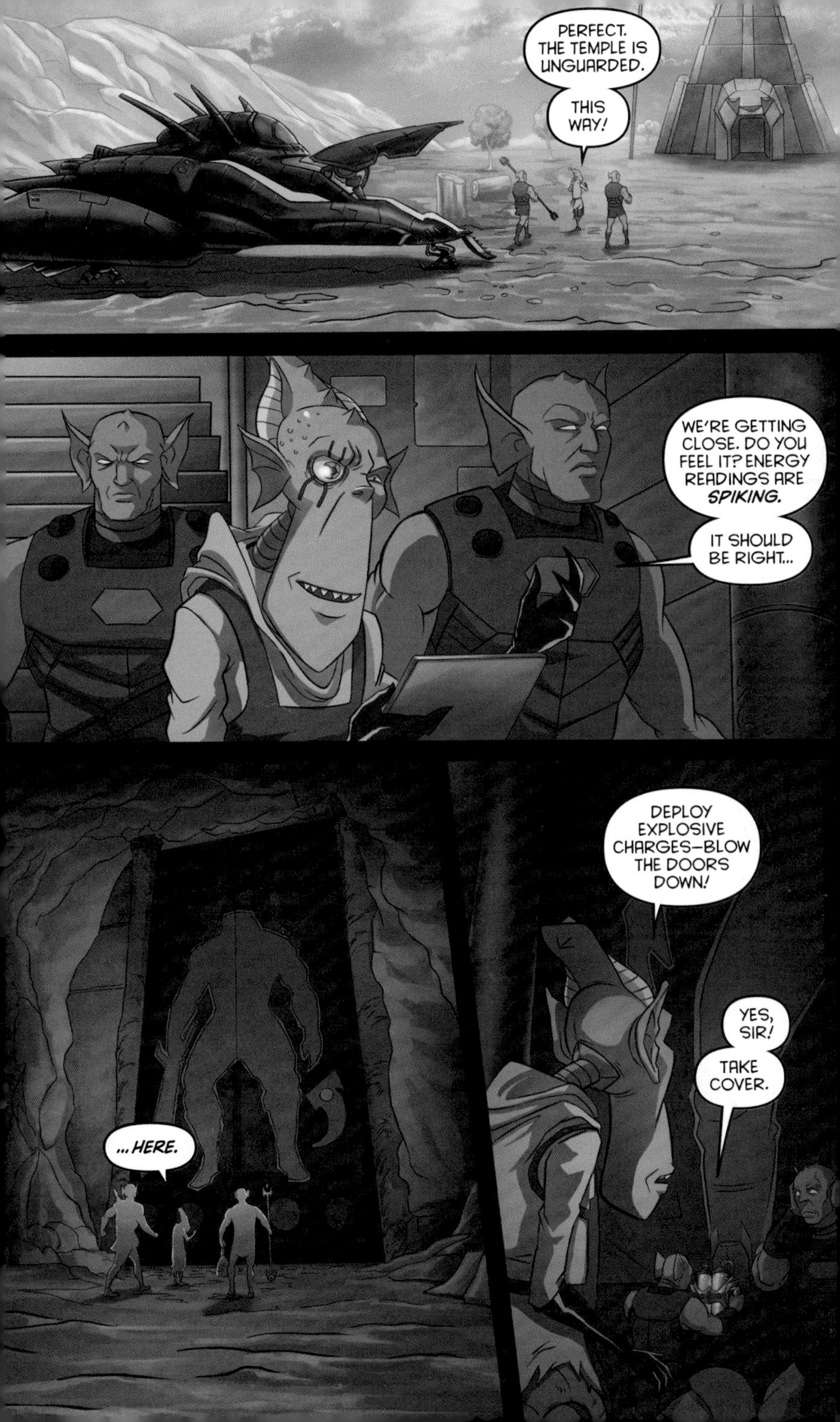
PERFECT. THE TEMPLE IS UNGUARDED.
THIS WAY!
WE'RE GETTING CLOSE. DO YOU FEEL IT? ENERGY READINGS ARE *SPIKING.*
IT SHOULD BE RIGHT...
...HERE.
DEPLOY EXPLOSIVE CHARGES—BLOW THE DOORS DOWN!
YES, SIR!
TAKE COVER.

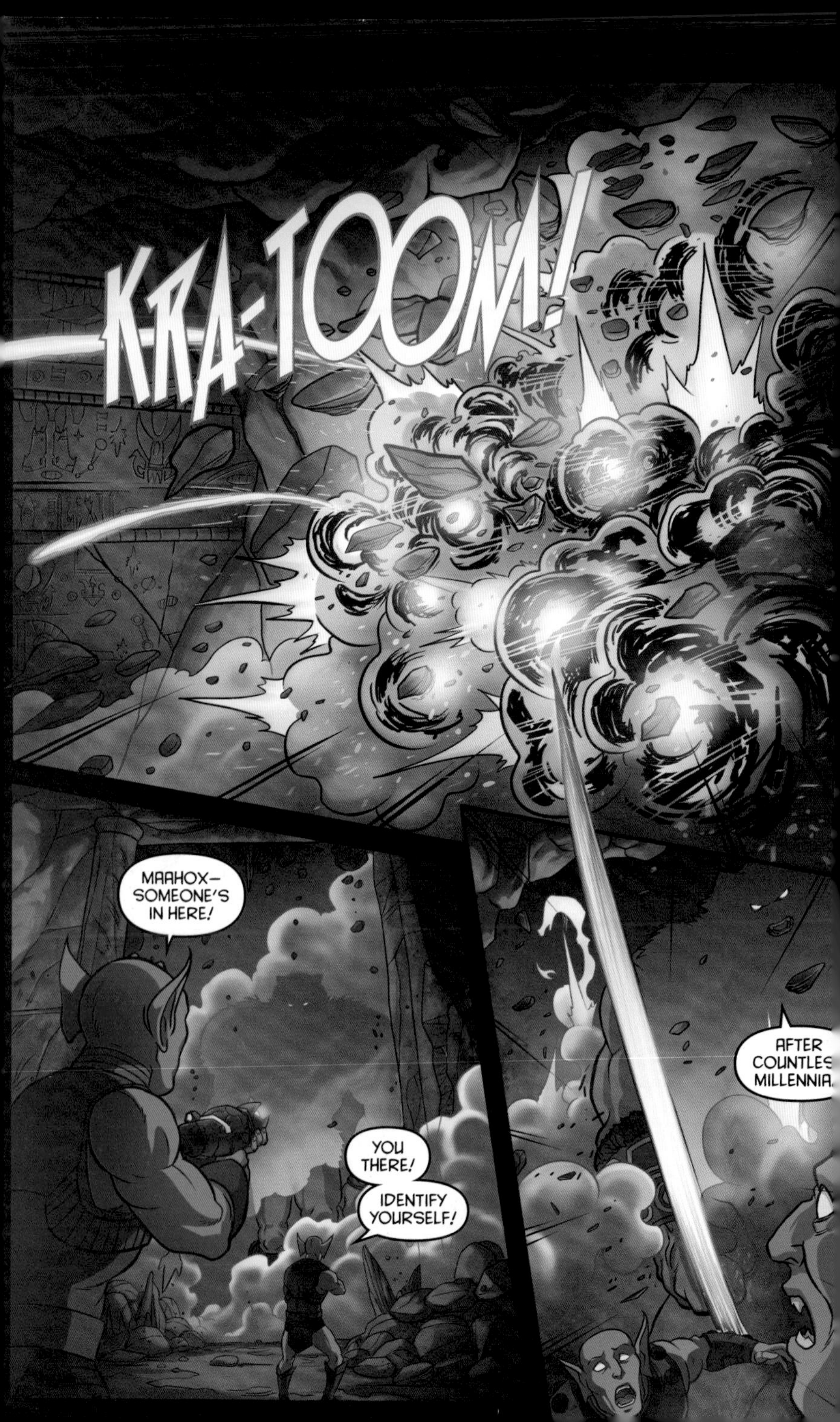
KRA-TOOM!
MAAHOX—SOMEONE'S IN HERE!
YOU THERE!
IDENTIFY YOURSELF!
AFTER COUNTLES MILLENNIA

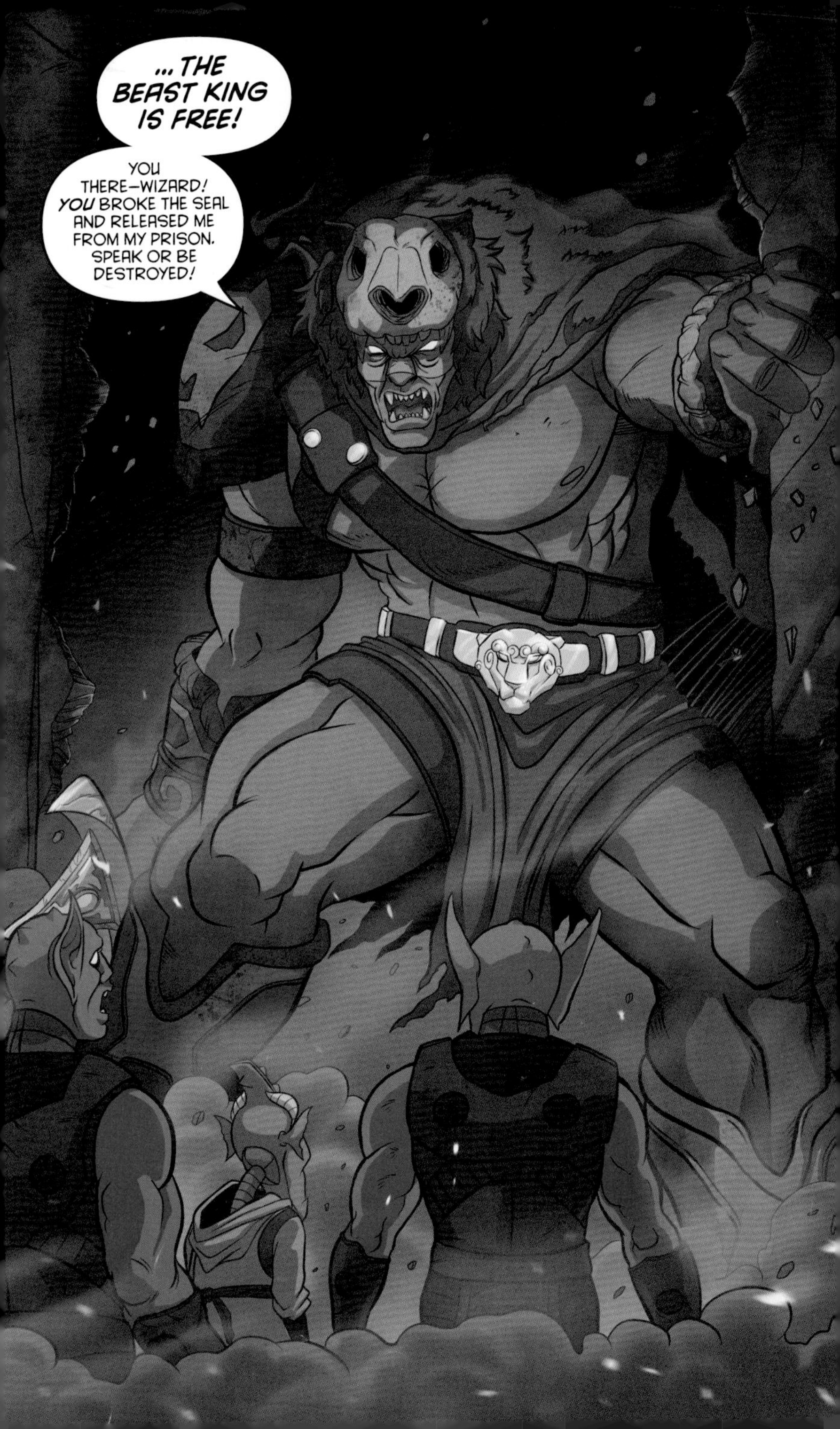
...THE BEAST KING IS FREE!
YOU THERE—WIZARD! YOU BROKE THE SEAL AND RELEASED ME FROM MY PRISON. SPEAK OR BE DESTROYED!

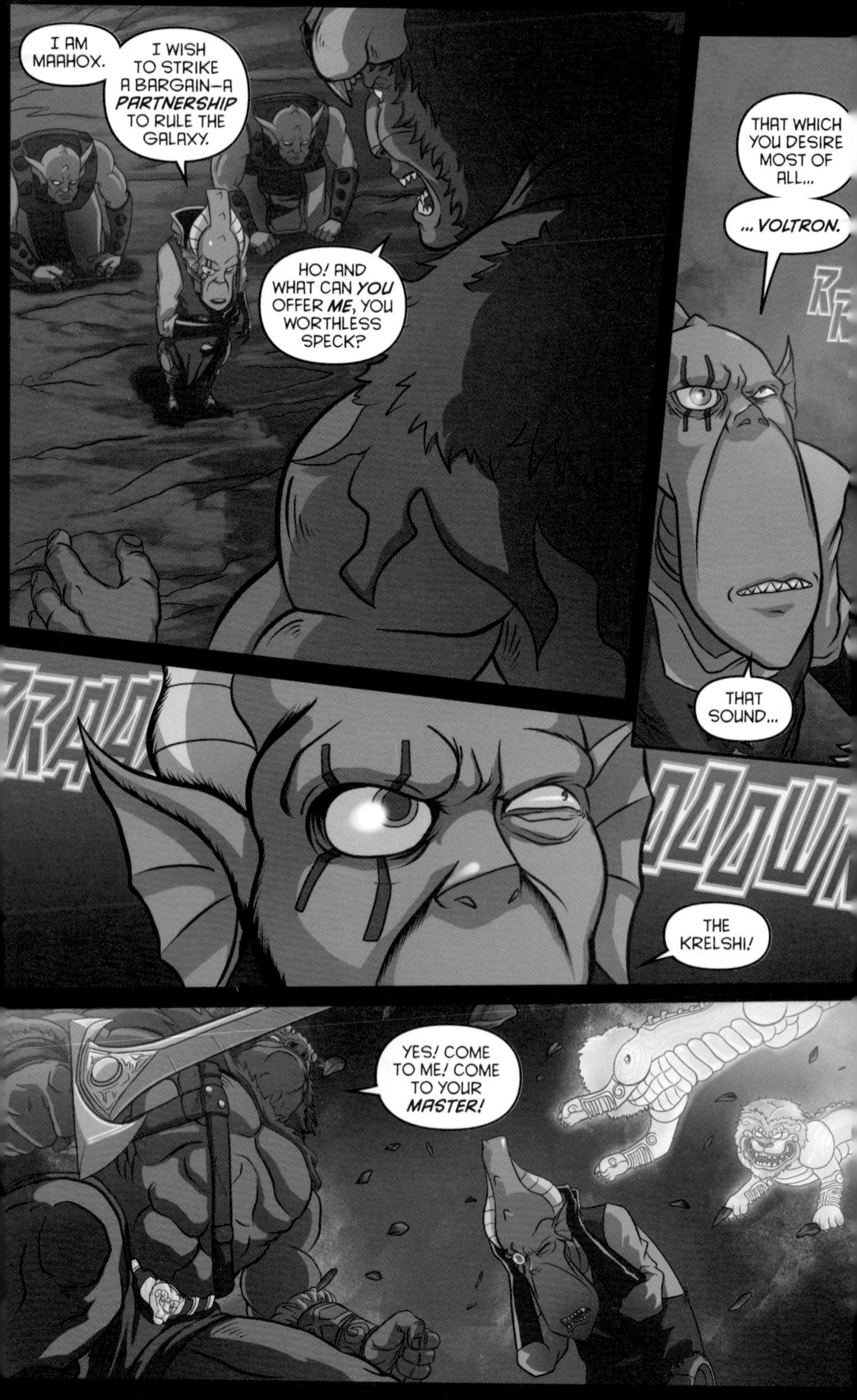
I AM MAAHOX.
I WISH TO STRIKE A BARGAIN—A *PARTNERSHIP* TO RULE THE GALAXY.
HO! AND WHAT CAN *YOU* OFFER *ME*, YOU WORTHLESS SPECK?
THAT WHICH YOU DESIRE MOST OF ALL...
...VOLTRON.
THAT SOUND...
THE KRELSHI!
YES! COME TO ME! COME TO YOUR *MASTER!*

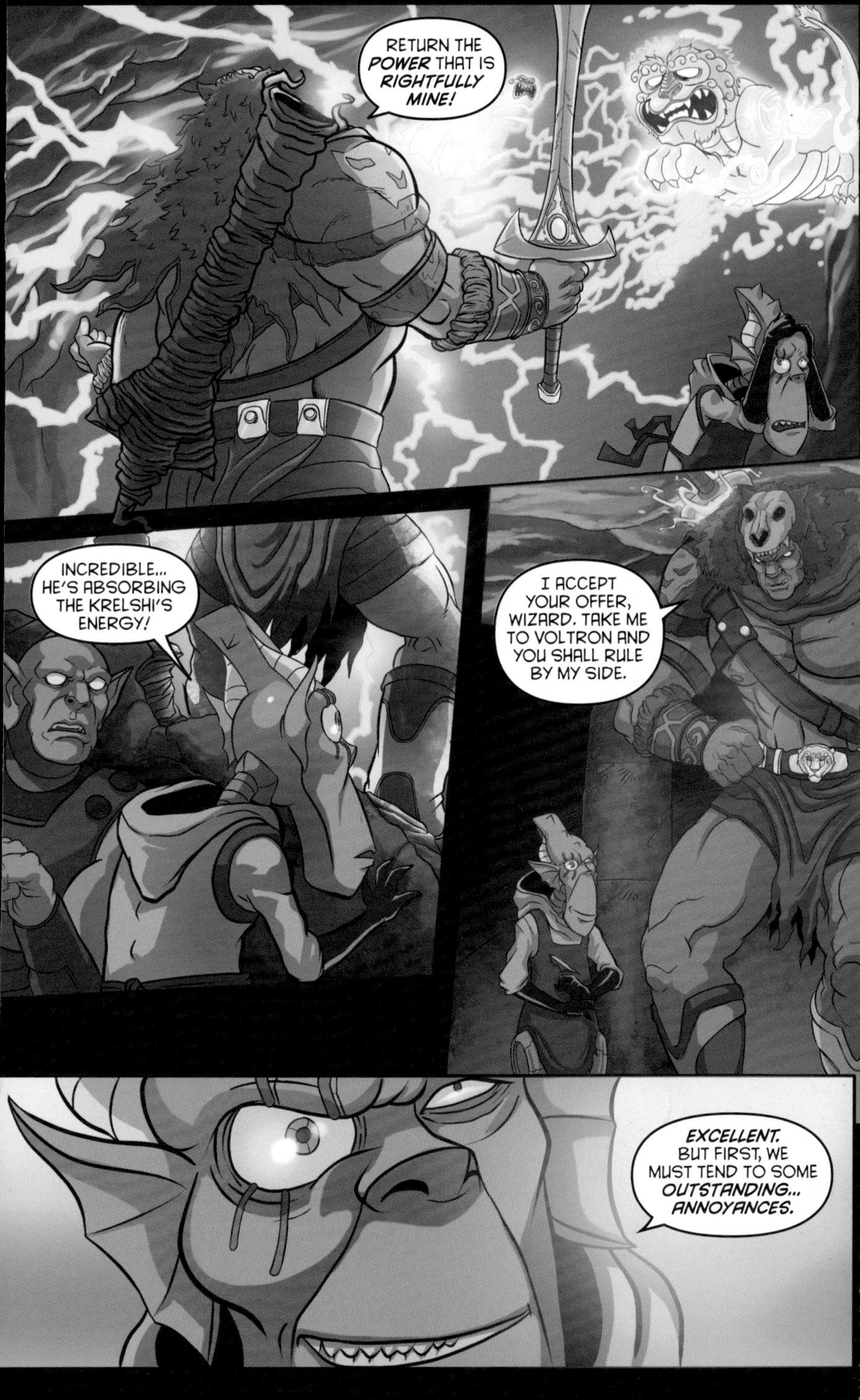
RETURN THE *POWER* THAT IS *RIGHTFULLY MINE!*
INCREDIBLE... HE'S ABSORBING THE KRELSHI'S ENERGY!
I ACCEPT YOUR OFFER, WIZARD. TAKE ME TO VOLTRON AND YOU SHALL RULE BY MY SIDE.
EXCELLENT. BUT FIRST, WE MUST TEND TO SOME *OUTSTANDING... ANNOYANCES.*

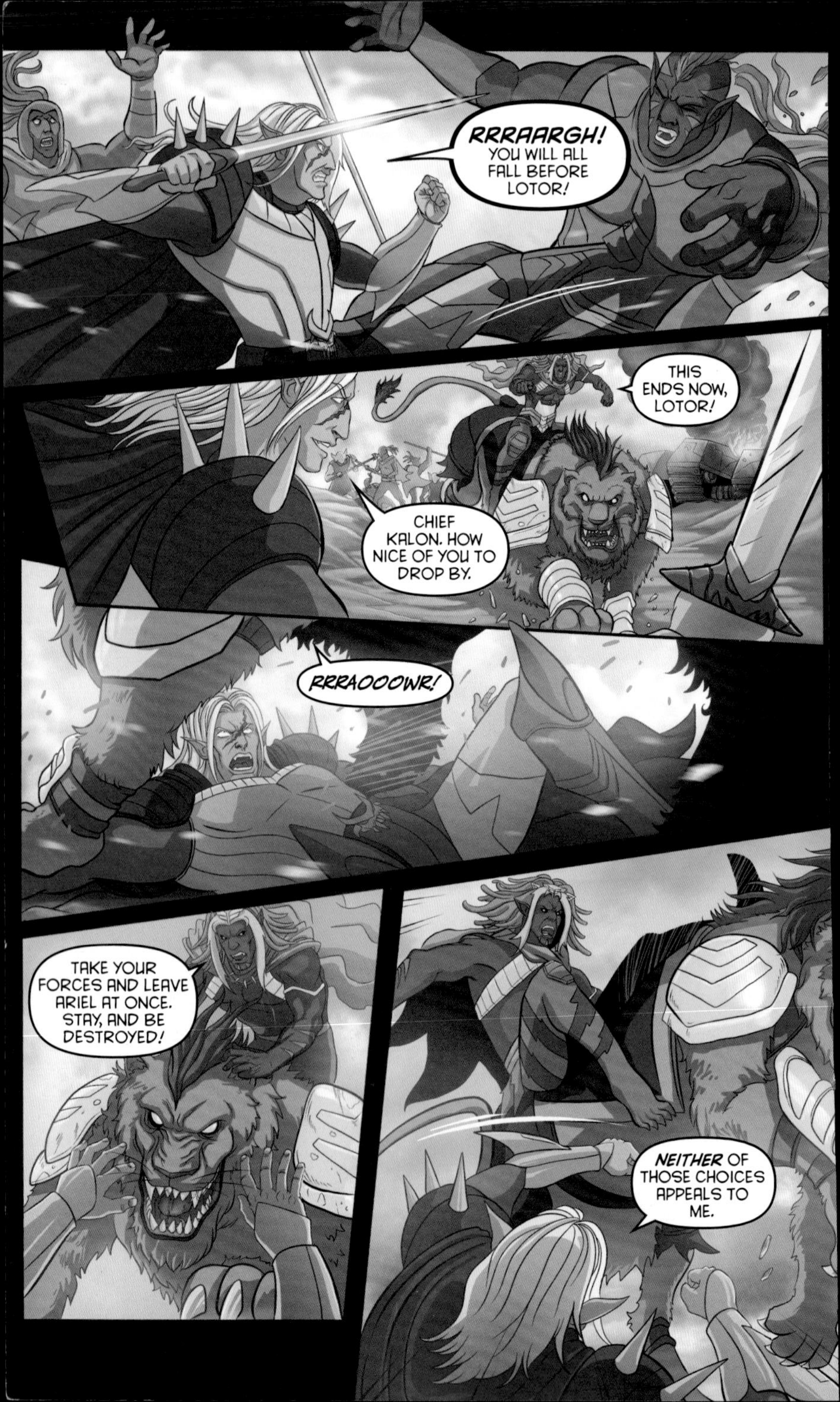
RRRAARGH! YOU WILL ALL FALL BEFORE LOTOR!
THIS ENDS NOW, LOTOR!
CHIEF KALON. HOW NICE OF YOU TO DROP BY.
RRRAOOOWR!
TAKE YOUR FORCES AND LEAVE ARIEL AT ONCE. STAY, AND BE DESTROYED!
NEITHER OF THOSE CHOICES APPEALS TO ME.

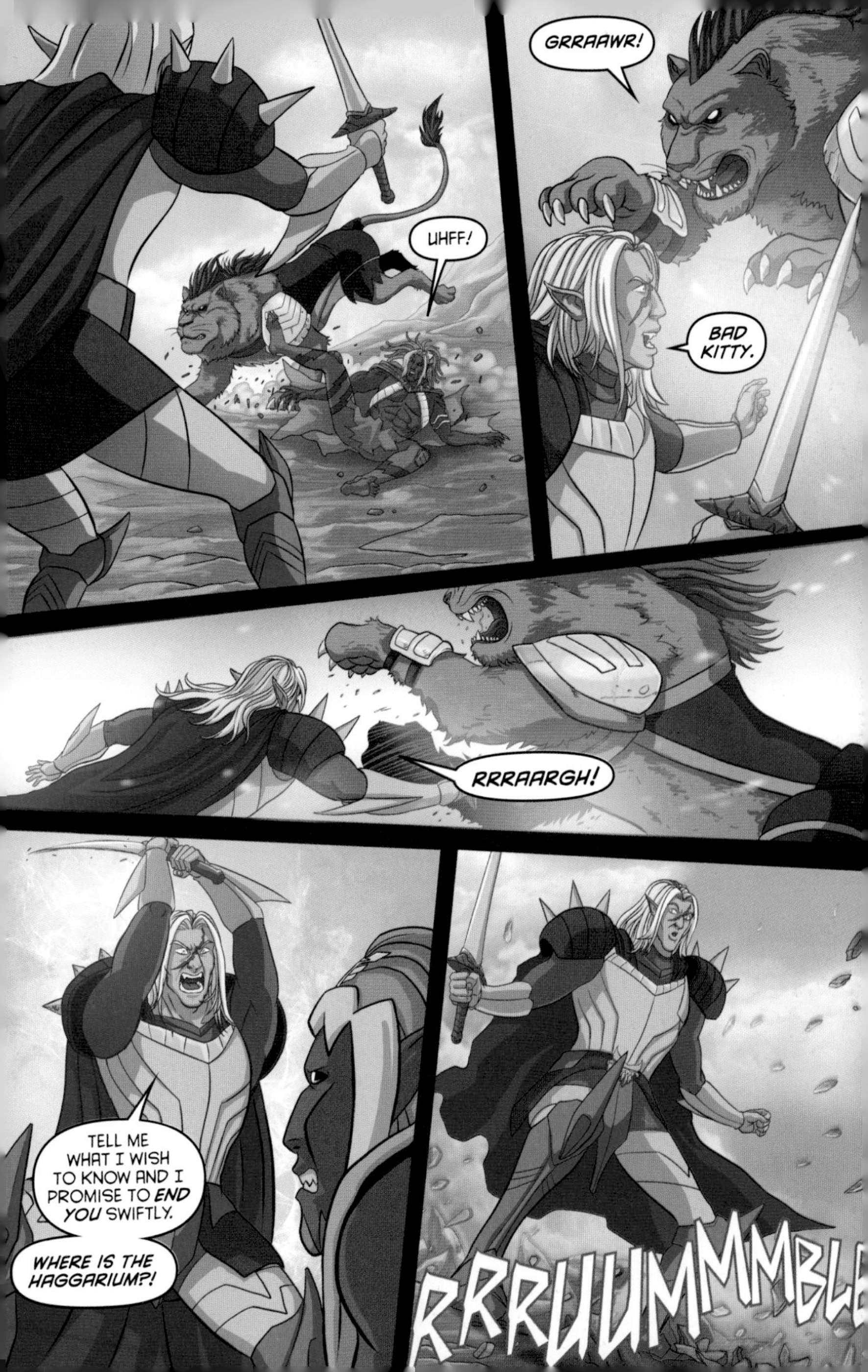
UHFF!
GRRAAWR!
BAD KITTY.
RRRAARGH!
TELL ME WHAT I WISH TO KNOW AND I PROMISE TO END YOU SWIFTLY.
WHERE IS THE HAGGARIUM?!
RRRUUMMMBLE

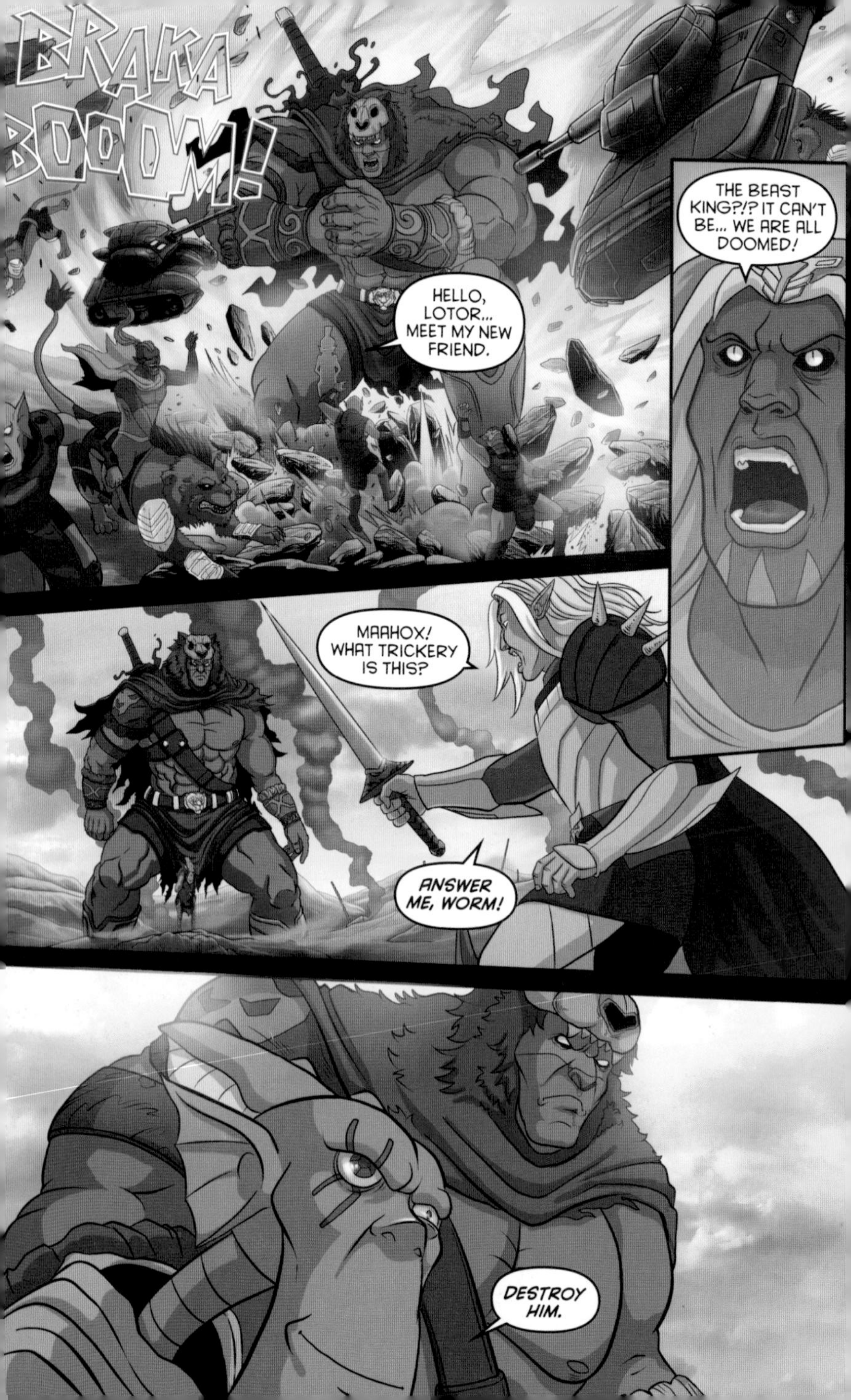
BRAKA BOOOM!
HELLO, LOTOR... MEET MY NEW FRIEND.
THE BEAST KING?!? IT CAN'T BE... WE ARE ALL DOOMED!
MAAHOX! WHAT TRICKERY IS THIS?
ANSWER ME, WORM!
DESTROY HIM.

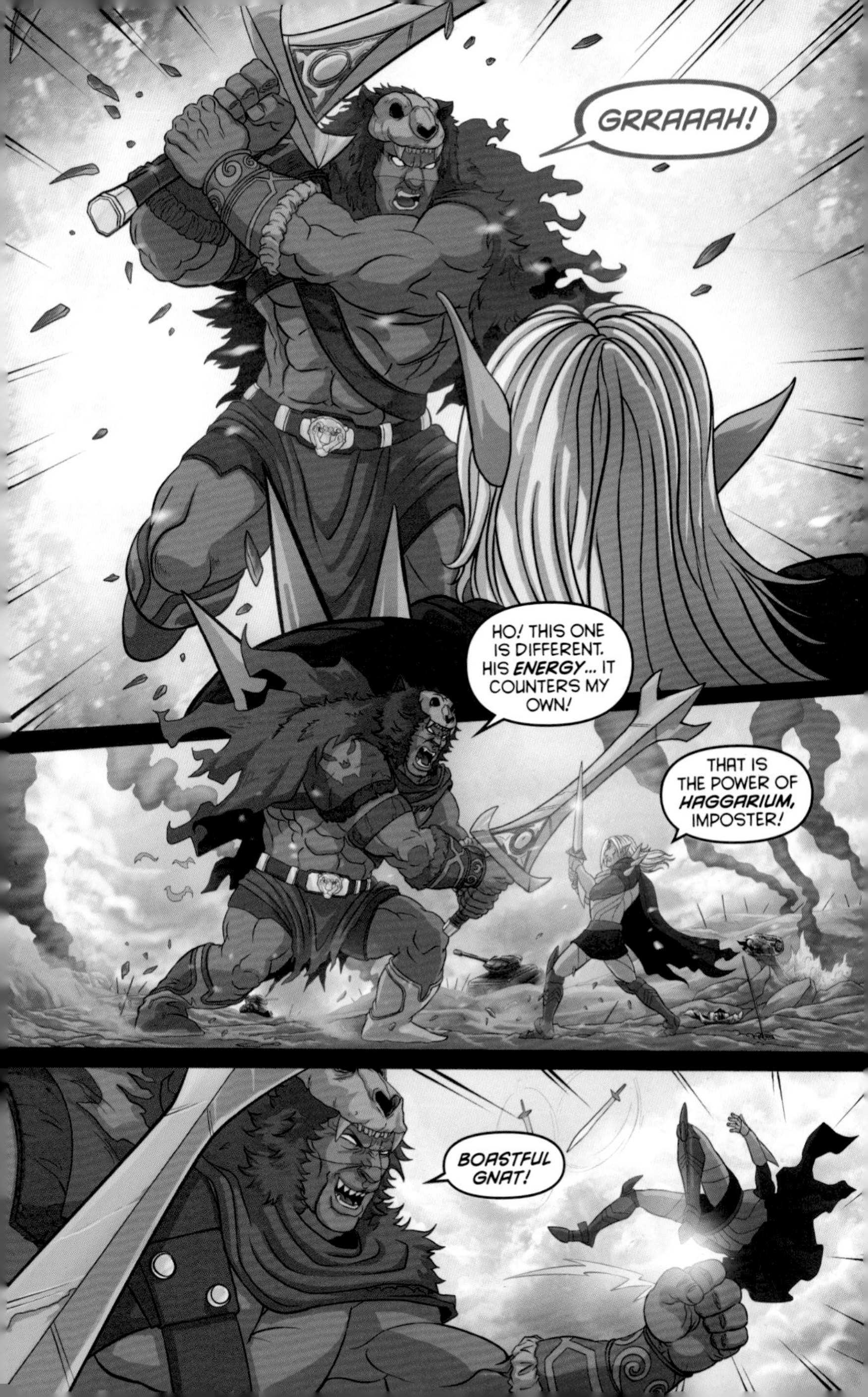
GRRAAAH!
HO! THIS ONE IS DIFFERENT. HIS ENERGY... IT COUNTERS MY OWN!
THAT IS THE POWER OF HAGGARIUM, IMPOSTER!
BOASTFUL GNAT!

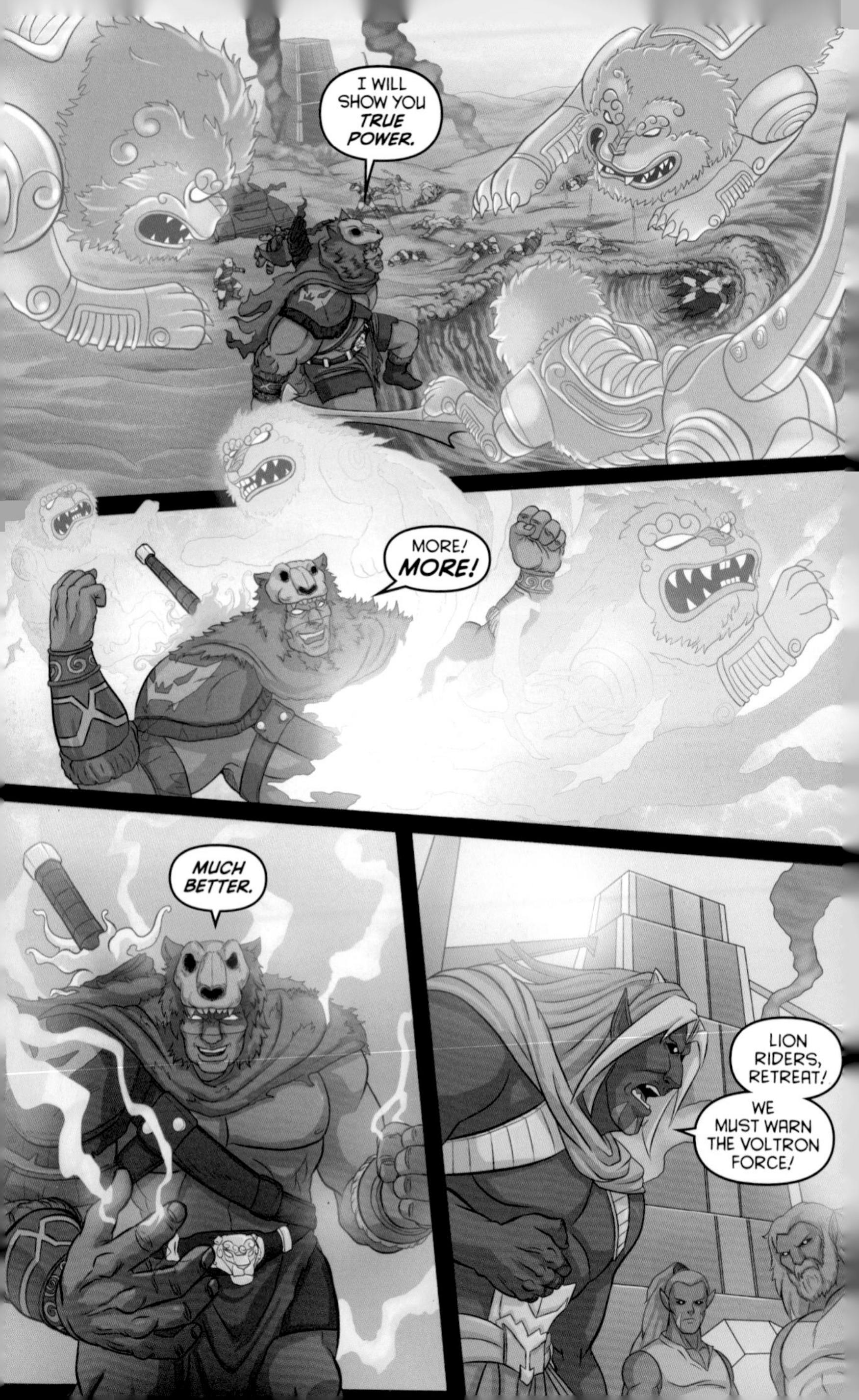
I WILL SHOW YOU *TRUE POWER.*
MORE! **MORE!**
MUCH BETTER.
LION RIDERS, RETREAT!
WE MUST WARN THE VOLTRON FORCE!

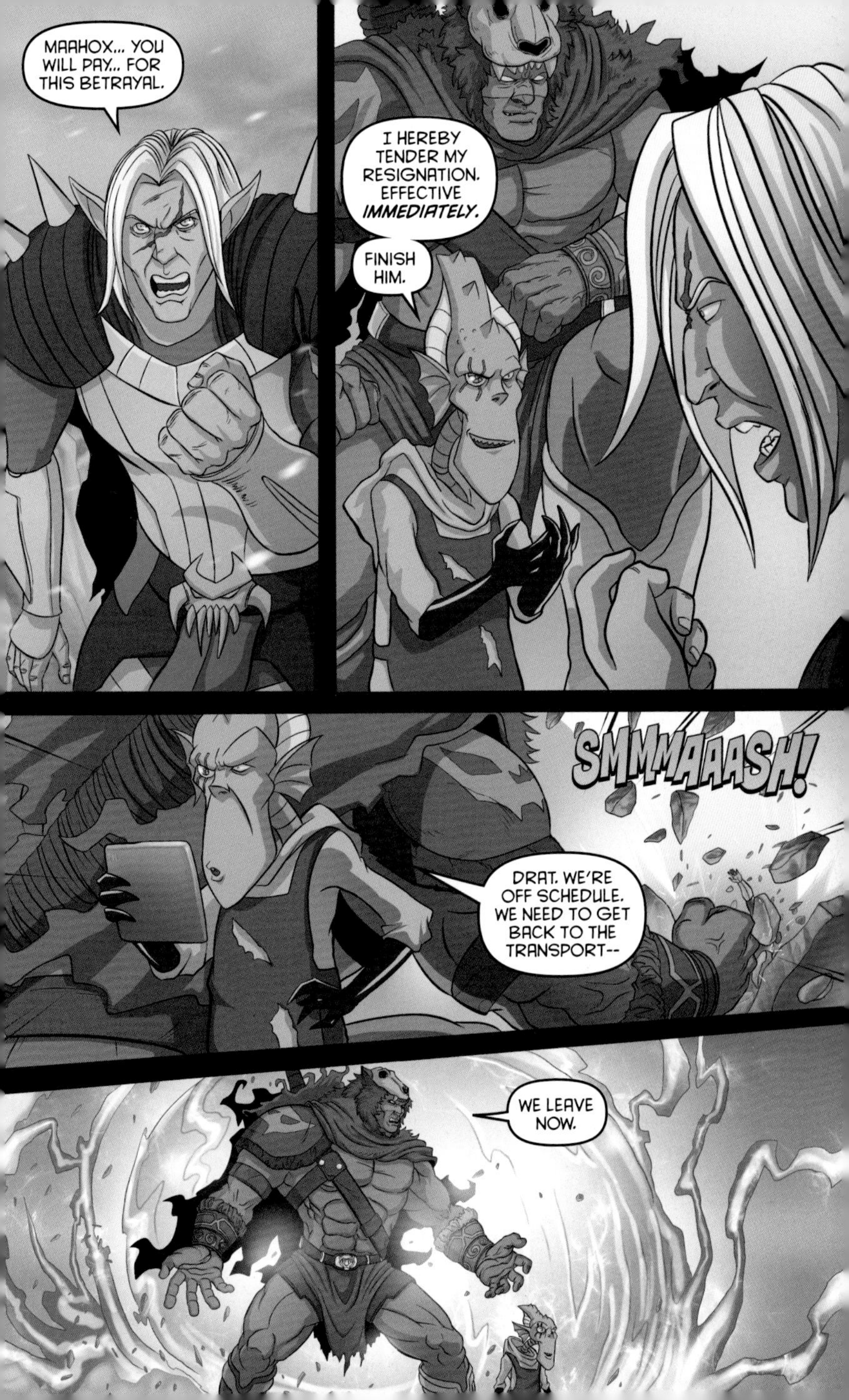
MAAHOX... YOU WILL PAY... FOR THIS BETRAYAL.
I HEREBY TENDER MY RESIGNATION. EFFECTIVE *IMMEDIATELY.*
FINISH HIM.
SMMMAAASH!
DRAT. WE'RE OFF SCHEDULE. WE NEED TO GET BACK TO THE TRANSPORT--
WE LEAVE NOW.

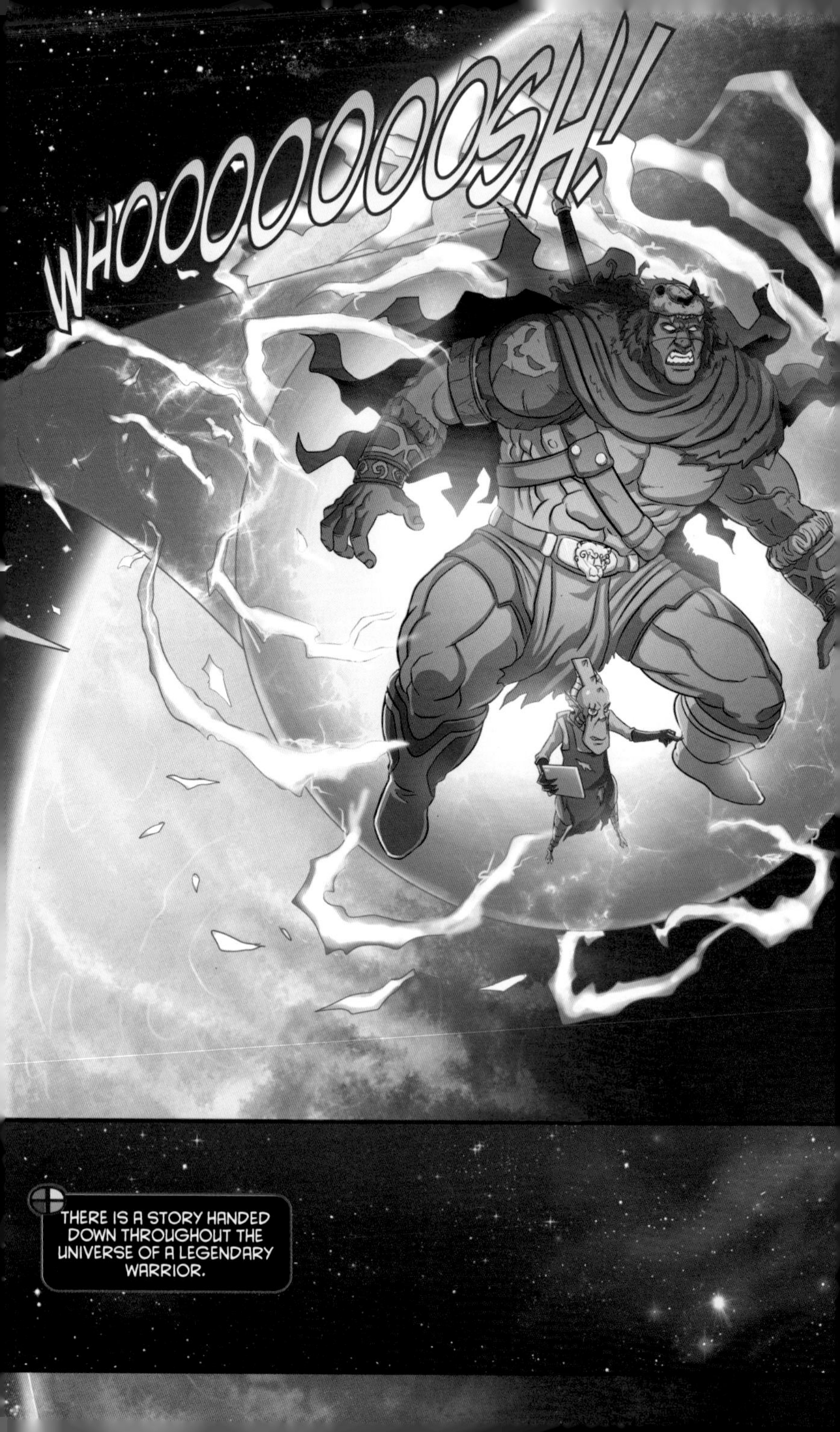
WHOOOOOOOSH!
THERE IS A STORY HANDED DOWN THROUGHOUT THE UNIVERSE OF A LEGENDARY WARRIOR.

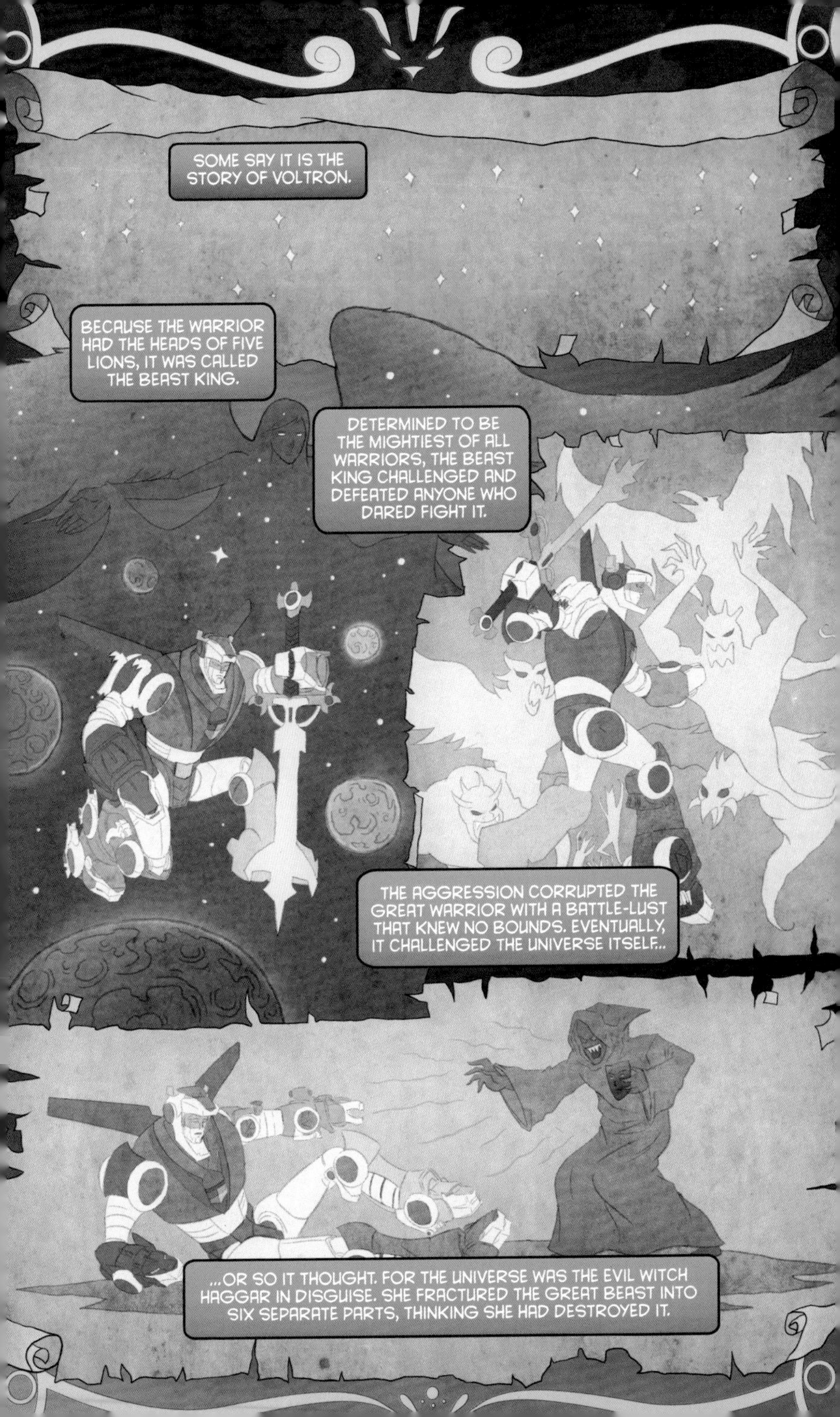
SOME SAY IT IS THE STORY OF VOLTRON.
BECAUSE THE WARRIOR HAD THE HEADS OF FIVE LIONS, IT WAS CALLED THE BEAST KING.
DETERMINED TO BE THE MIGHTIEST OF ALL WARRIORS, THE BEAST KING CHALLENGED AND DEFEATED ANYONE WHO DARED FIGHT IT.
THE AGGRESSION CORRUPTED THE GREAT WARRIOR WITH A BATTLE-LUST THAT KNEW NO BOUNDS. EVENTUALLY, IT CHALLENGED THE UNIVERSE ITSELF...
...OR SO IT THOUGHT. FOR THE UNIVERSE WAS THE EVIL WITCH HAGGAR IN DISGUISE. SHE FRACTURED THE GREAT BEAST INTO SIX SEPARATE PARTS, THINKING SHE HAD DESTROYED IT.

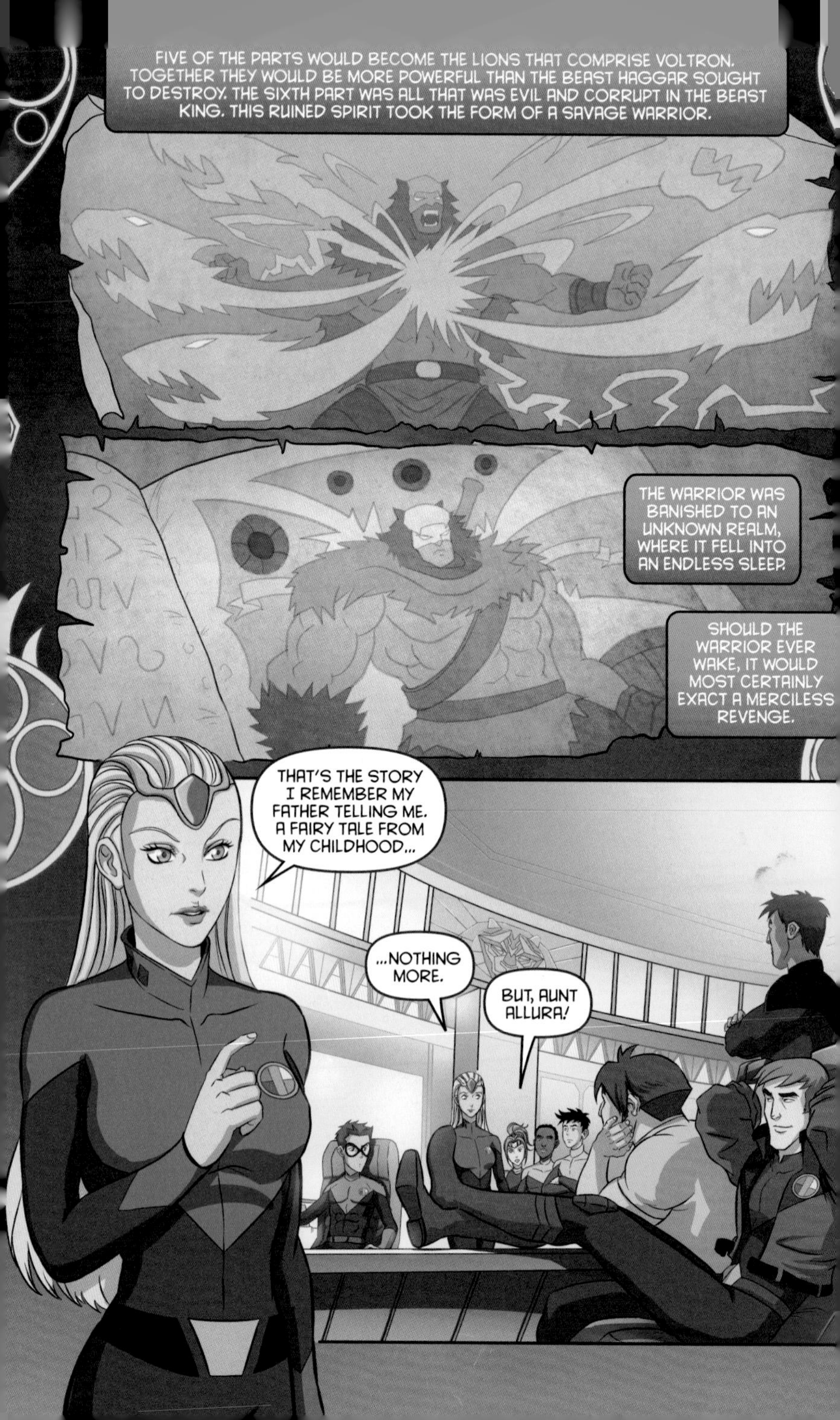
FIVE OF THE PARTS WOULD BECOME THE LIONS THAT COMPRISE VOLTRON. TOGETHER THEY WOULD BE MORE POWERFUL THAN THE BEAST HAGGAR SOUGHT TO DESTROY. THE SIXTH PART WAS ALL THAT WAS EVIL AND CORRUPT IN THE BEAST KING. THIS RUINED SPIRIT TOOK THE FORM OF A SAVAGE WARRIOR.
THE WARRIOR WAS BANISHED TO AN UNKNOWN REALM, WHERE IT FELL INTO AN ENDLESS SLEEP.
SHOULD THE WARRIOR EVER WAKE, IT WOULD MOST CERTAINLY EXACT A MERCILESS REVENGE.
THAT'S THE STORY I REMEMBER MY FATHER TELLING ME. A FAIRY TALE FROM MY CHILDHOOD...
...NOTHING MORE.
BUT, AUNT ALLURA!

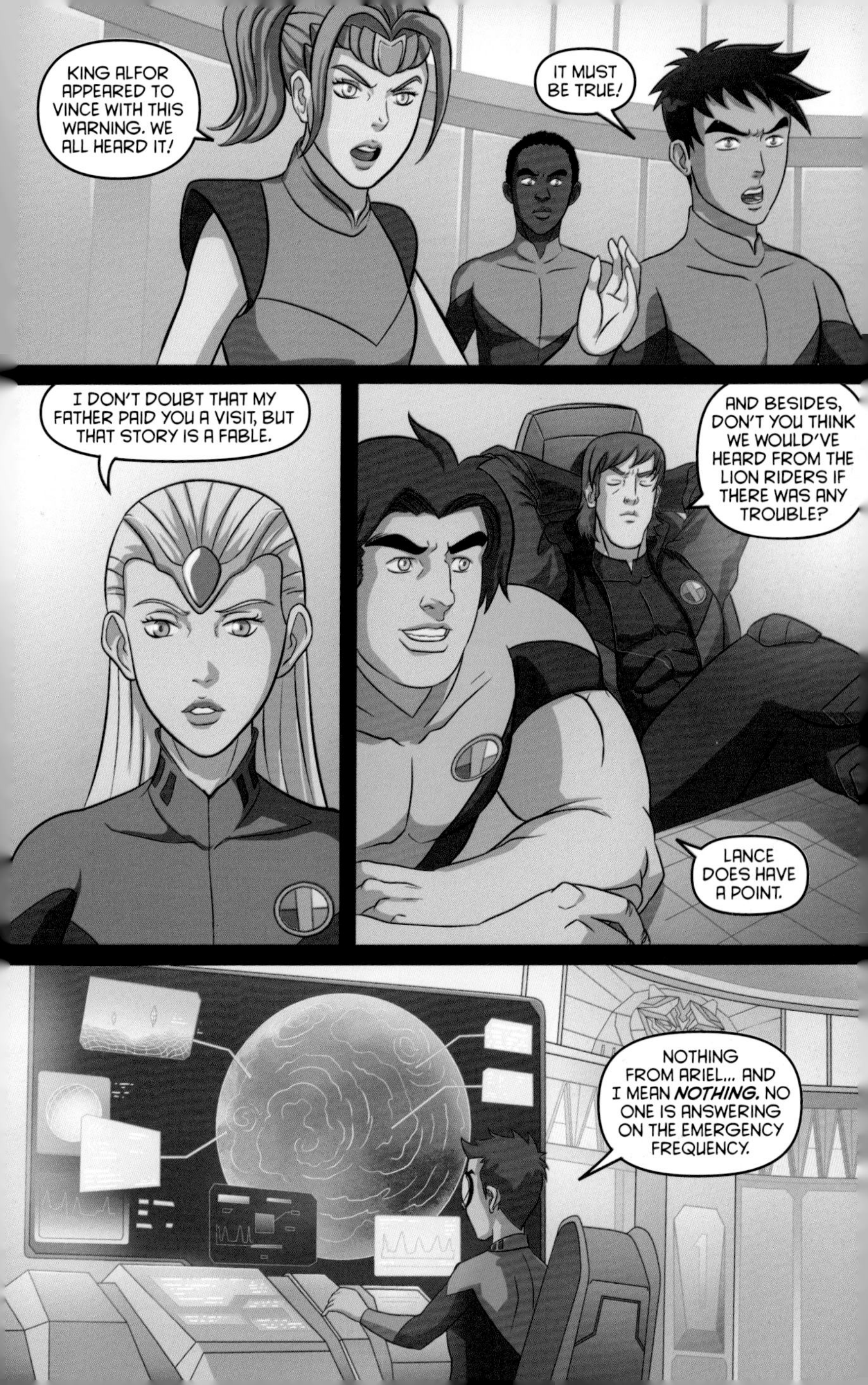
KING ALFOR APPEARED TO VINCE WITH THIS WARNING. WE ALL HEARD IT!
IT MUST BE TRUE!
I DON'T DOUBT THAT MY FATHER PAID YOU A VISIT, BUT THAT STORY IS A FABLE.
AND BESIDES, DON'T YOU THINK WE WOULD'VE HEARD FROM THE LION RIDERS IF THERE WAS ANY TROUBLE?
LANCE DOES HAVE A POINT.
NOTHING FROM ARIEL... AND I MEAN ***NOTHING.*** NO ONE IS ANSWERING ON THE EMERGENCY FREQUENCY.

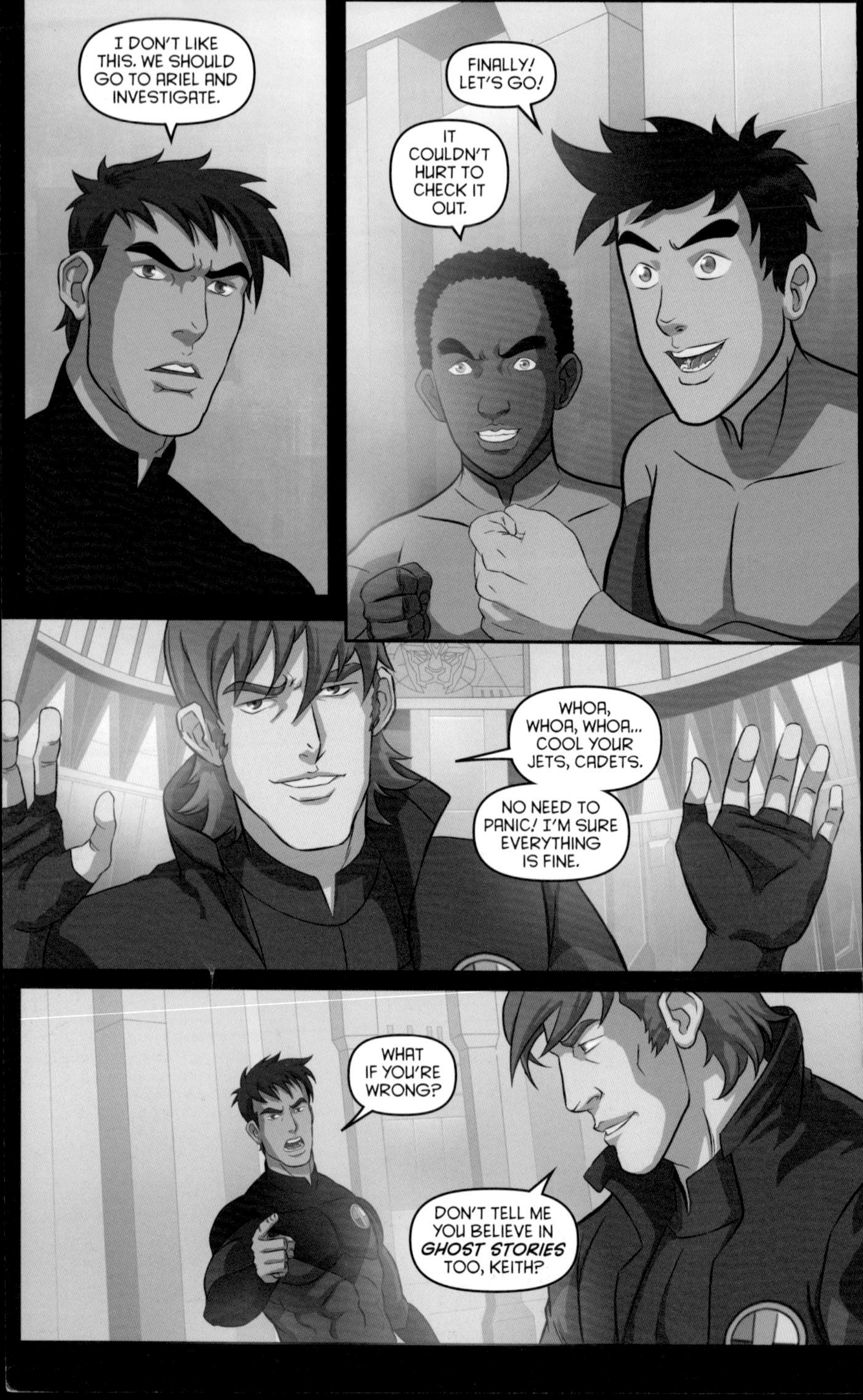
I DON'T LIKE THIS. WE SHOULD GO TO ARIEL AND INVESTIGATE.
FINALLY! LET'S GO!
IT COULDN'T HURT TO CHECK IT OUT.
WHOA, WHOA, WHOA... COOL YOUR JETS, CADETS.
NO NEED TO PANIC! I'M SURE EVERYTHING IS FINE.
WHAT IF YOU'RE WRONG?
DON'T TELL ME YOU BELIEVE IN *GHOST STORIES* TOO, KEITH?

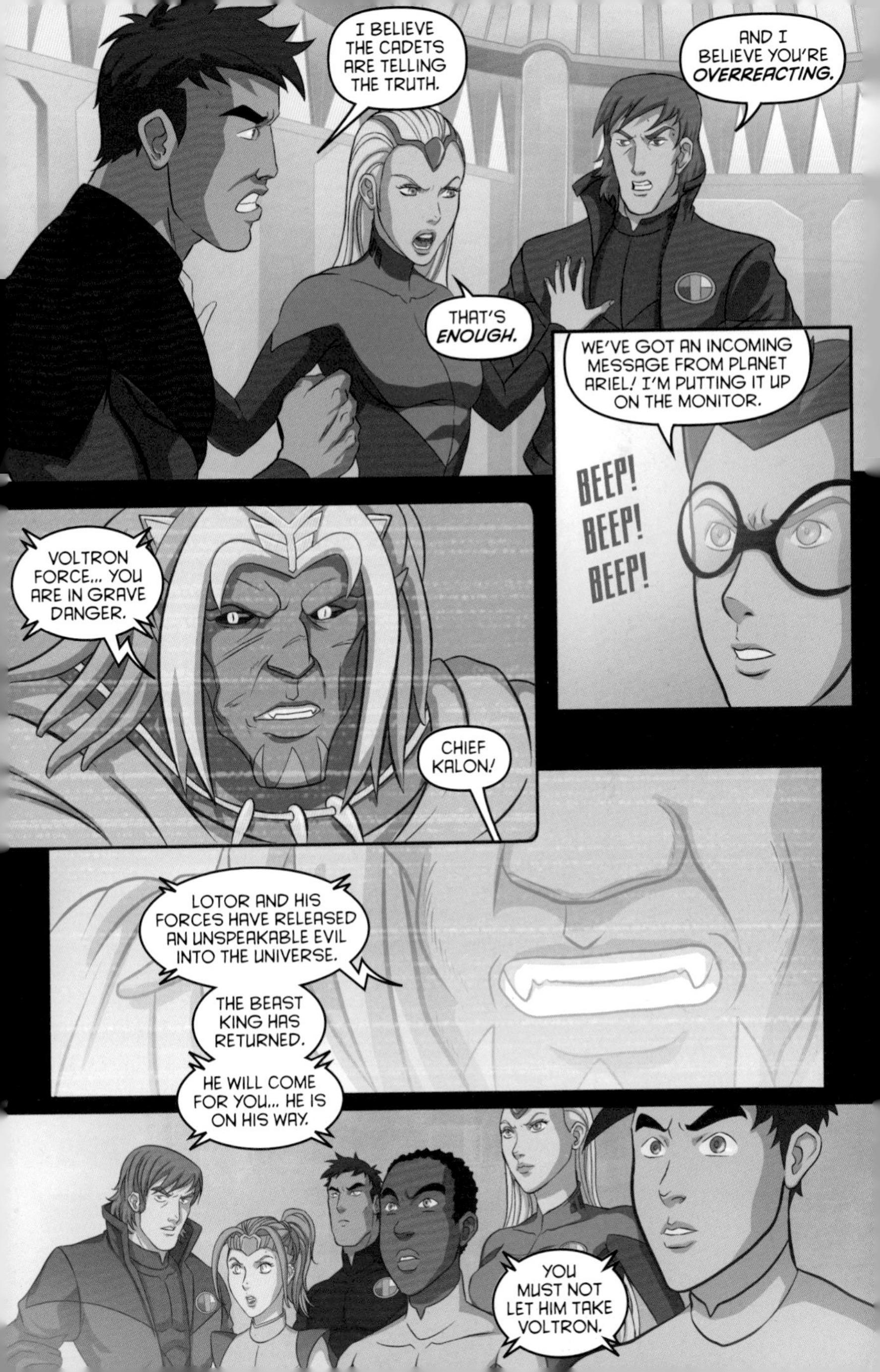
I BELIEVE THE CADETS ARE TELLING THE TRUTH.
AND I BELIEVE YOU'RE OVERREACTING.
THAT'S ENOUGH.
WE'VE GOT AN INCOMING MESSAGE FROM PLANET ARIEL! I'M PUTTING IT UP ON THE MONITOR.
BEEP! BEEP! BEEP!
VOLTRON FORCE... YOU ARE IN GRAVE DANGER.
CHIEF KALON!
LOTOR AND HIS FORCES HAVE RELEASED AN UNSPEAKABLE EVIL INTO THE UNIVERSE.
THE BEAST KING HAS RETURNED.
HE WILL COME FOR YOU... HE IS ON HIS WAY.
YOU MUST NOT LET HIM TAKE VOLTRON.

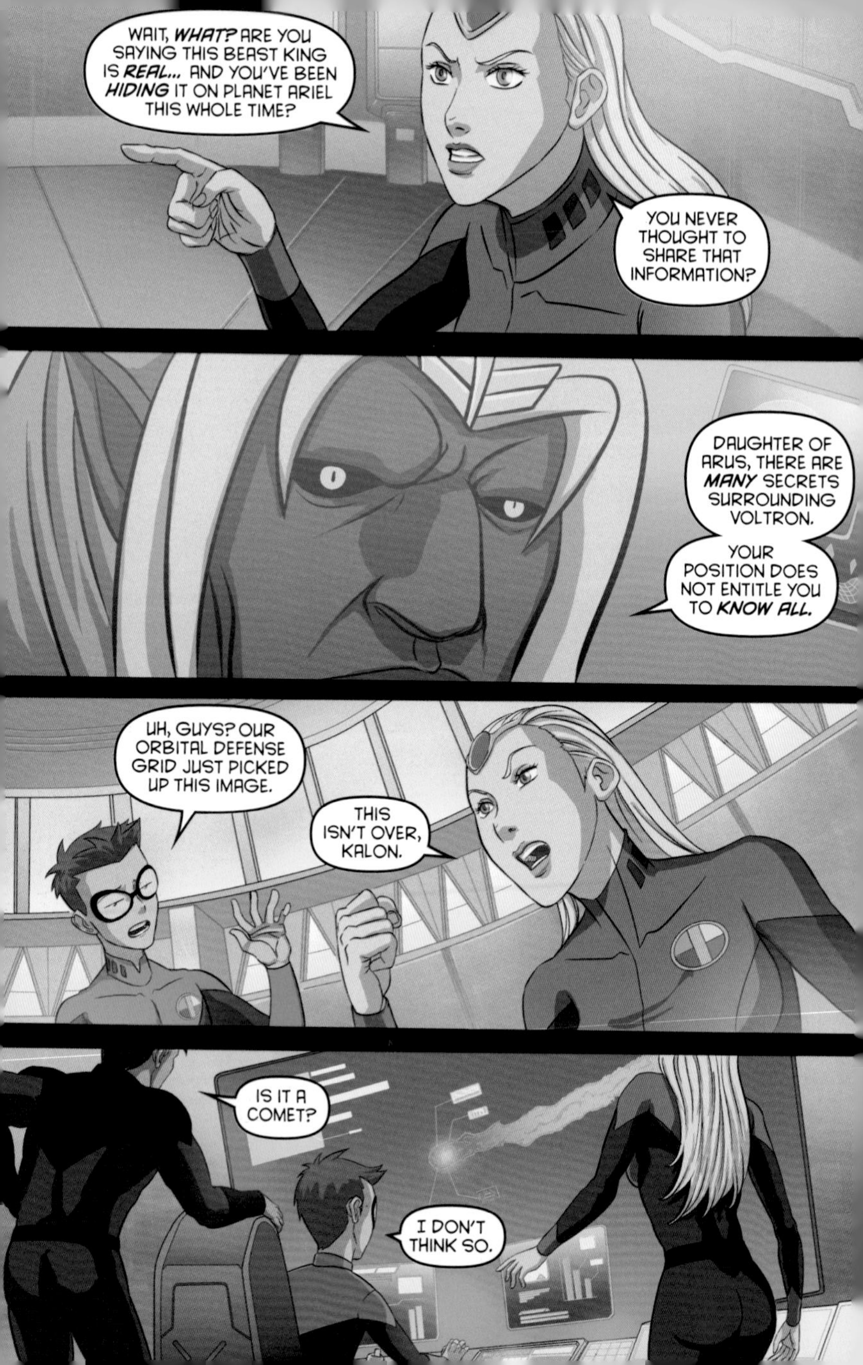
WAIT, WHAT? ARE YOU SAYING THIS BEAST KING IS REAL... AND YOU'VE BEEN HIDING IT ON PLANET ARIEL THIS WHOLE TIME?
YOU NEVER THOUGHT TO SHARE THAT INFORMATION?
DAUGHTER OF ARUS, THERE ARE MANY SECRETS SURROUNDING VOLTRON.
YOUR POSITION DOES NOT ENTITLE YOU TO KNOW ALL.
UH, GUYS? OUR ORBITAL DEFENSE GRID JUST PICKED UP THIS IMAGE.
THIS ISN'T OVER, KALON.
IS IT A COMET?
I DON'T THINK SO.

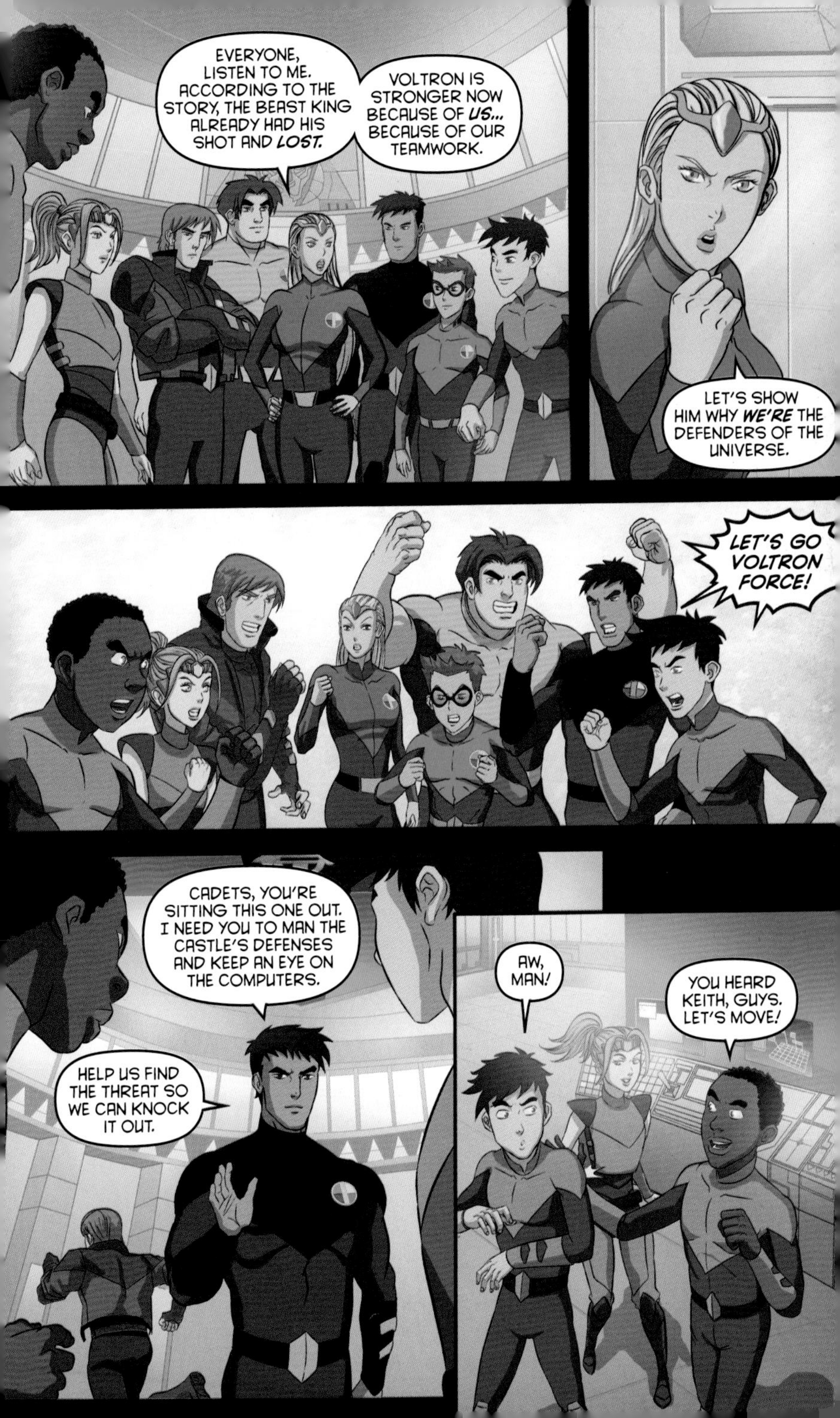
EVERYONE, LISTEN TO ME. ACCORDING TO THE STORY, THE BEAST KING ALREADY HAD HIS SHOT AND *LOST.*
VOLTRON IS STRONGER NOW BECAUSE OF *US...* BECAUSE OF OUR TEAMWORK.
LET'S SHOW HIM WHY *WE'RE* THE DEFENDERS OF THE UNIVERSE.
LET'S GO VOLTRON FORCE!
CADETS, YOU'RE SITTING THIS ONE OUT. I NEED YOU TO MAN THE CASTLE'S DEFENSES AND KEEP AN EYE ON THE COMPUTERS.
HELP US FIND THE THREAT SO WE CAN KNOCK IT OUT.
AW, MAN!
YOU HEARD KEITH, GUYS. LET'S MOVE!

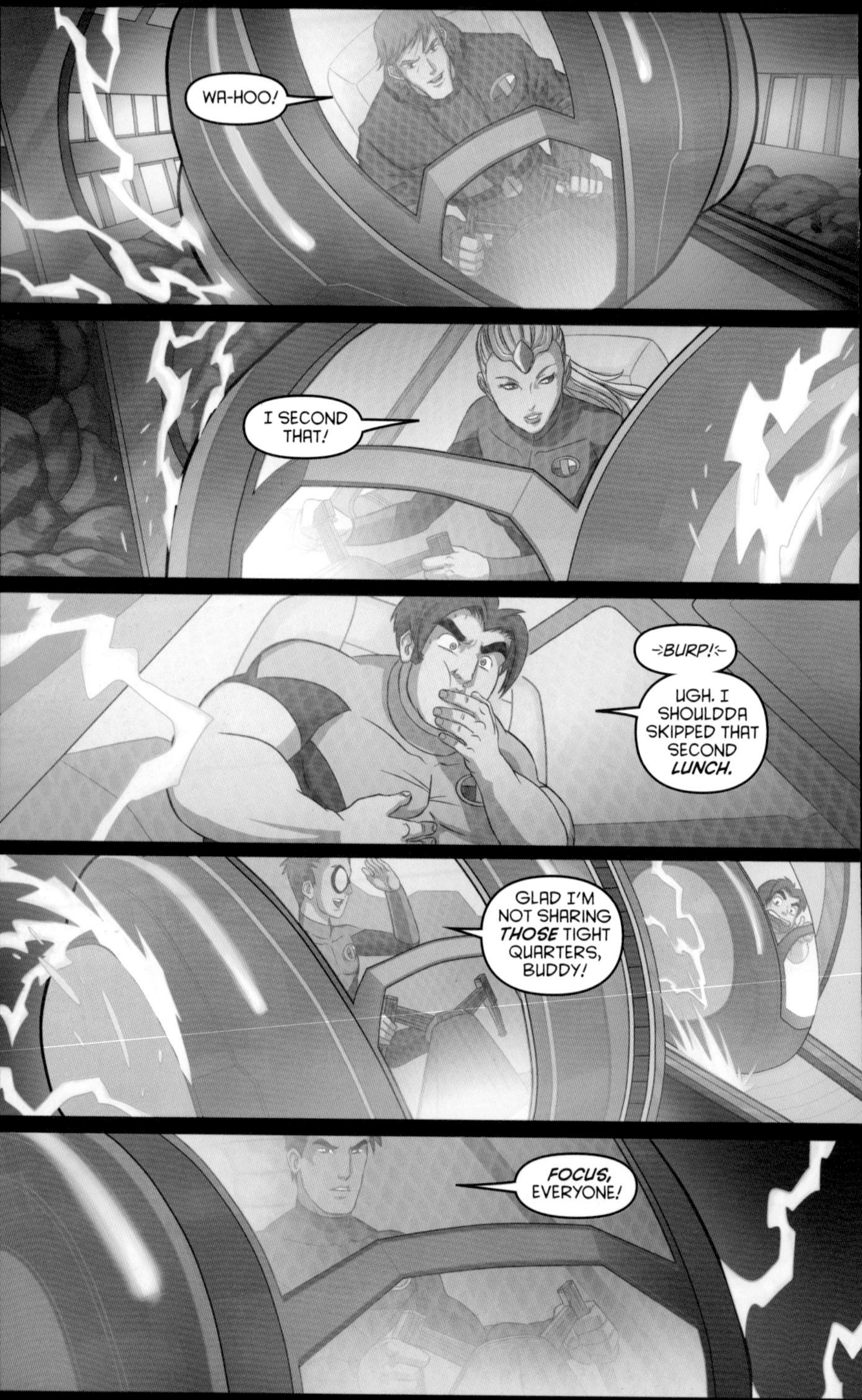
WA-HOO!
I SECOND THAT!
BURP!
UGH. I SHOULDDA SKIPPED THAT SECOND LUNCH.
GLAD I'M NOT SHARING THOSE TIGHT QUARTERS, BUDDY!
FOCUS, EVERYONE!

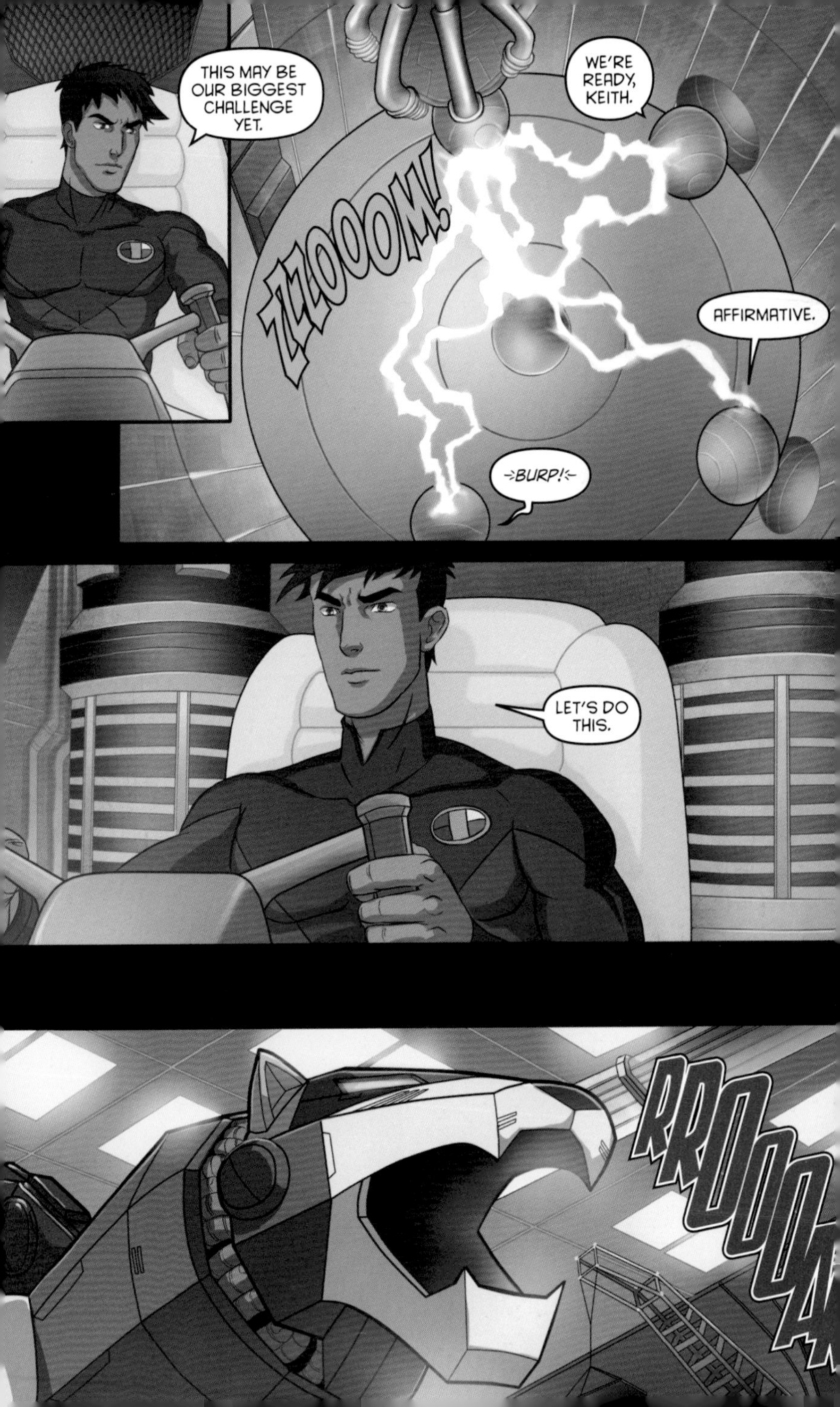
THIS MAY BE OUR BIGGEST CHALLENGE YET.
WE'RE READY, KEITH.
ZZZOOOM!
AFFIRMATIVE.
-BURP!-
LET'S DO THIS.
RROOOA

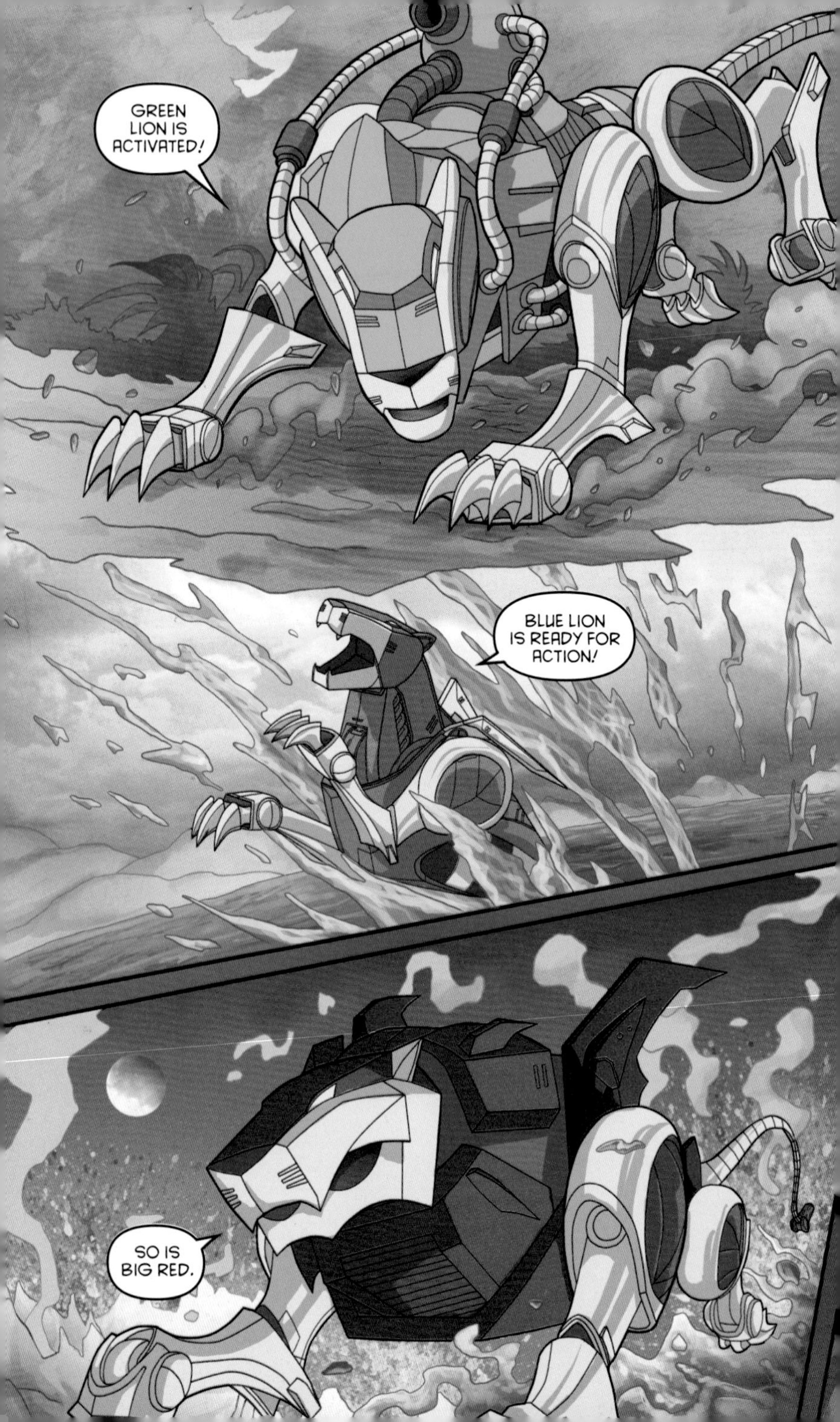
GREEN LION IS ACTIVATED!
BLUE LION IS READY FOR ACTION!
SO IS BIG RED.

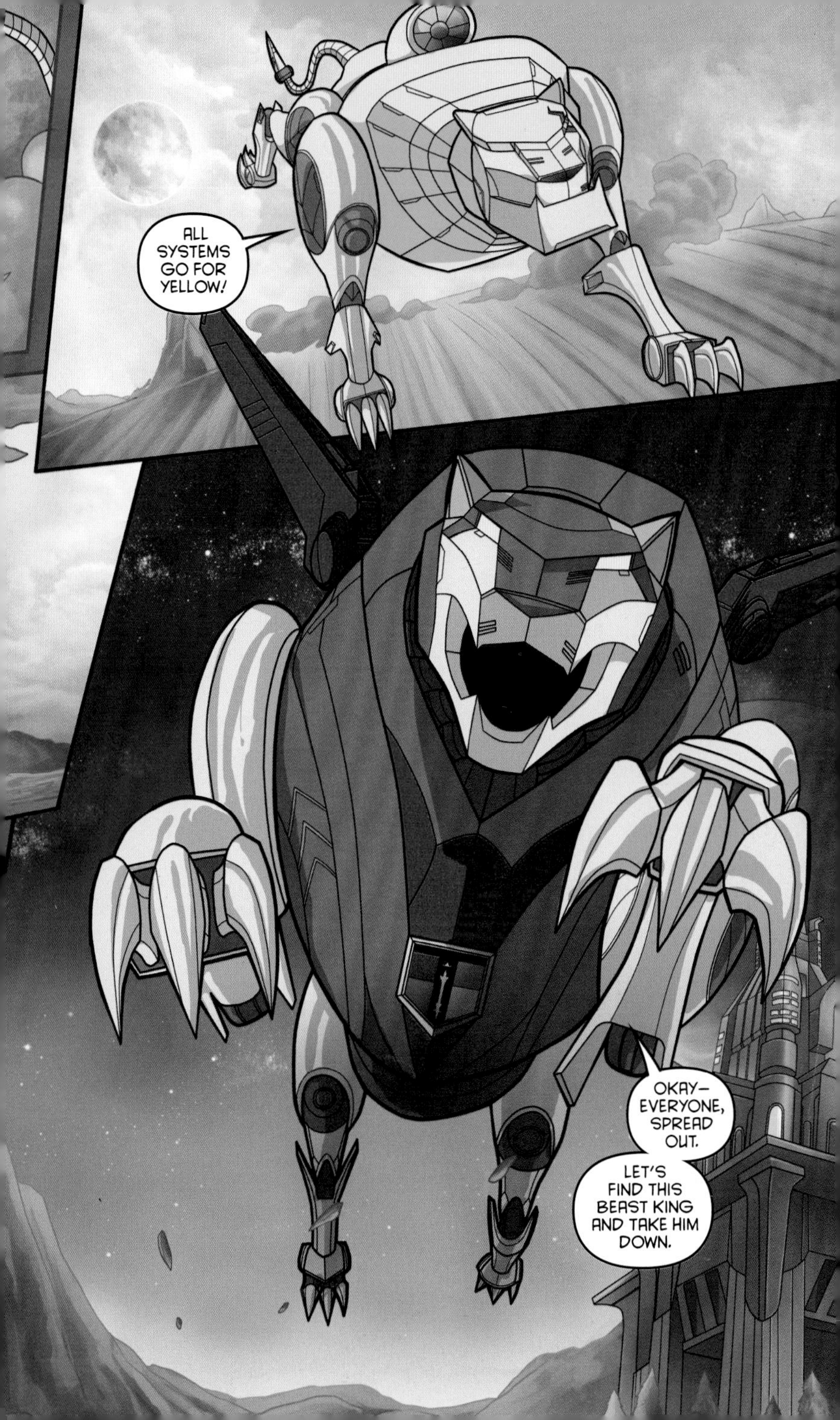
ALL SYSTEMS GO FOR YELLOW!
OKAY— EVERYONE, SPREAD OUT.
LET'S FIND THIS BEAST KING AND TAKE HIM DOWN.

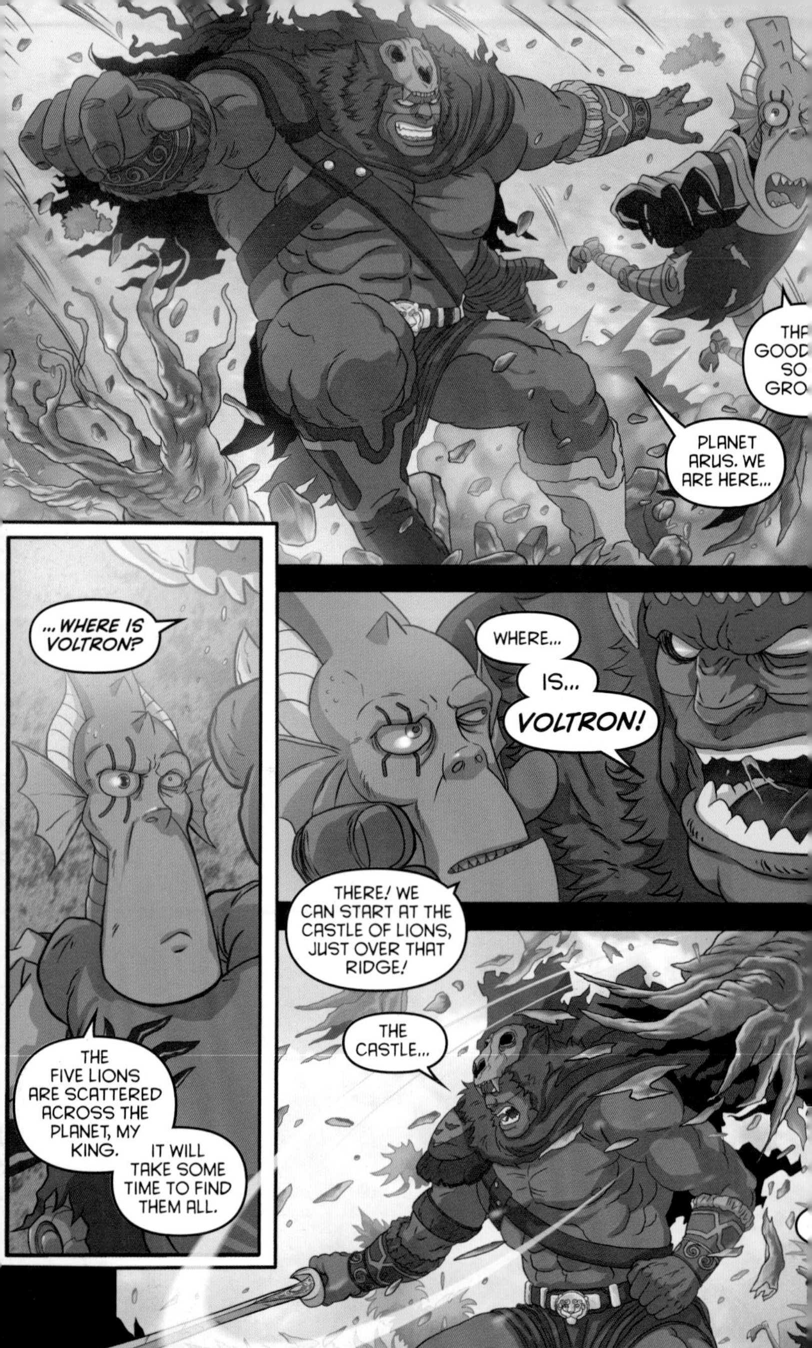

PLANET ARUS. WE ARE HERE...
...WHERE IS VOLTRON?
THE FIVE LIONS ARE SCATTERED ACROSS THE PLANET, MY KING.
IT WILL TAKE SOME TIME TO FIND THEM ALL.
WHERE...
IS...
VOLTRON!
THERE! WE CAN START AT THE CASTLE OF LIONS, JUST OVER THAT RIDGE!
THE CASTLE...

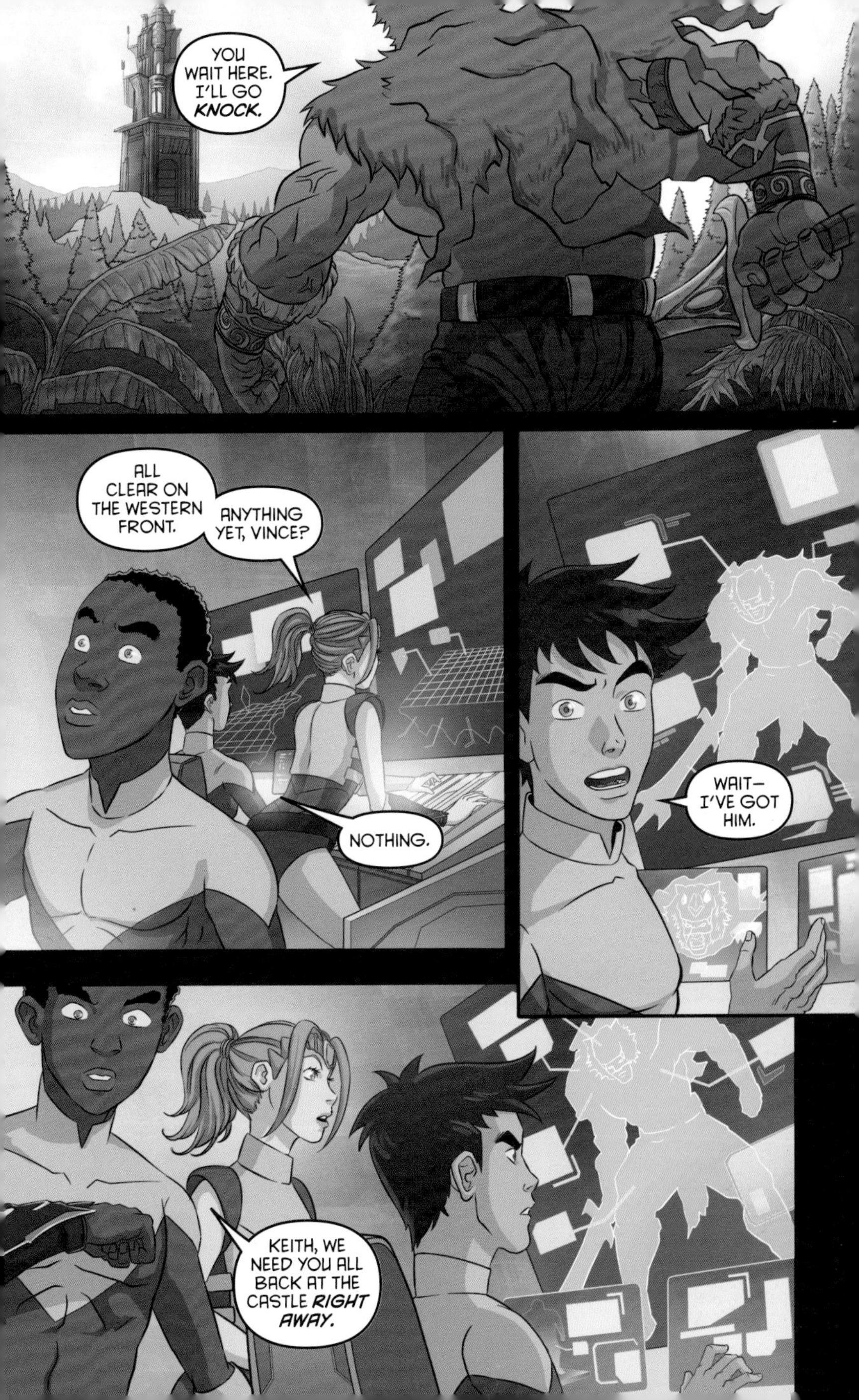
YOU WAIT HERE. I'LL GO KNOCK.
ALL CLEAR ON THE WESTERN FRONT.
ANYTHING YET, VINCE?
NOTHING.
WAIT— I'VE GOT HIM.
KEITH, WE NEED YOU ALL BACK AT THE CASTLE RIGHT AWAY.

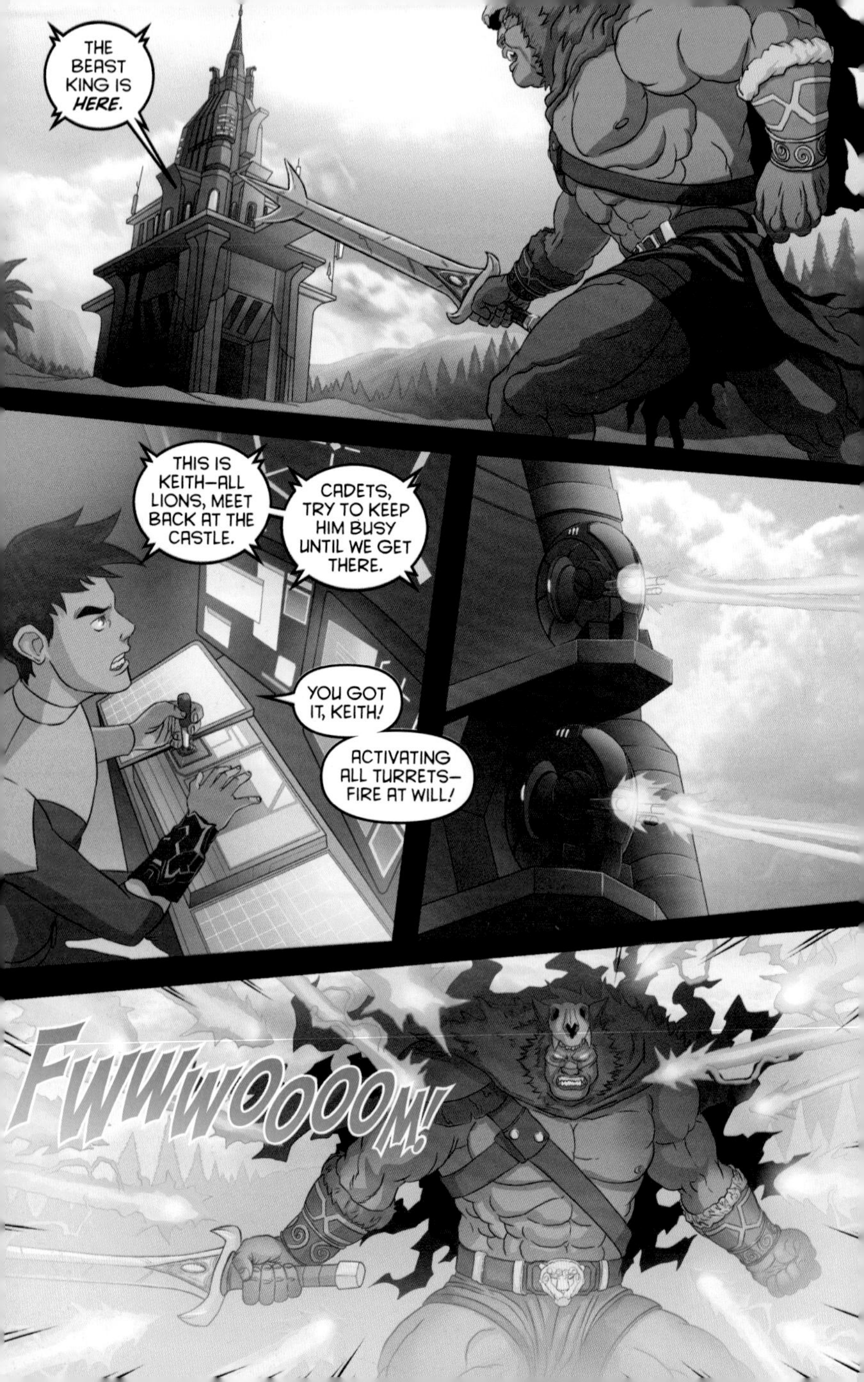
THE BEAST KING IS *HERE.*
THIS IS KEITH—ALL LIONS, MEET BACK AT THE CASTLE.
CADETS, TRY TO KEEP HIM BUSY UNTIL WE GET THERE.
YOU GOT IT, KEITH!
ACTIVATING ALL TURRETS—FIRE AT WILL!
FWWWOOOOM!

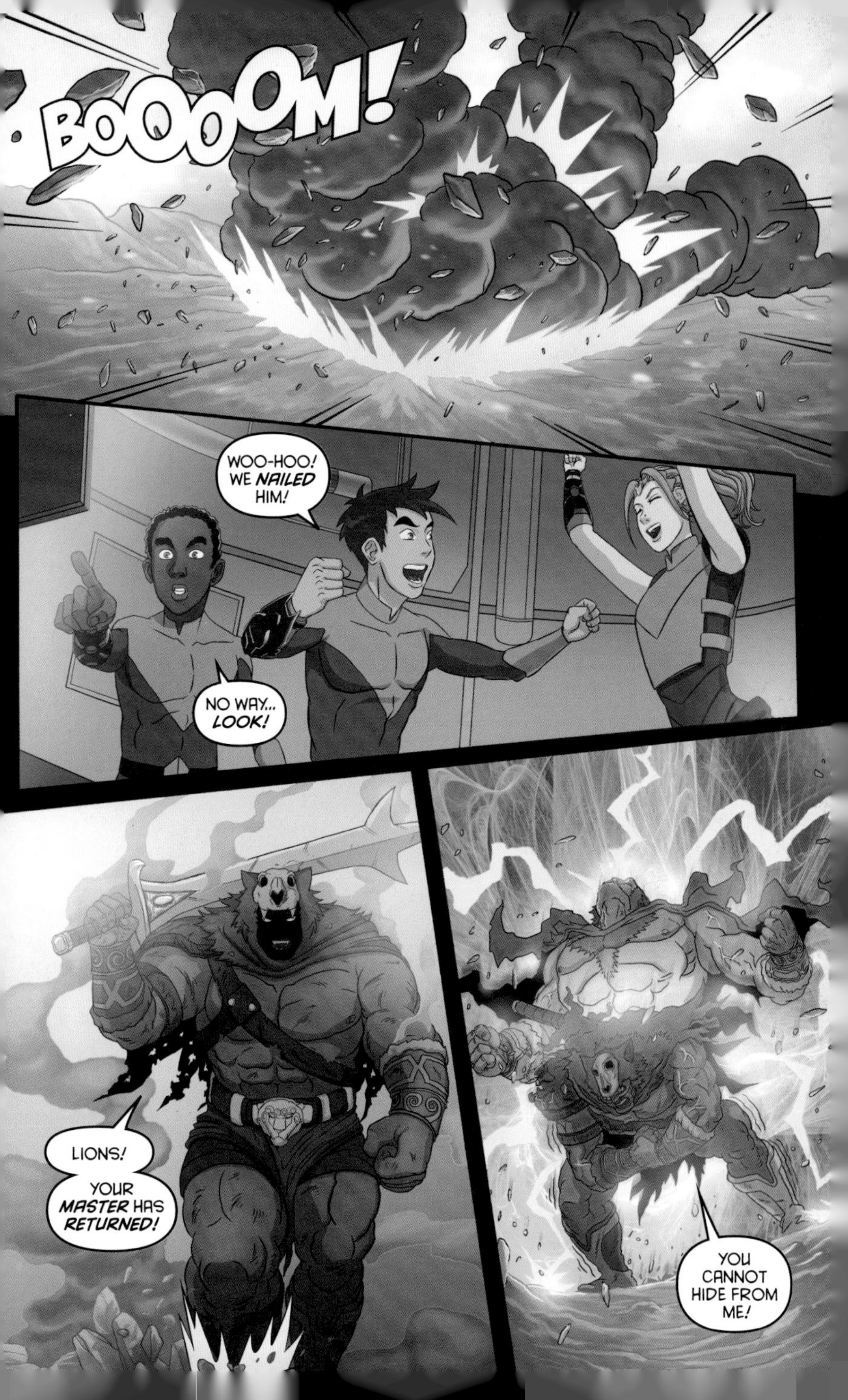
BOOOOM!
WOO-HOO! WE NAILED HIM!
NO WAY... LOOK!
LIONS!
YOUR MASTER HAS RETURNED!
YOU CANNOT HIDE FROM ME!

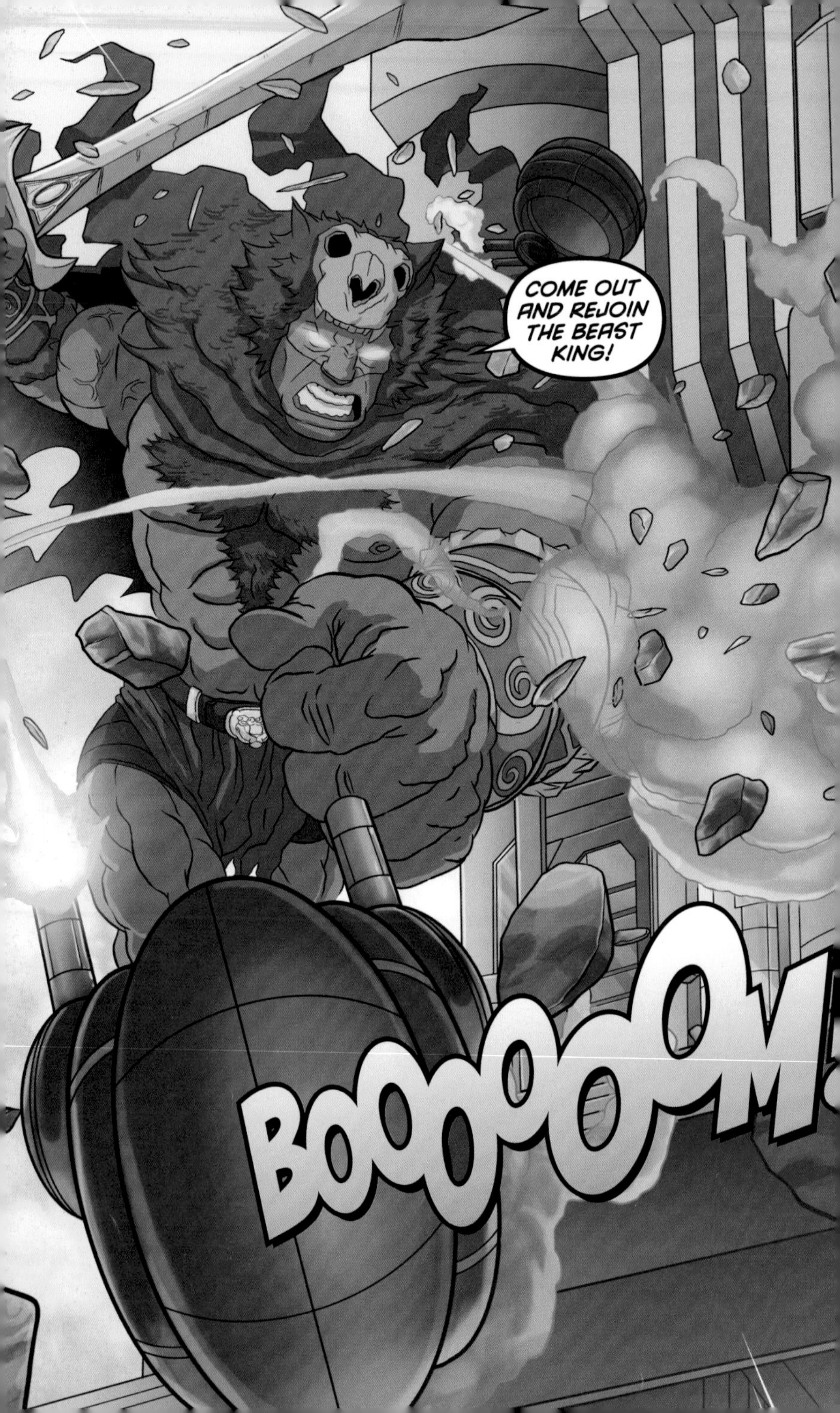
COME OUT AND REJOIN THE BEAST KING!
BOOOOOOM!

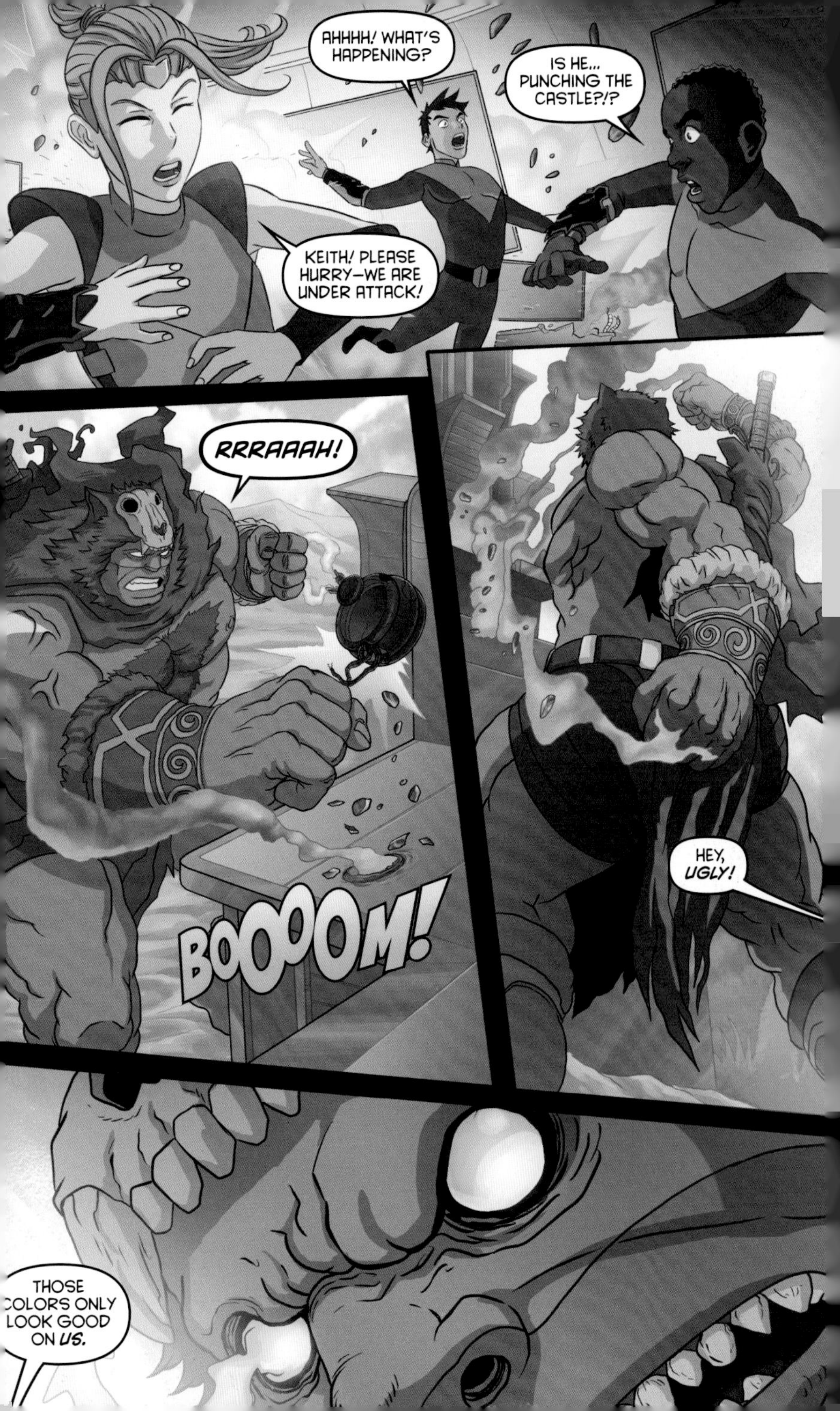
AHHHH! WHAT'S HAPPENING?
IS HE... PUNCHING THE CASTLE?!?
KEITH! PLEASE HURRY—WE ARE UNDER ATTACK!
RRRAAAH!
BOOOOM!
HEY, UGLY!
THOSE COLORS ONLY LOOK GOOD ON US.

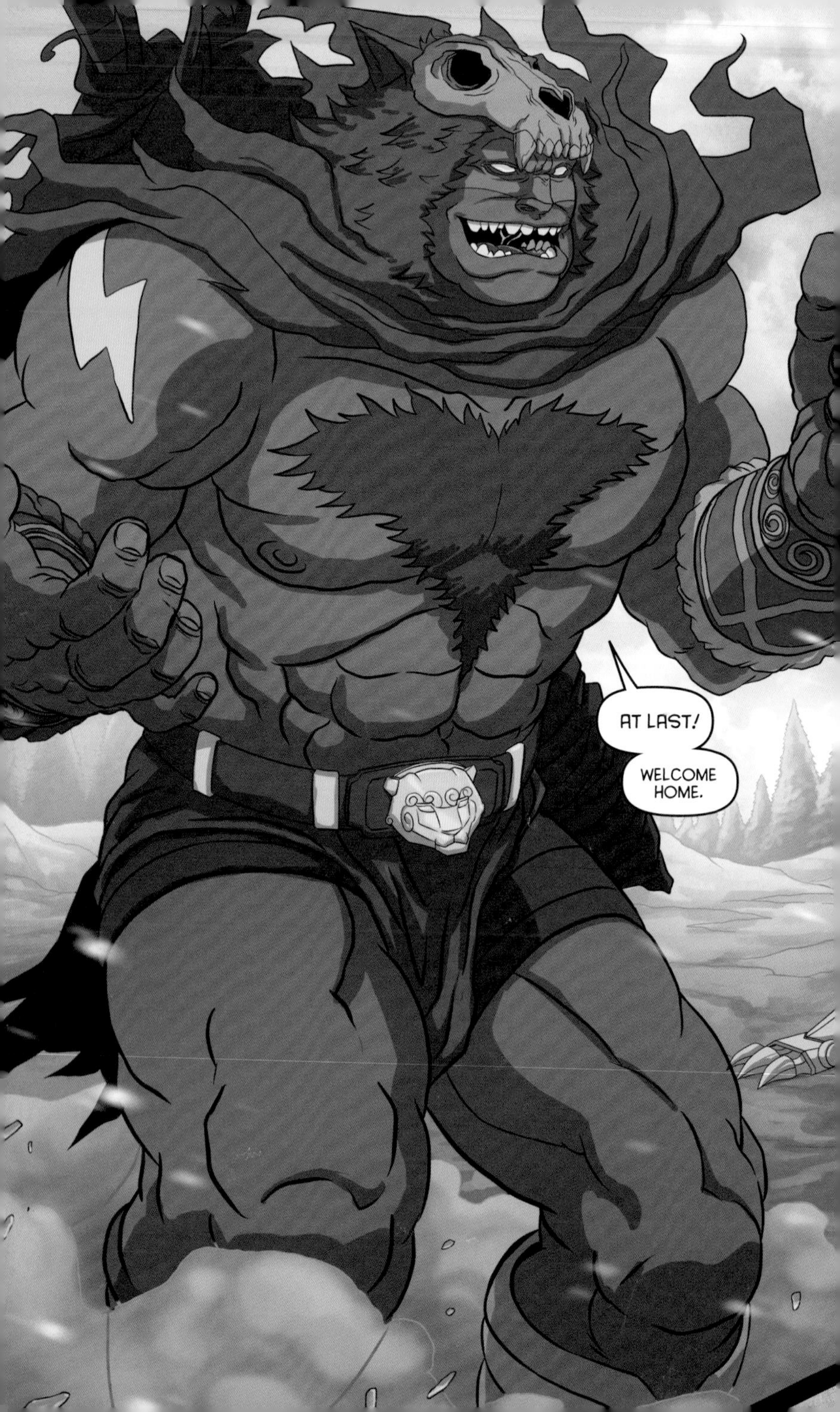
AT LAST!
WELCOME HOME.

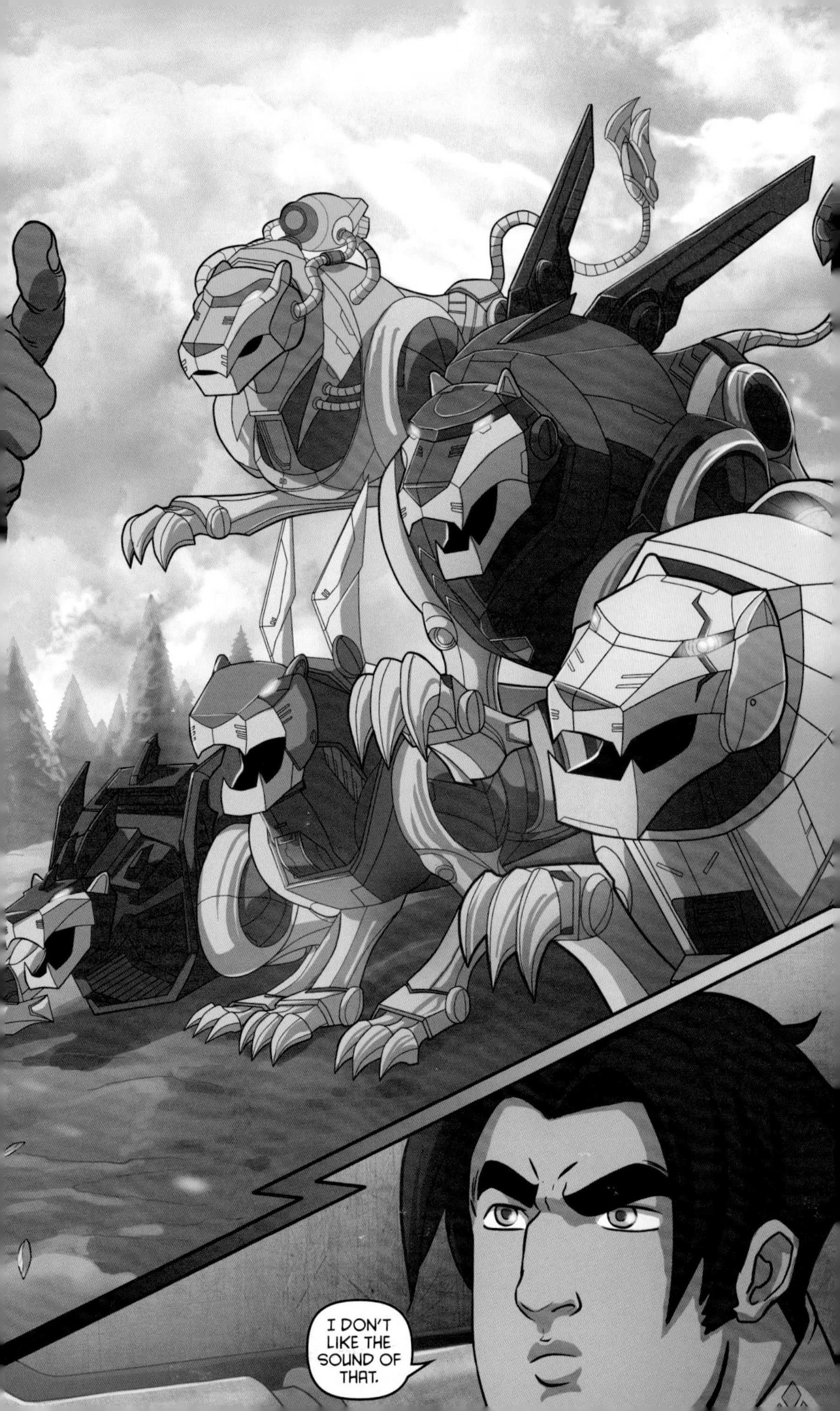
I DON'T LIKE THE SOUND OF THAT.

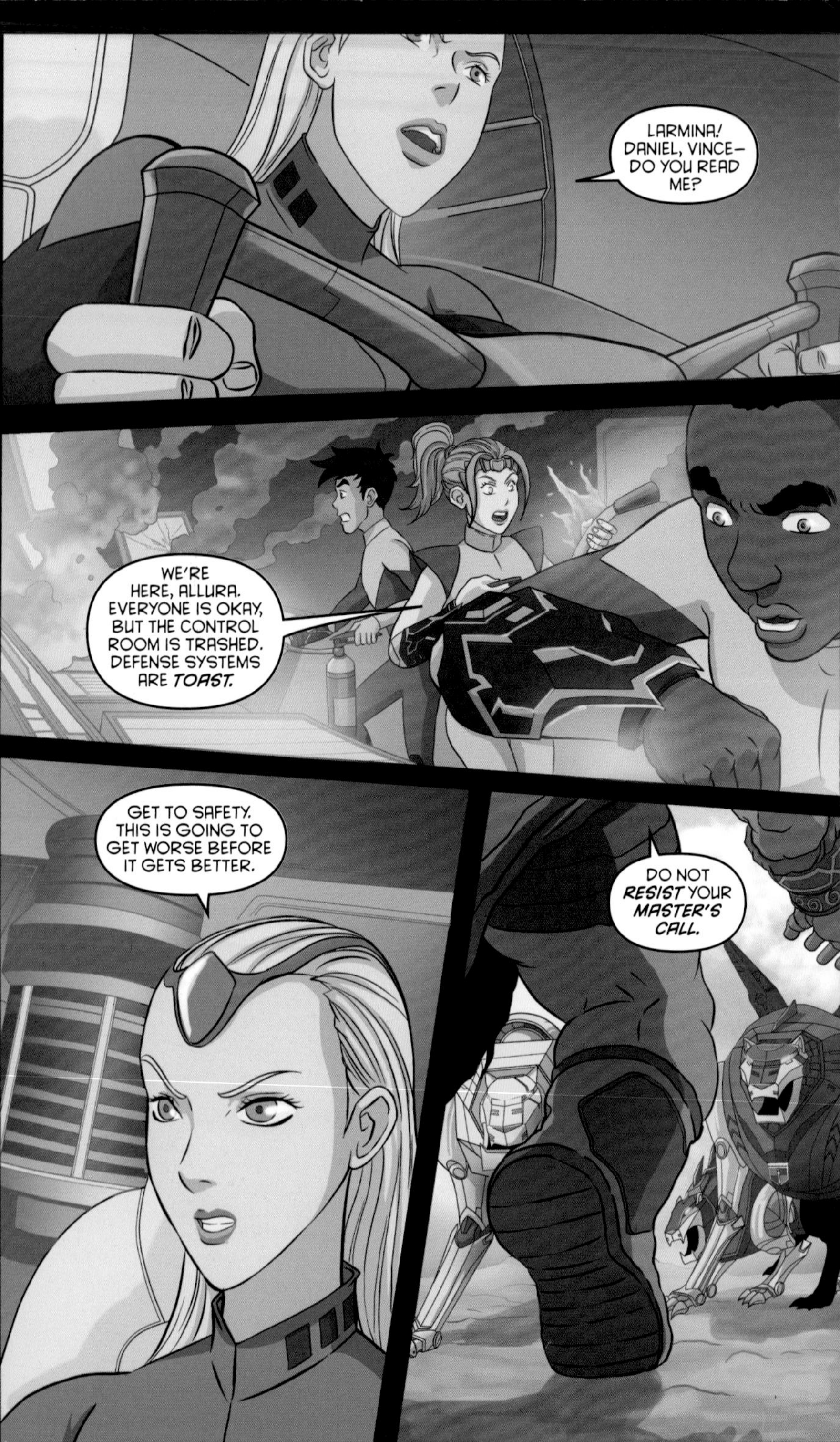
LARMINA! DANIEL, VINCE— DO YOU READ ME?
WE'RE HERE, ALLURA. EVERYONE IS OKAY, BUT THE CONTROL ROOM IS TRASHED. DEFENSE SYSTEMS ARE *TOAST.*
GET TO SAFETY. THIS IS GOING TO GET WORSE BEFORE IT GETS BETTER.
DO NOT *RESIST* YOUR *MASTER'S CALL.*

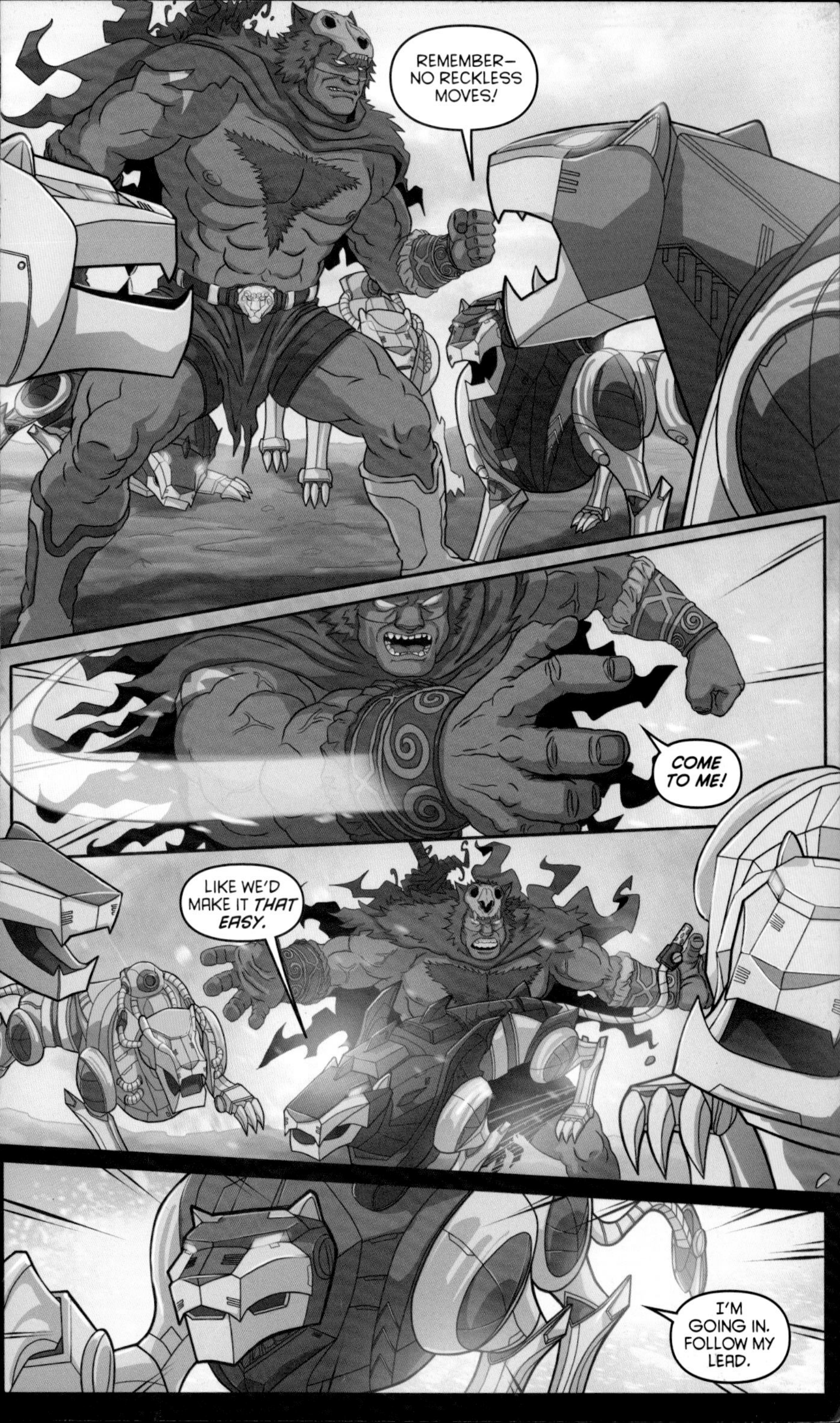
REMEMBER—NO RECKLESS MOVES!
COME TO ME!
LIKE WE'D MAKE IT *THAT EASY.*
I'M GOING IN. FOLLOW MY LEAD.

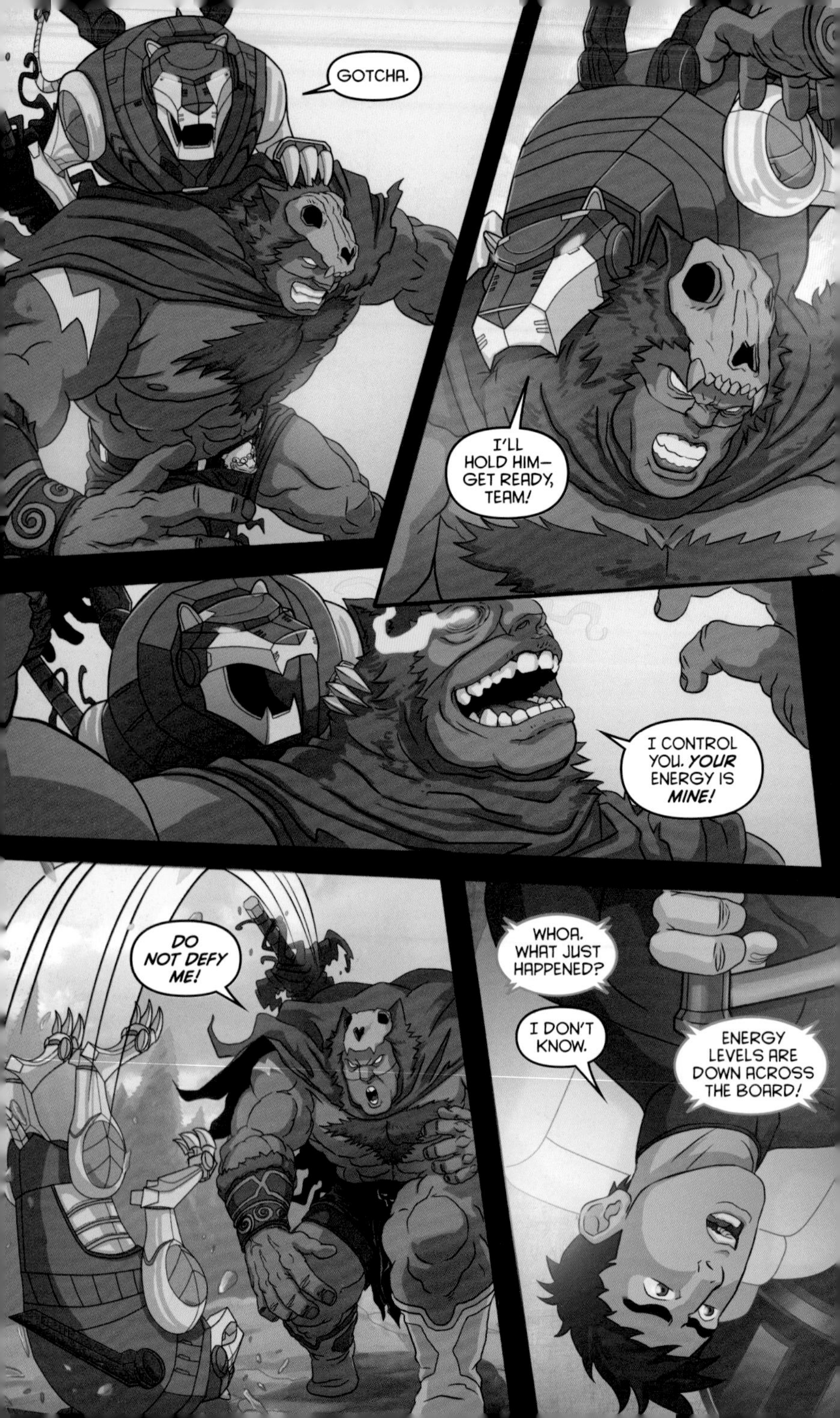
GOTCHA.
I'LL HOLD HIM— GET READY, TEAM!
I CONTROL YOU. *YOUR* ENERGY IS *MINE!*
DO NOT DEFY ME!
WHOA. WHAT JUST HAPPENED?
I DON'T KNOW.
ENERGY LEVELS ARE DOWN ACROSS THE BOARD!

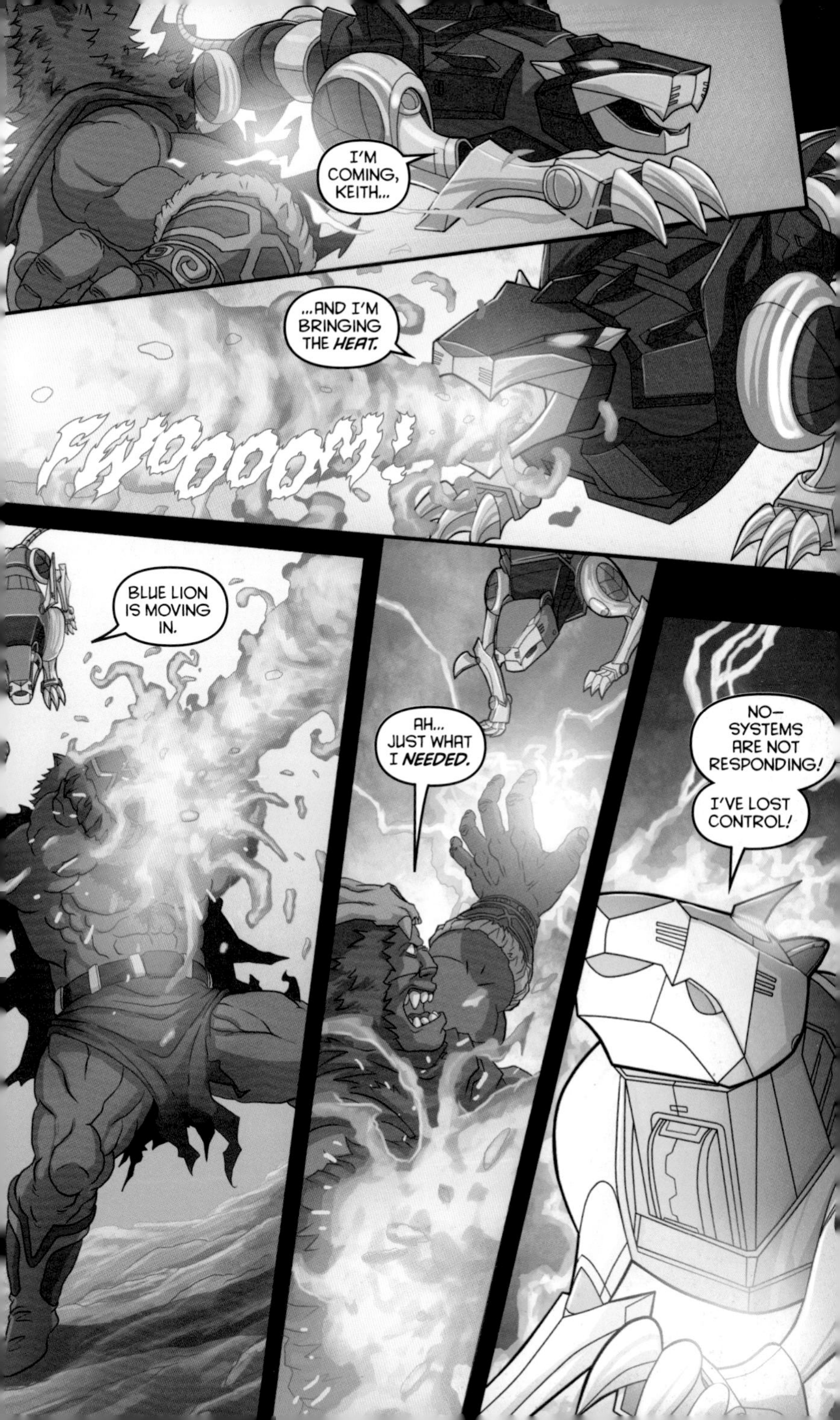
I'M COMING, KEITH...
...AND I'M BRINGING THE HEAT.
FWOOOOM!
BLUE LION IS MOVING IN.
AH... JUST WHAT I NEEDED.
NO— SYSTEMS ARE NOT RESPONDING!
I'VE LOST CONTROL!

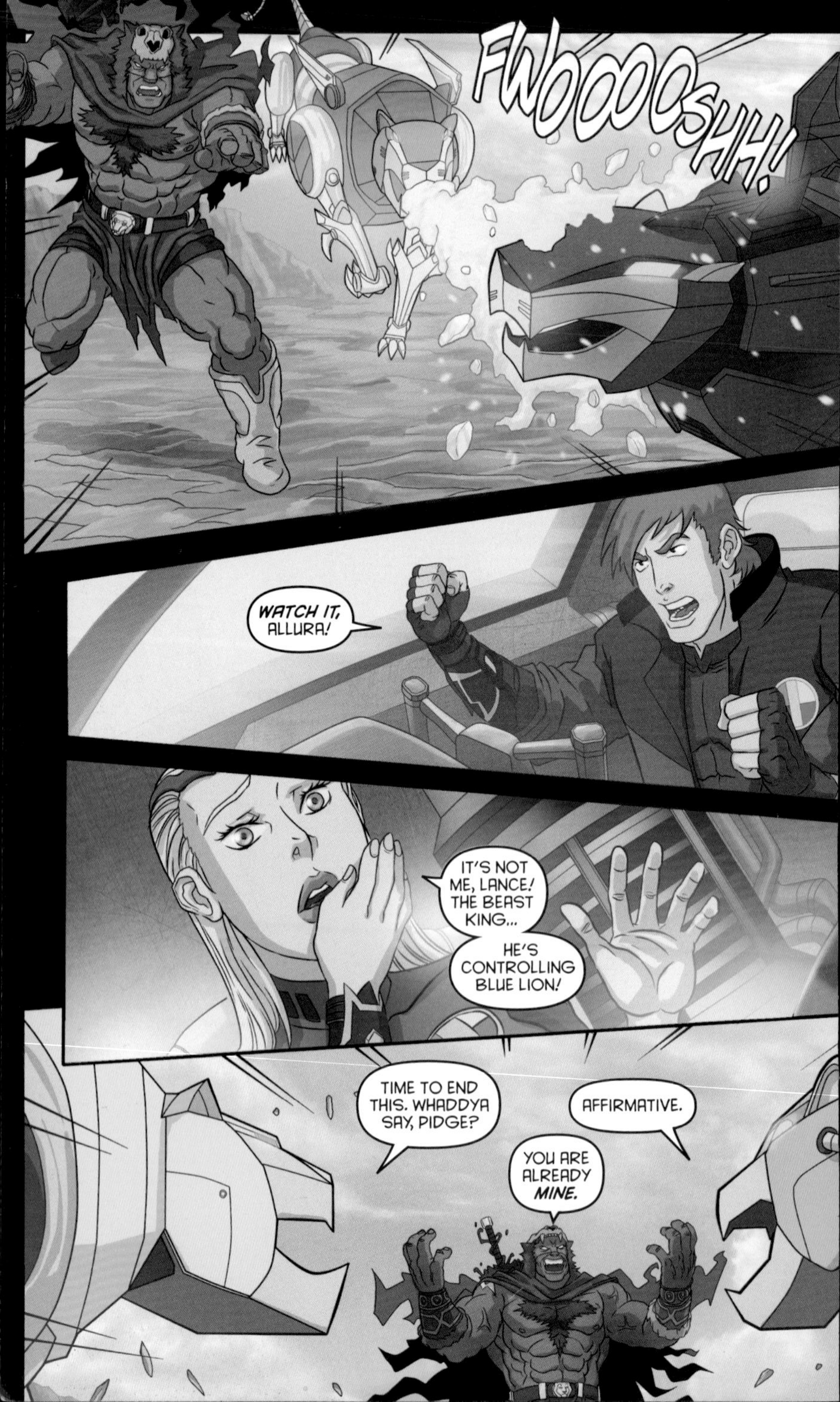
FWOOOOSHH!
WATCH IT, ALLURA!
IT'S NOT ME, LANCE! THE BEAST KING...
HE'S CONTROLLING BLUE LION!
TIME TO END THIS. WHADDYA SAY, PIDGE?
AFFIRMATIVE.
YOU ARE ALREADY MINE.

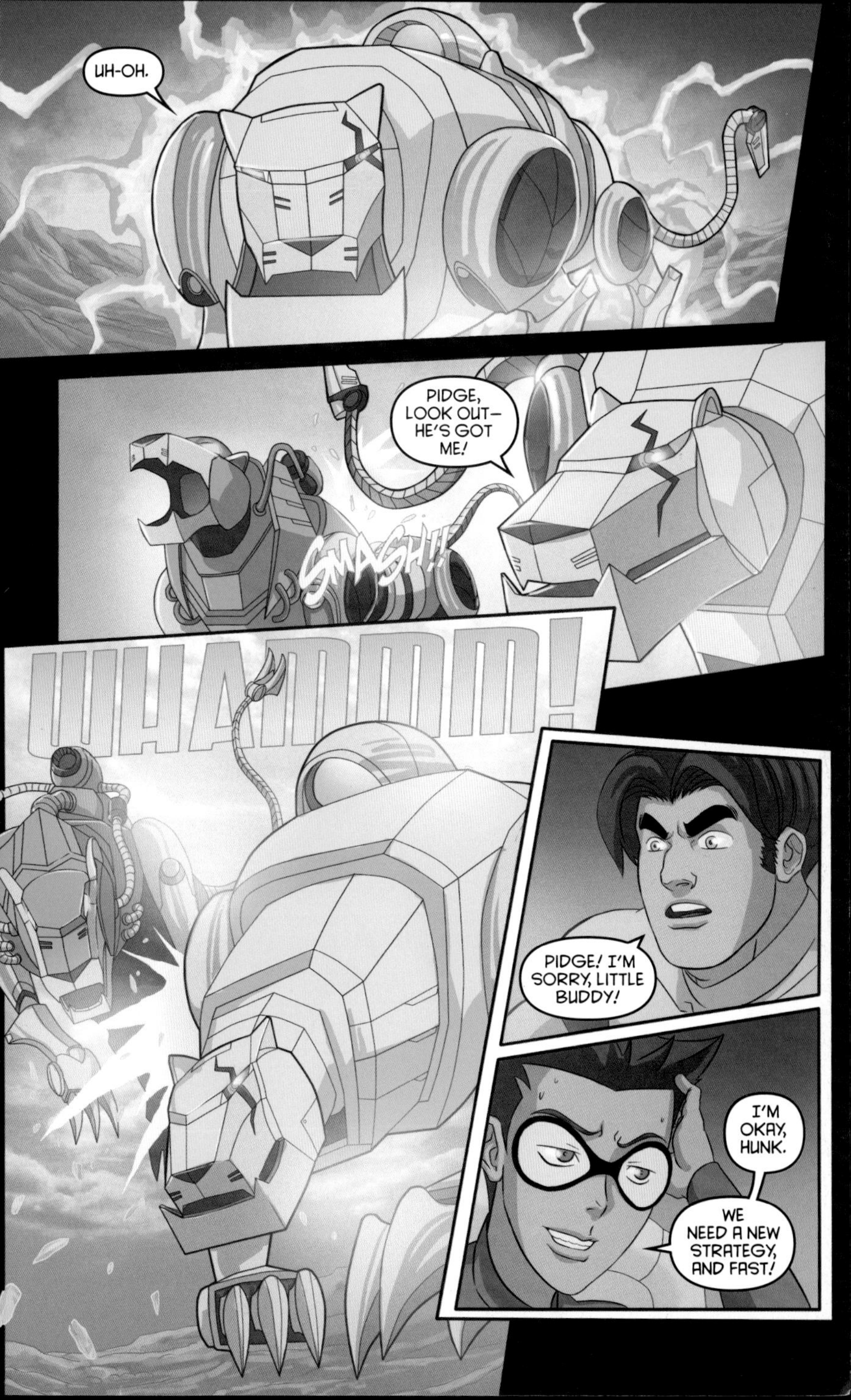
UH-OH.
PIDGE, LOOK OUT— HE'S GOT ME!
SMASH!!
WHAMMM!
PIDGE! I'M SORRY, LITTLE BUDDY!
I'M OKAY, HUNK.
WE NEED A NEW STRATEGY, AND FAST!

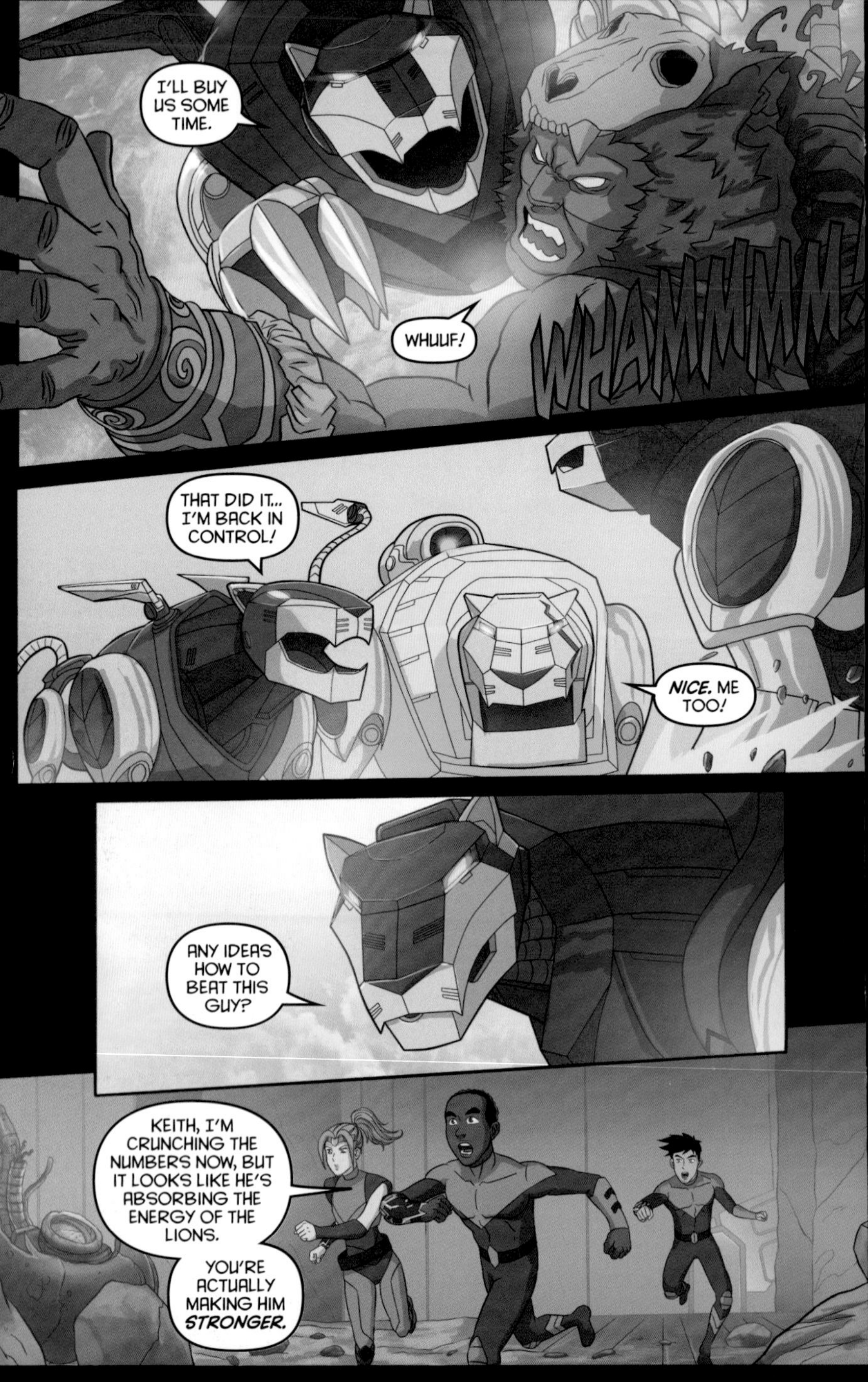

I'LL BUY US SOME TIME.
WHUUF!
WHAMMMMM!
THAT DID IT... I'M BACK IN CONTROL!
NICE. ME TOO!
ANY IDEAS HOW TO BEAT THIS GUY?
KEITH, I'M CRUNCHING THE NUMBERS NOW, BUT IT LOOKS LIKE HE'S ABSORBING THE ENERGY OF THE LIONS.
YOU'RE ACTUALLY MAKING HIM STRONGER.

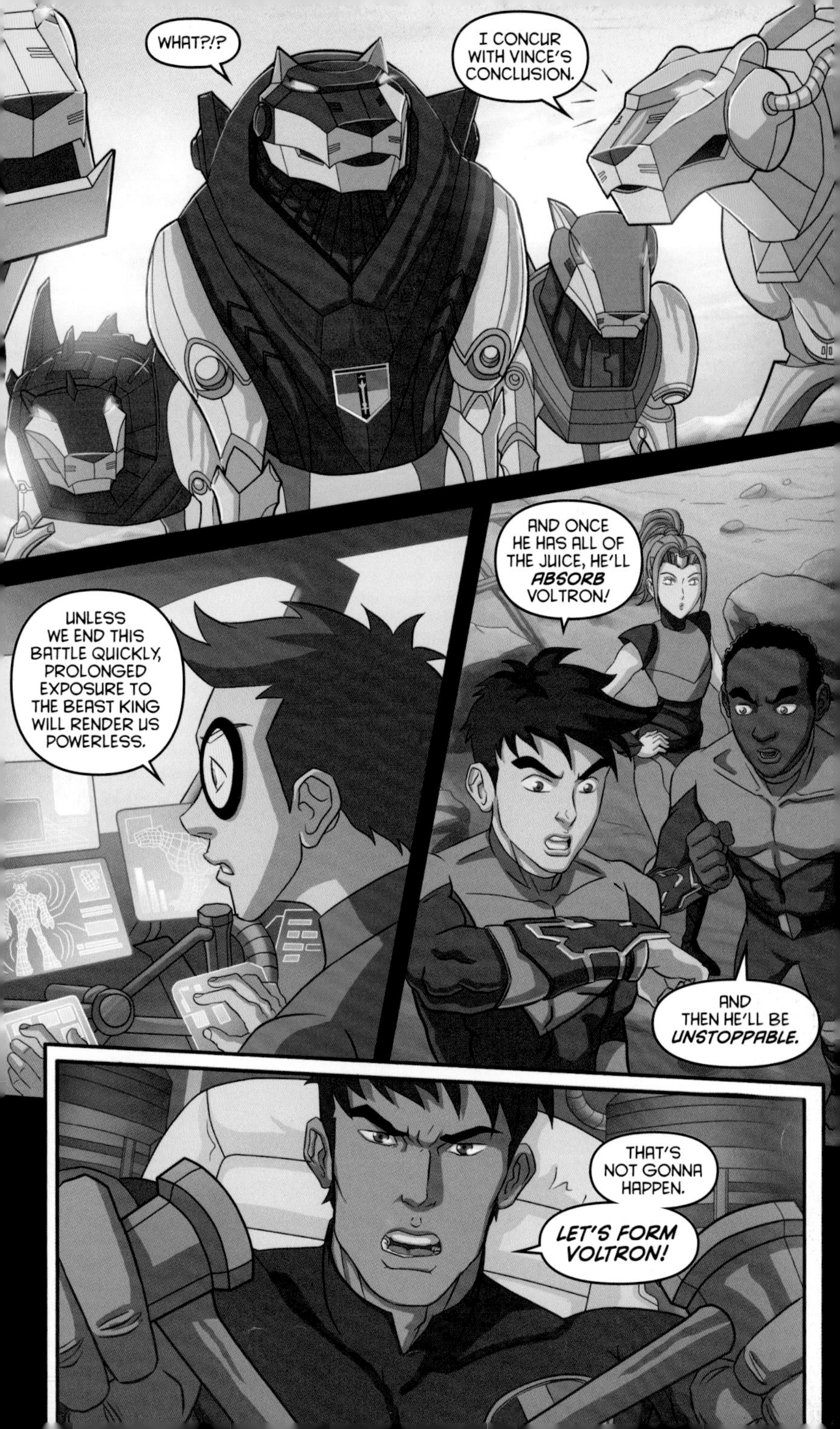
WHAT?!?
I CONCUR WITH VINCE'S CONCLUSION.
UNLESS WE END THIS BATTLE QUICKLY, PROLONGED EXPOSURE TO THE BEAST KING WILL RENDER US POWERLESS.
AND ONCE HE HAS ALL OF THE JUICE, HE'LL ABSORB VOLTRON!
AND THEN HE'LL BE UNSTOPPABLE.
THAT'S NOT GONNA HAPPEN.
LET'S FORM VOLTRON!

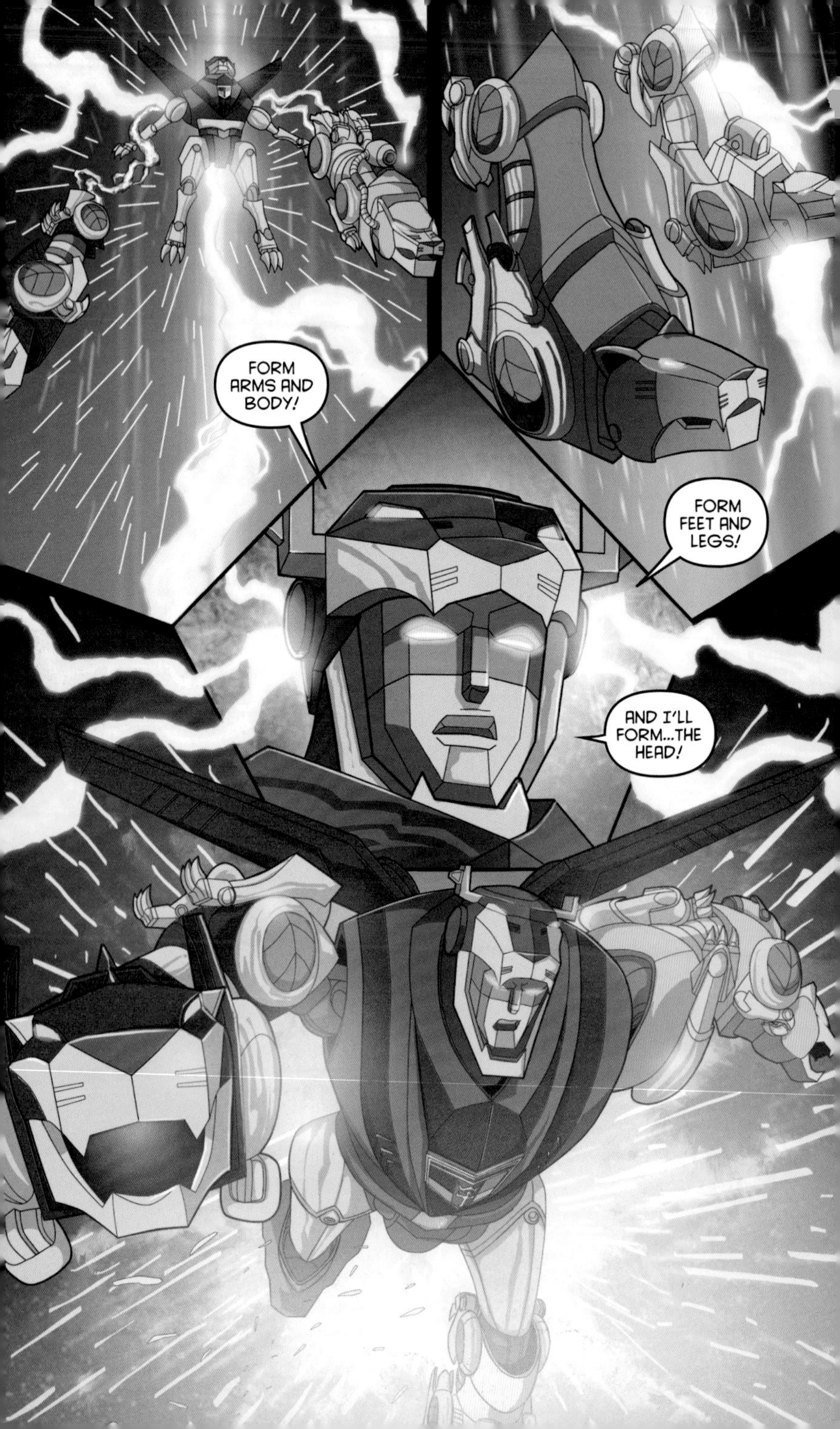
FORM ARMS AND BODY!
FORM FEET AND LEGS!
AND I'LL FORM...THE HEAD!

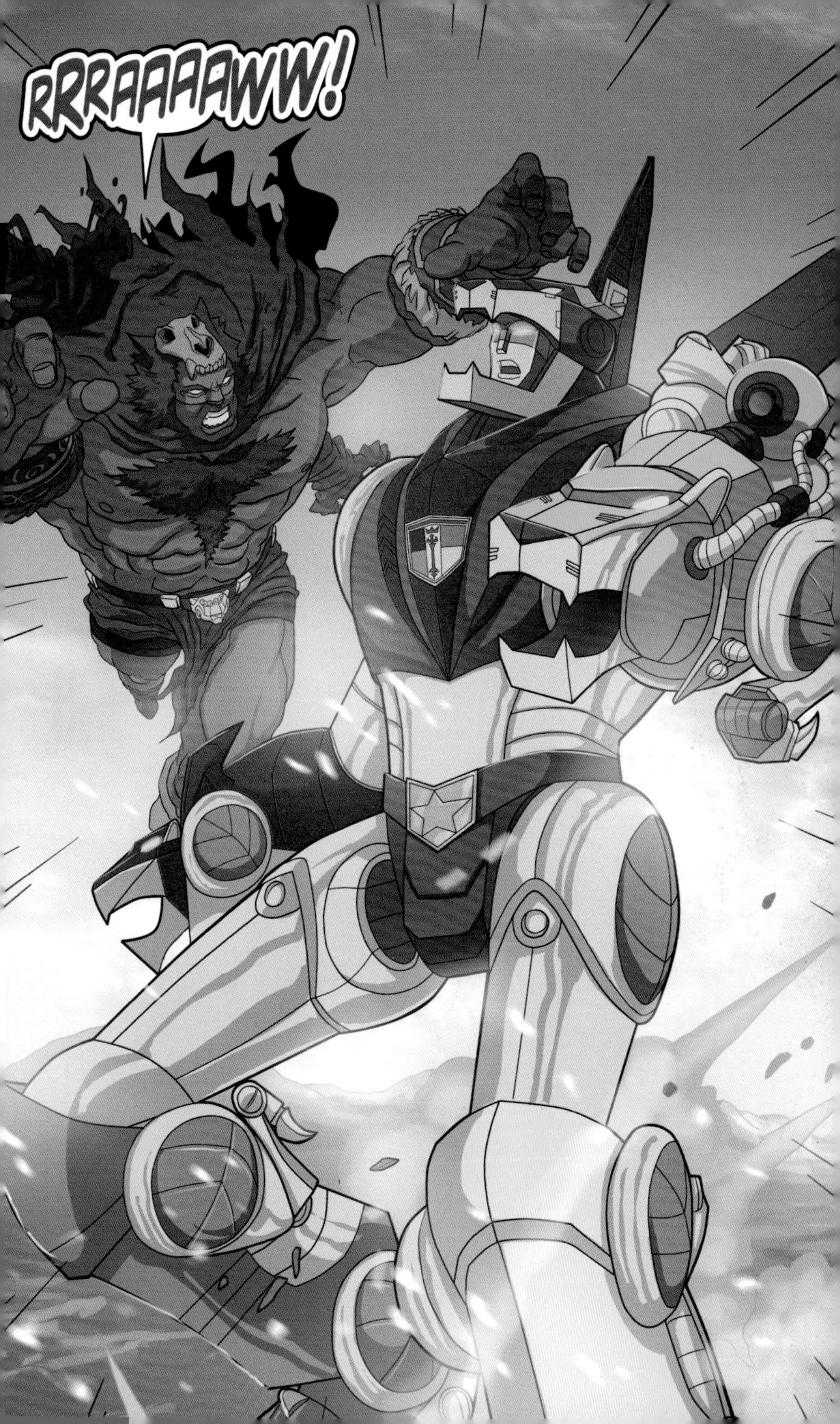
RRRAAAAAWW!

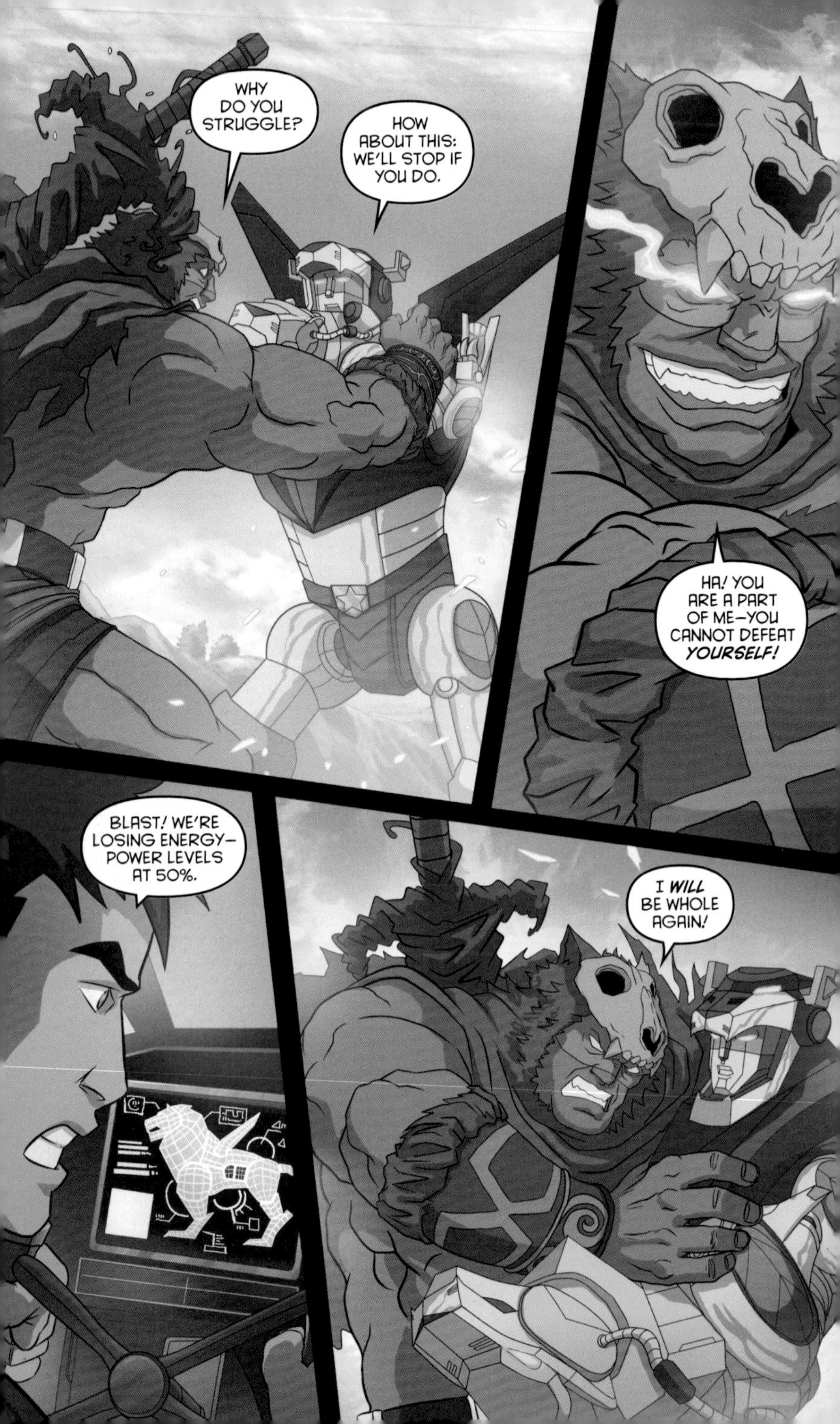
WHY DO YOU STRUGGLE?
HOW ABOUT THIS: WE'LL STOP IF YOU DO.
HA! YOU ARE A PART OF ME—YOU CANNOT DEFEAT *YOURSELF!*
BLAST! WE'RE LOSING ENERGY— POWER LEVELS AT 50%.
I *WILL* BE WHOLE AGAIN!

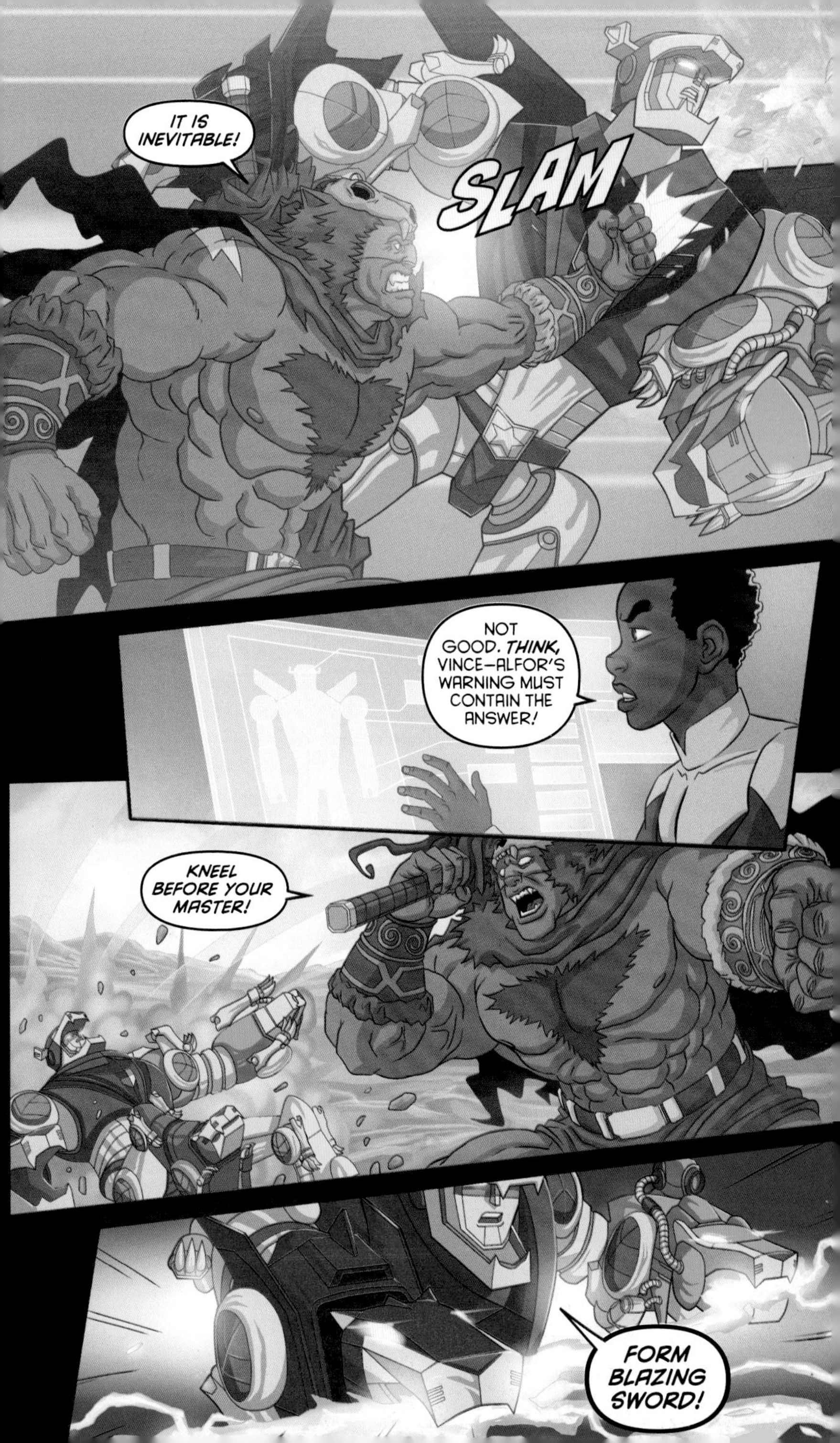
IT IS INEVITABLE!
SLAM
NOT GOOD. THINK, VINCE—ALFOR'S WARNING MUST CONTAIN THE ANSWER!
KNEEL BEFORE YOUR MASTER!
FORM BLAZING SWORD!

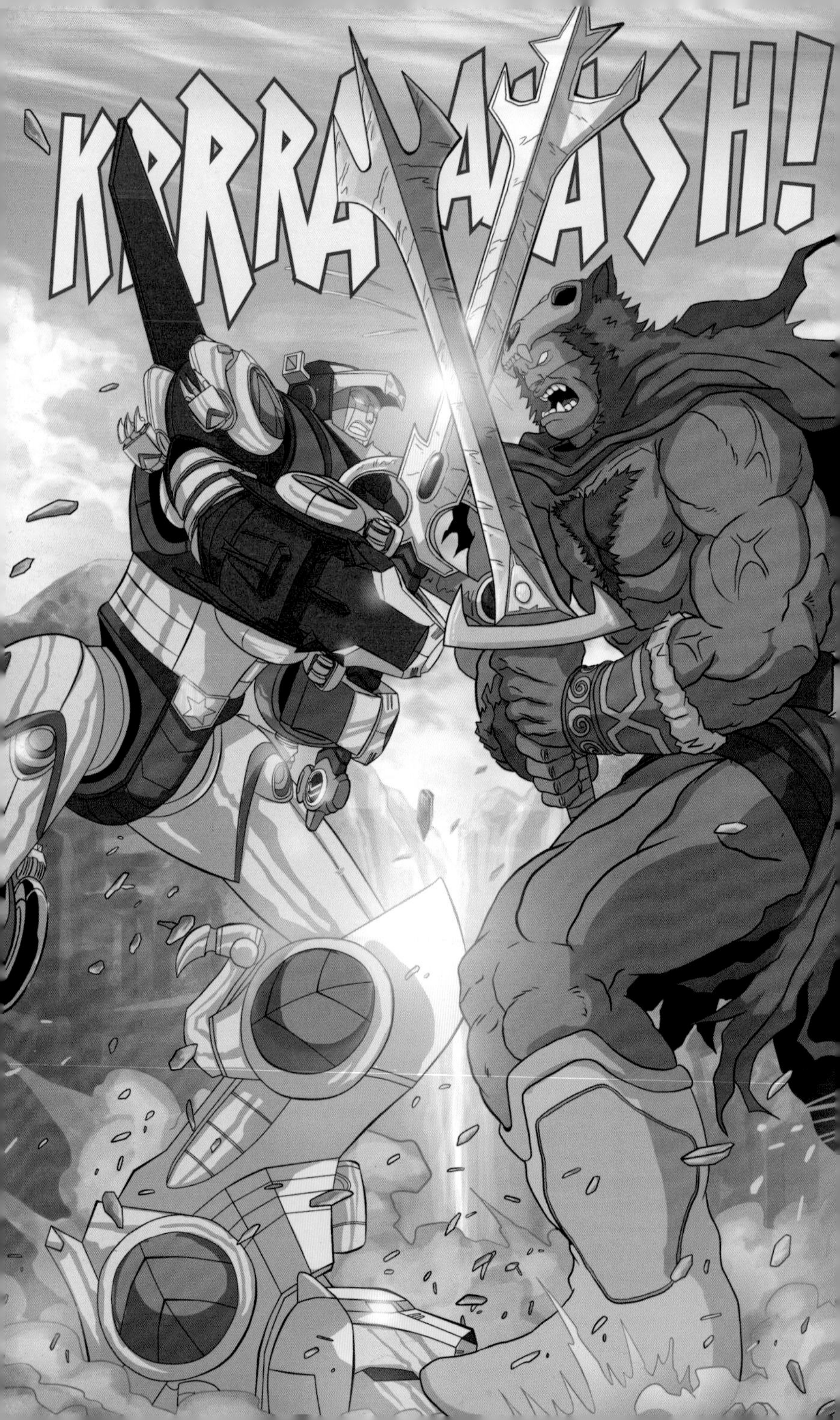
KRRRAAASH!

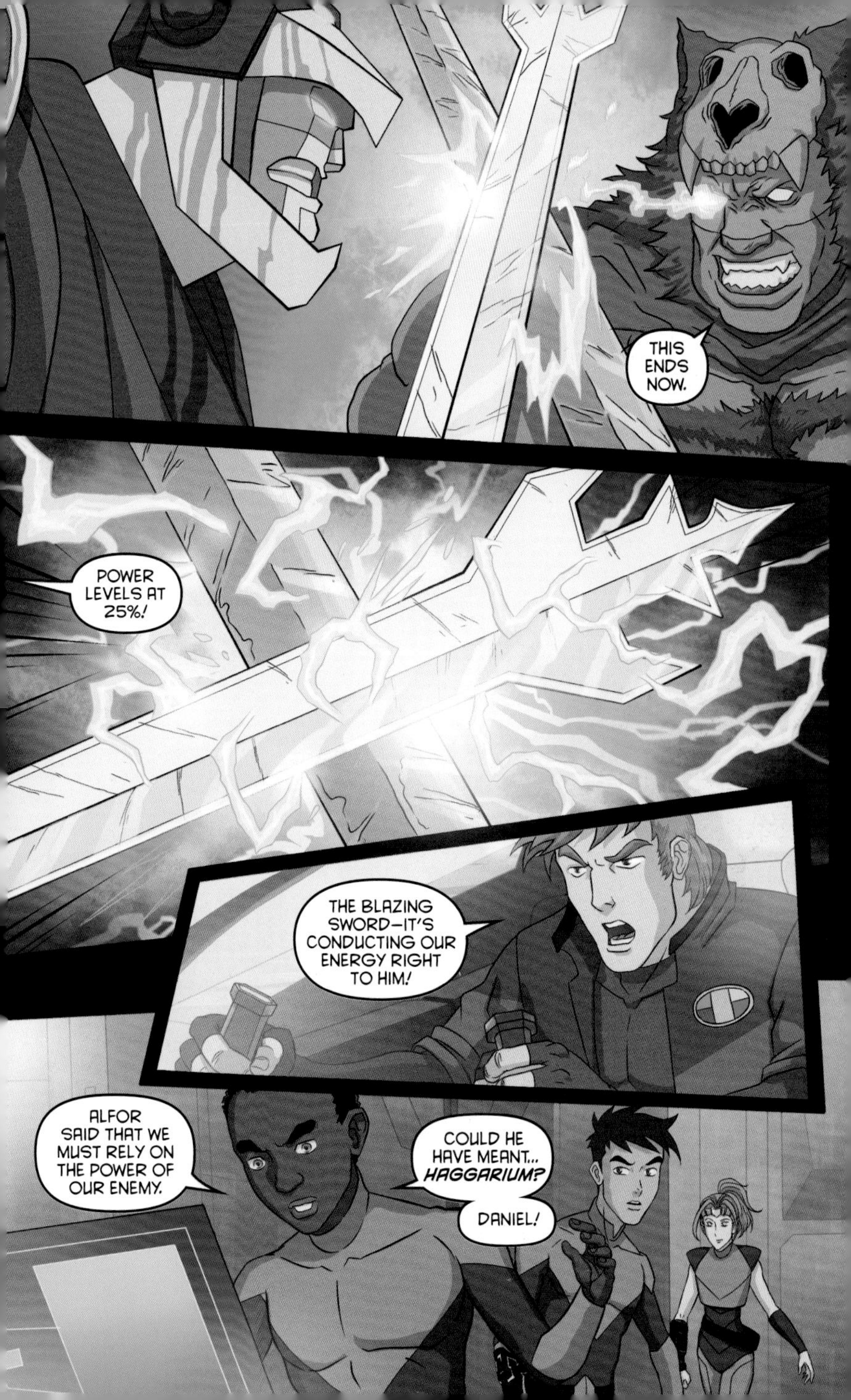
THIS ENDS NOW.
POWER LEVELS AT 25%!
THE BLAZING SWORD—IT'S CONDUCTING OUR ENERGY RIGHT TO HIM!
ALFOR SAID THAT WE MUST RELY ON THE POWER OF OUR ENEMY.
COULD HE HAVE MEANT... *HAGGARIUM?*
DANIEL!

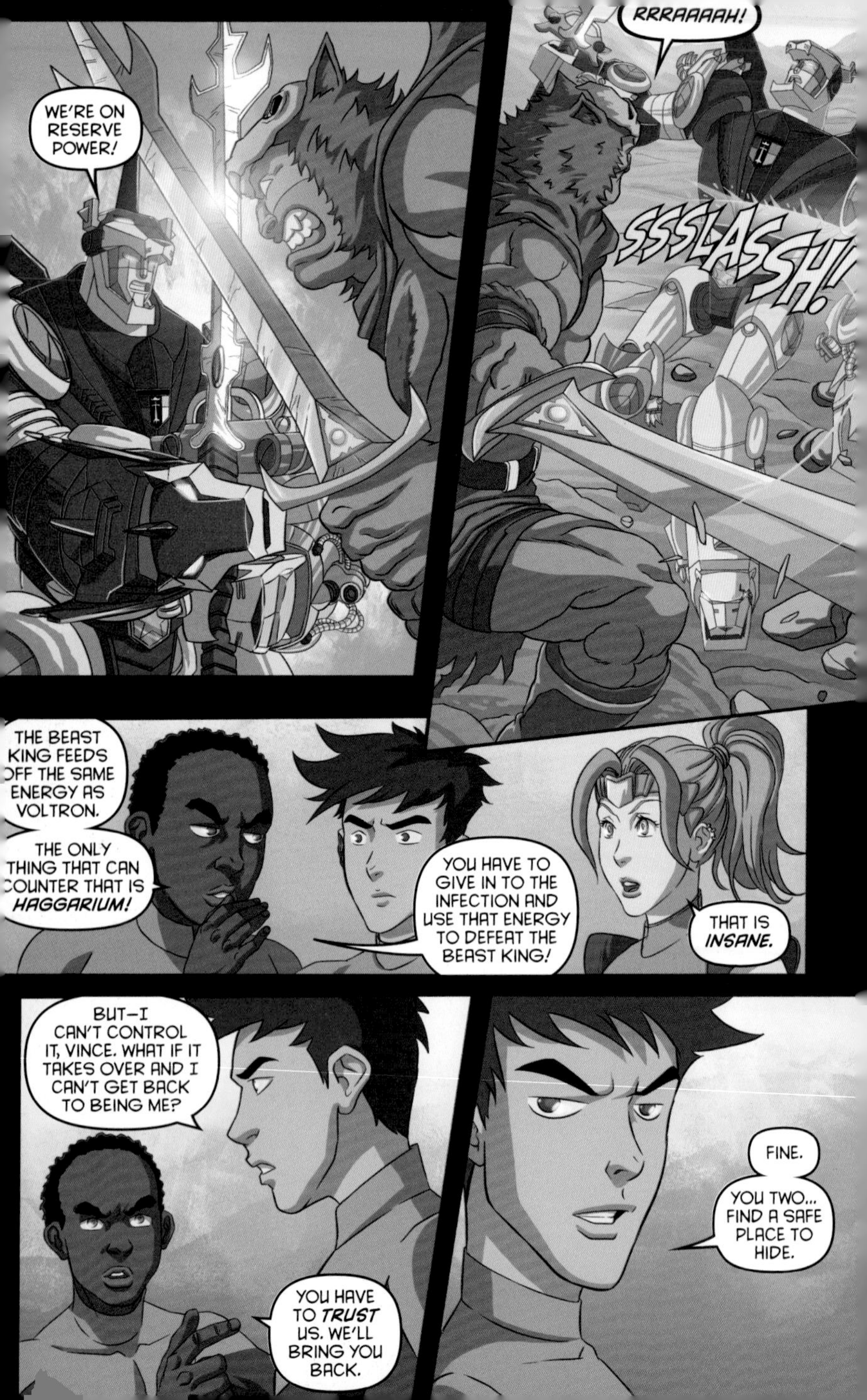
WE'RE ON RESERVE POWER!
RRRAAAAH!
SSSLASSH!
THE BEAST KING FEEDS OFF THE SAME ENERGY AS VOLTRON.
THE ONLY THING THAT CAN COUNTER THAT IS *HAGGARIUM!*
YOU HAVE TO GIVE IN TO THE INFECTION AND USE THAT ENERGY TO DEFEAT THE BEAST KING!
THAT IS *INSANE.*
BUT—I CAN'T CONTROL IT, VINCE. WHAT IF IT TAKES OVER AND I CAN'T GET BACK TO BEING ME?
YOU HAVE TO *TRUST* US. WE'LL BRING YOU BACK.
FINE.
YOU TWO... FIND A SAFE PLACE TO HIDE.

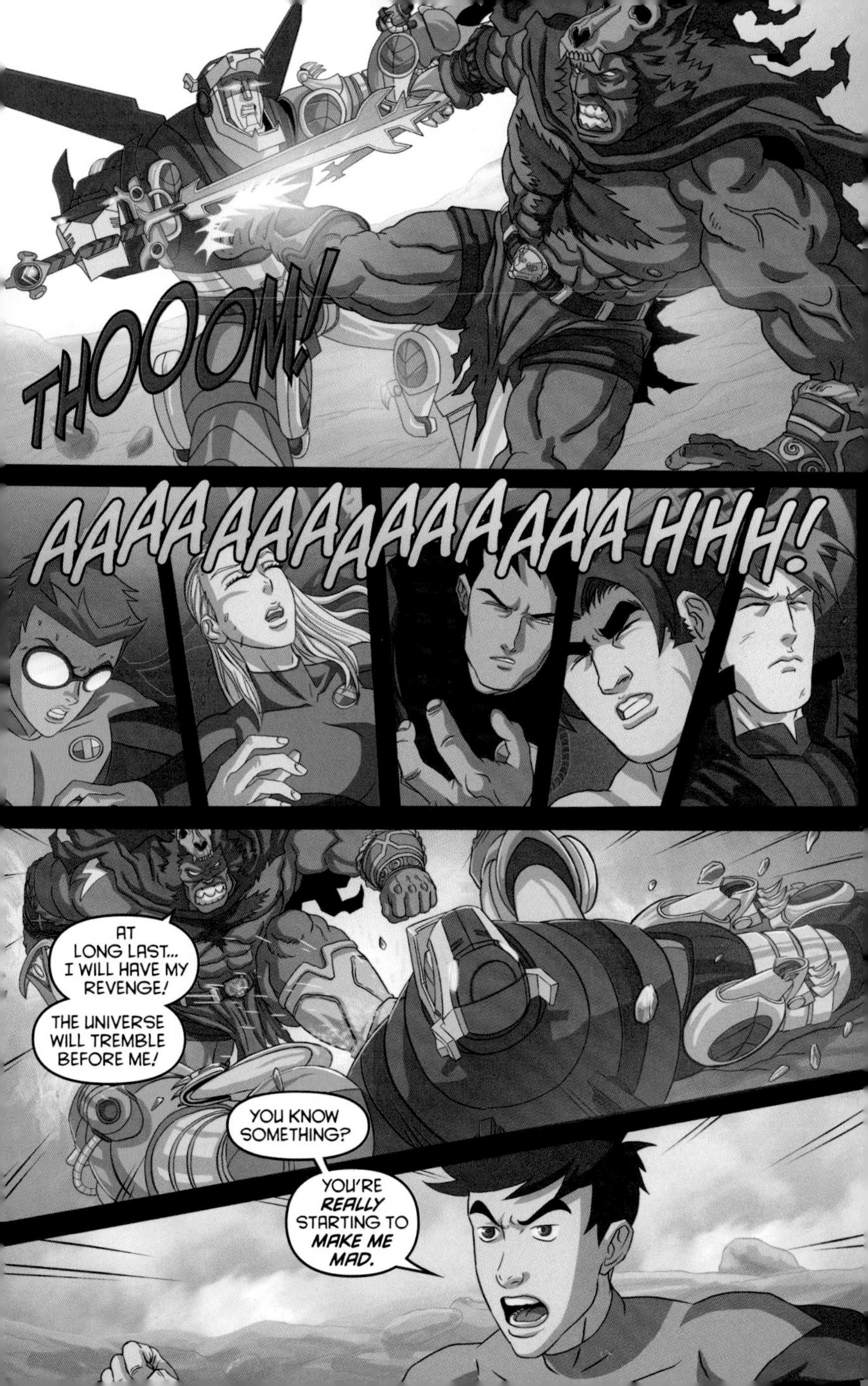
THOOOOM!
AAAAAAAAAAAAAAHHH!
AT LONG LAST... I WILL HAVE MY REVENGE!
THE UNIVERSE WILL TREMBLE BEFORE ME!
YOU KNOW SOMETHING?
YOU'RE *REALLY* STARTING TO *MAKE ME MAD.*

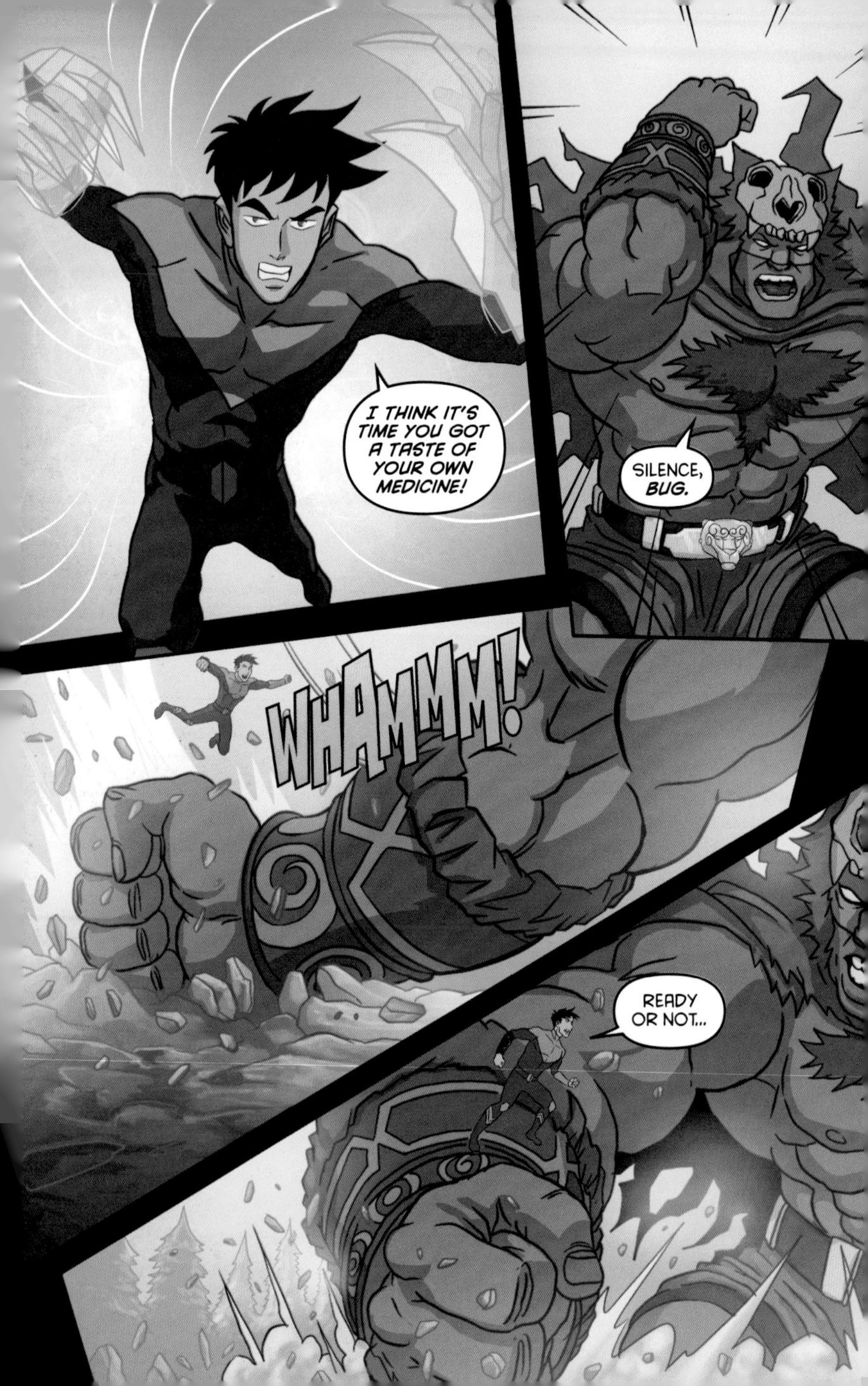
I THINK IT'S TIME YOU GOT A TASTE OF YOUR OWN MEDICINE!
SILENCE, BUG.
WHAMMM!
READY OR NOT...

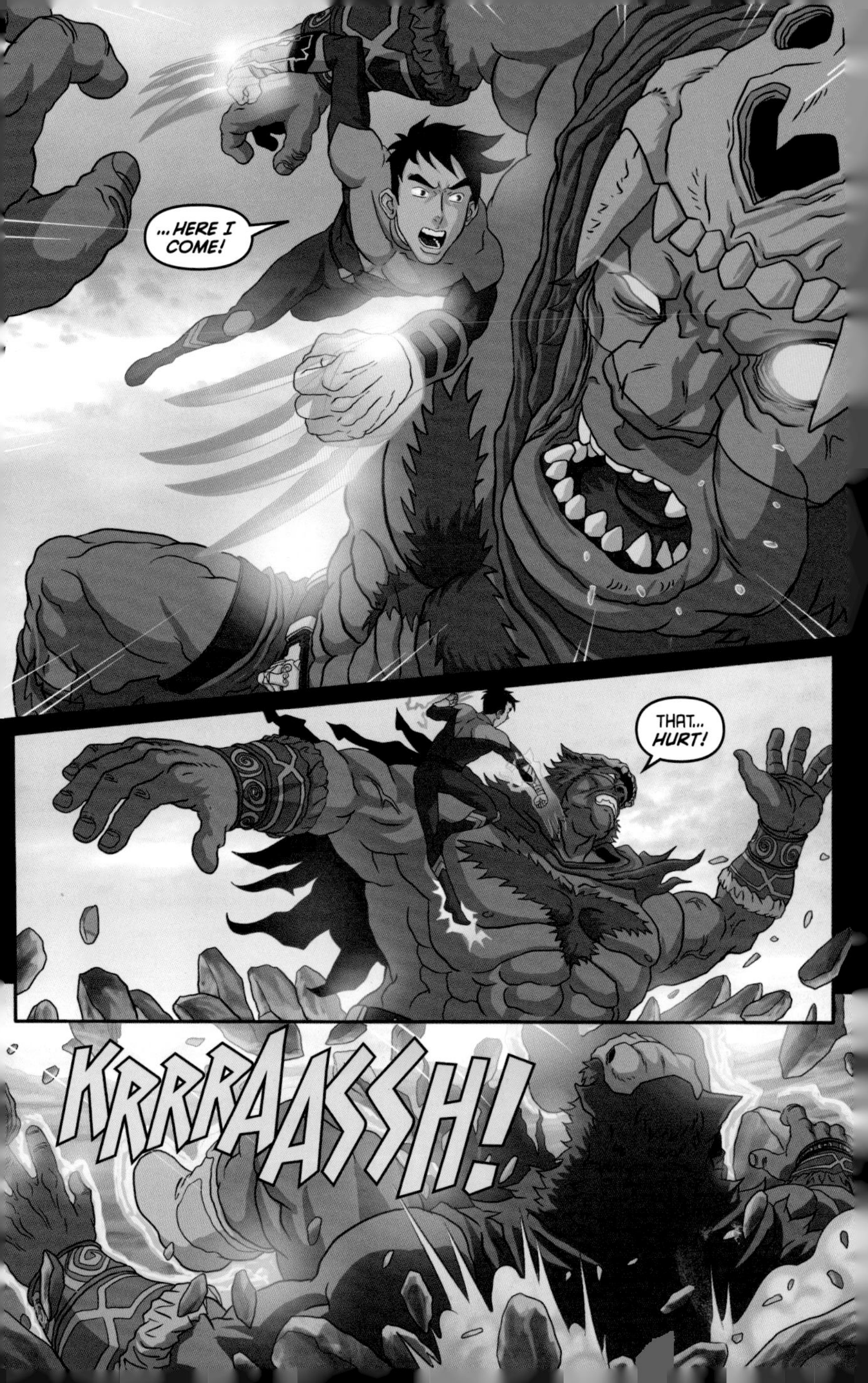
...HERE I COME!
THAT... HURT!
KRRRAASSH!

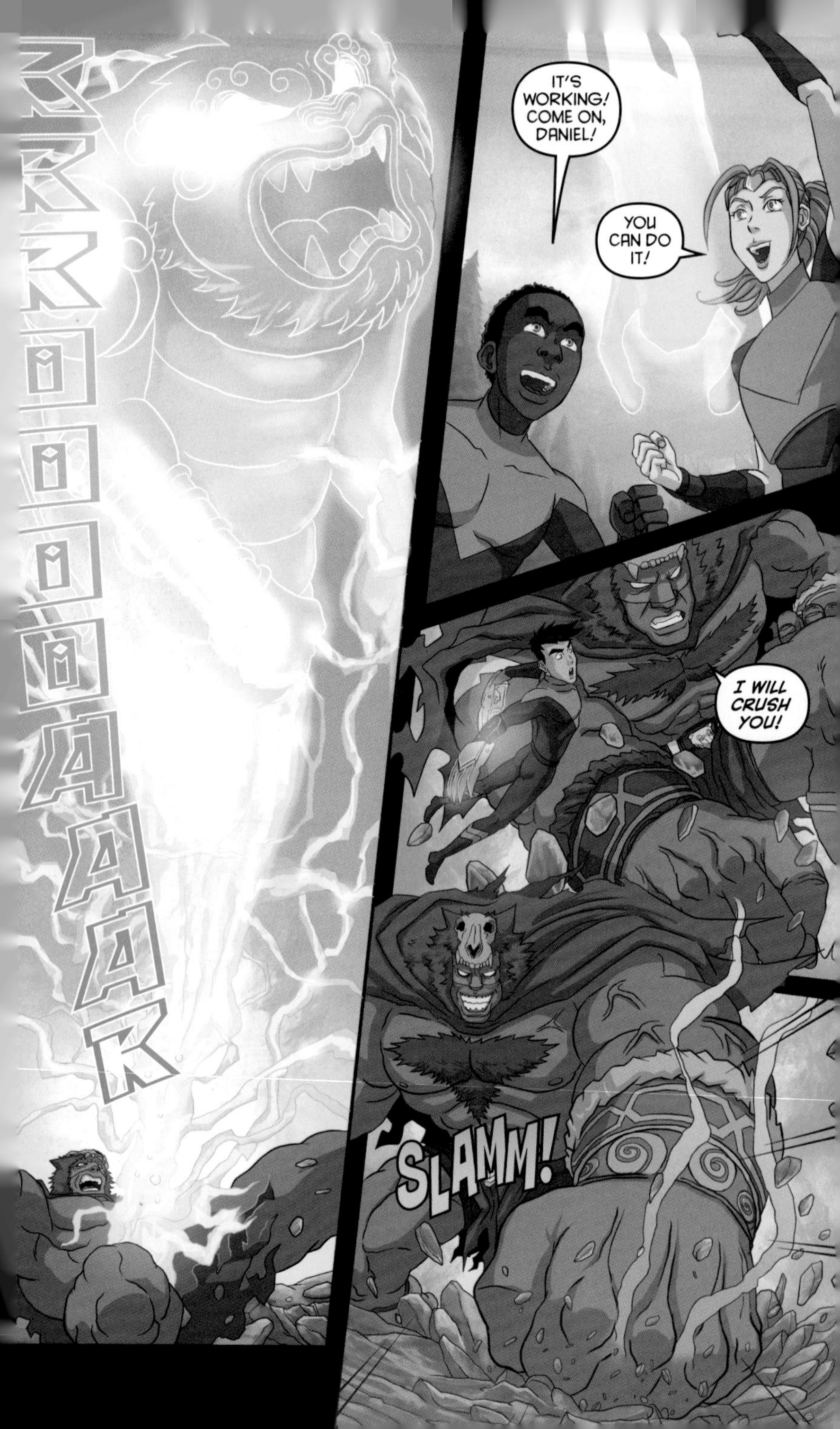
RRROOOOOAAAAR
IT'S WORKING! COME ON, DANIEL!
YOU CAN DO IT!
I WILL CRUSH YOU!
SLAMM!

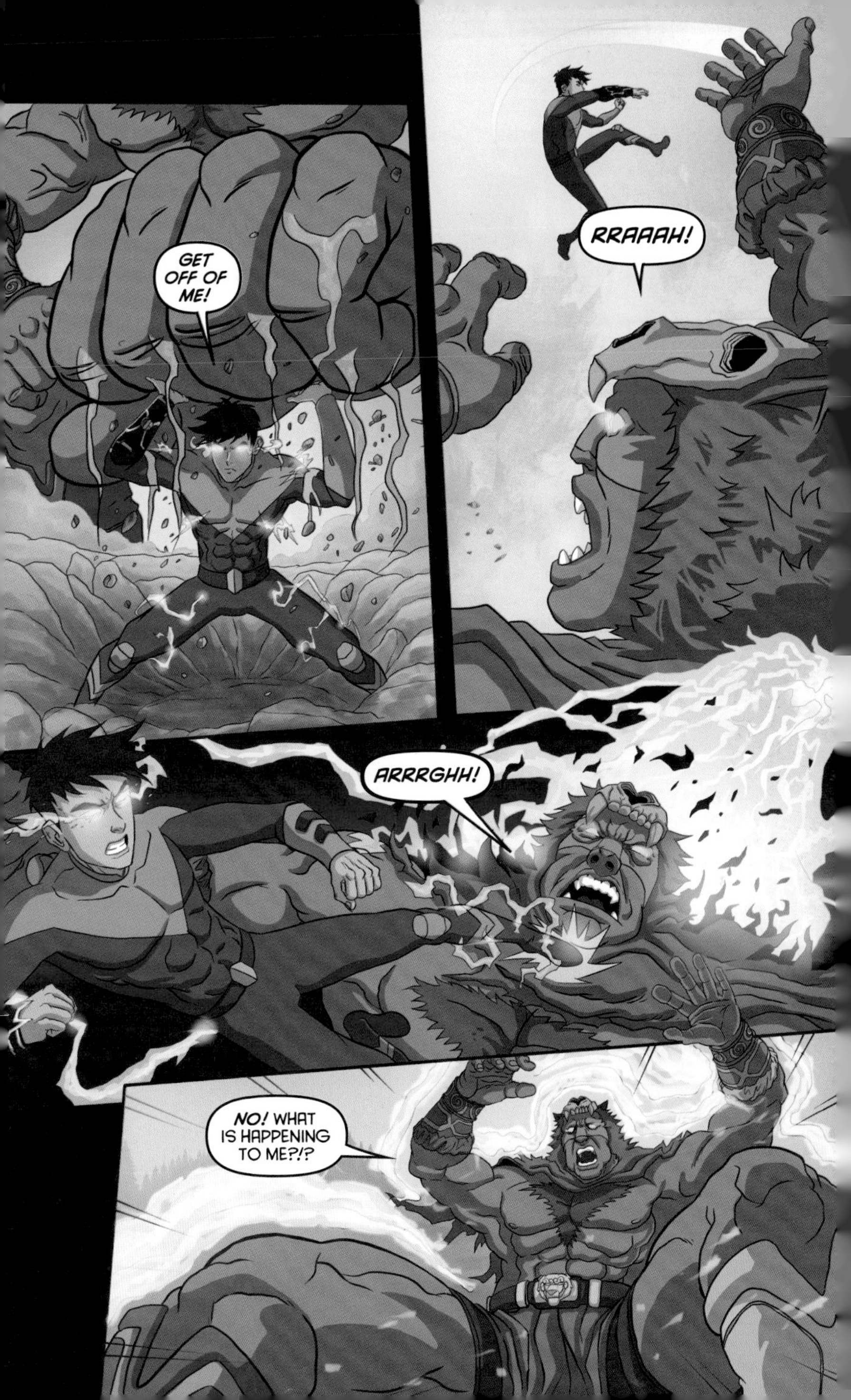
GET OFF OF ME!
RRAAAH!
ARRRGHH!
NO! WHAT IS HAPPENING TO ME?!?

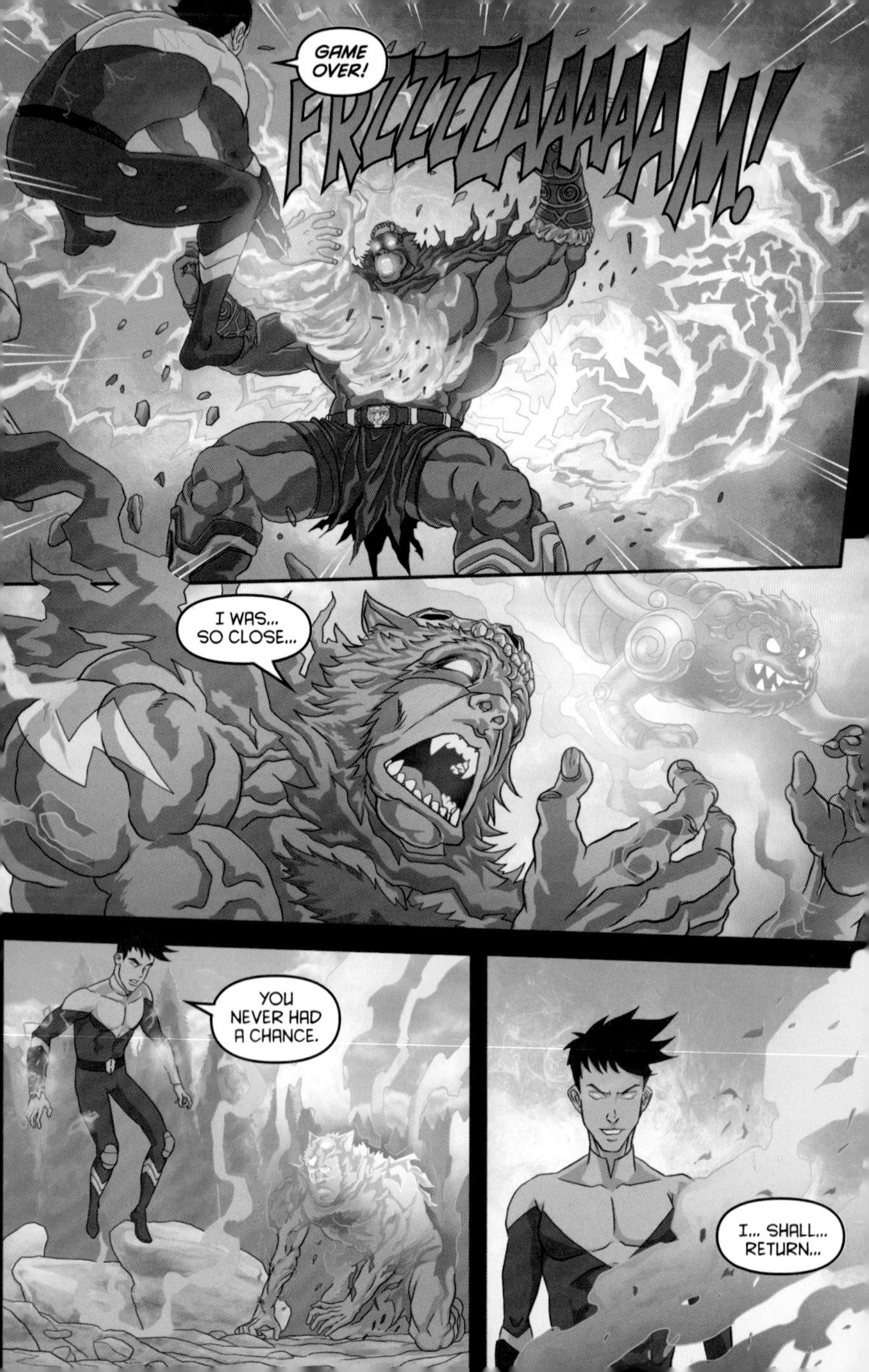
GAME OVER!
FRZZZZAAAAAM!
I WAS... SO CLOSE...
YOU NEVER HAD A CHANCE.
I... SHALL... RETURN...

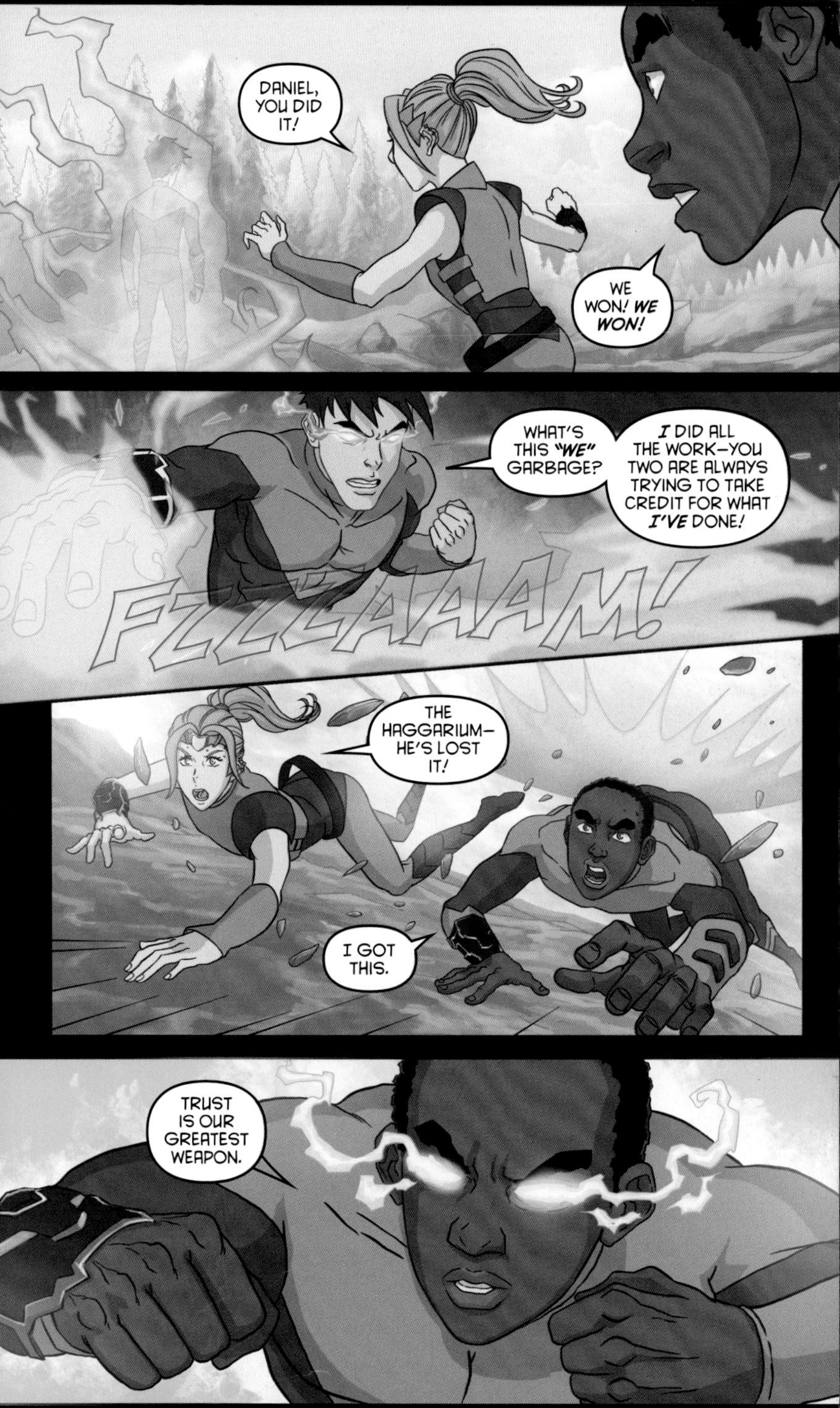
DANIEL, YOU DID IT!
WE WON! WE WON!
WHAT'S THIS "WE" GARBAGE?
I DID ALL THE WORK—YOU TWO ARE ALWAYS TRYING TO TAKE CREDIT FOR WHAT I'VE DONE!
FZZZAAAM!
THE HAGGARIUM—HE'S LOST IT!
I GOT THIS.
TRUST IS OUR GREATEST WEAPON.

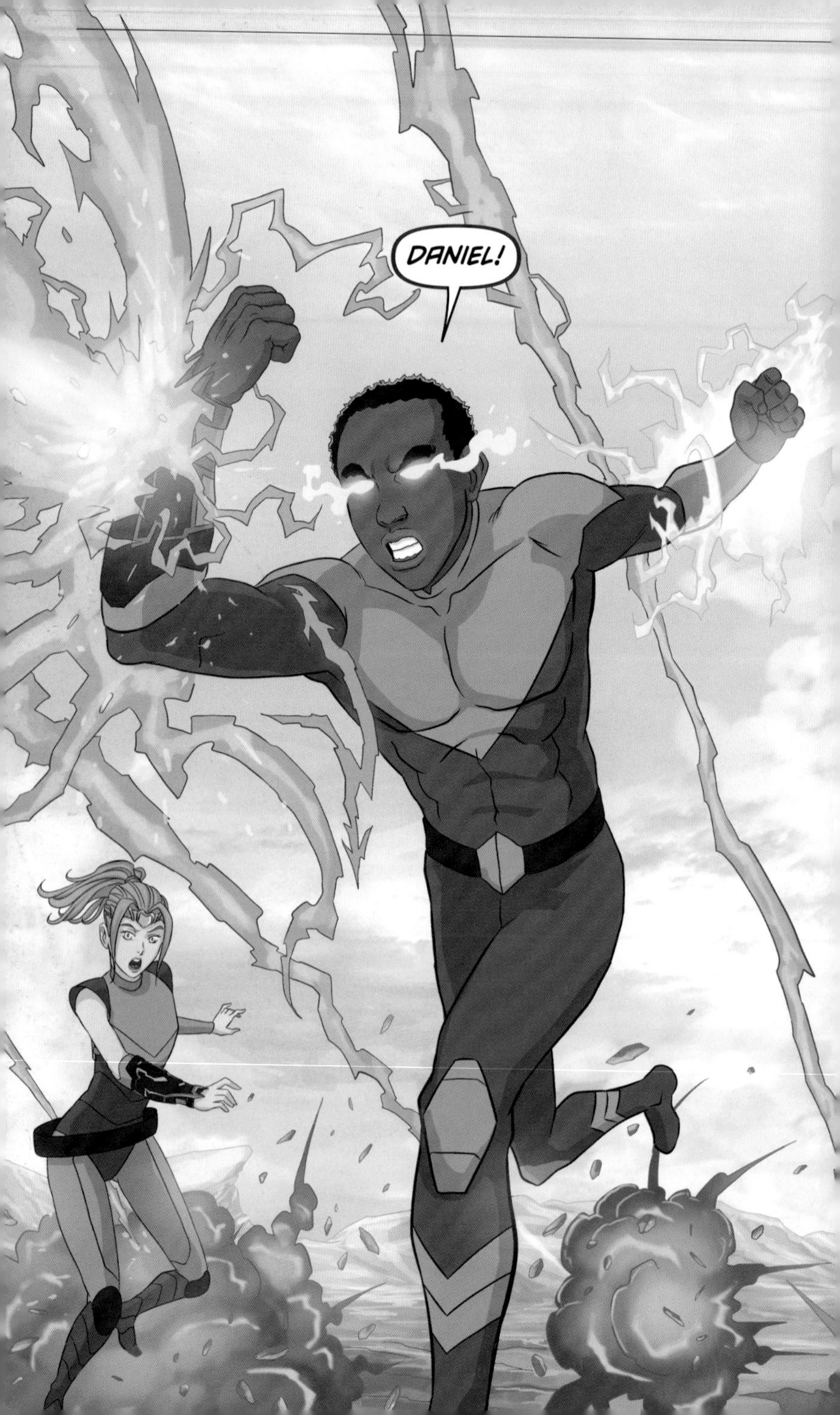
DANIEL!

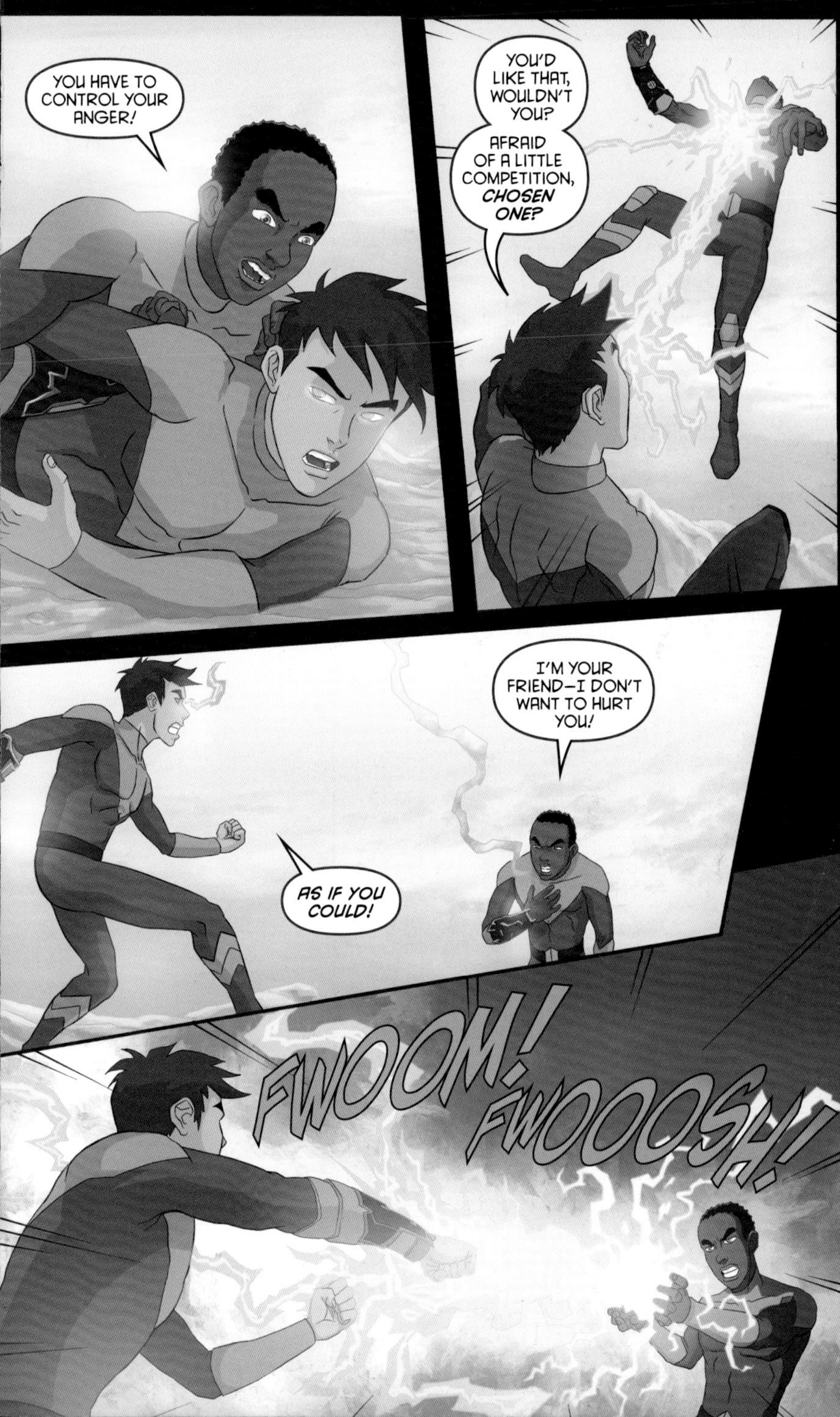

YOU HAVE TO CONTROL YOUR ANGER!
YOU'D LIKE THAT, WOULDN'T YOU?
AFRAID OF A LITTLE COMPETITION, *CHOSEN ONE?*
I'M YOUR FRIEND—I DON'T WANT TO HURT YOU!
AS IF YOU COULD!
FWOOM!
FWOOOSH!

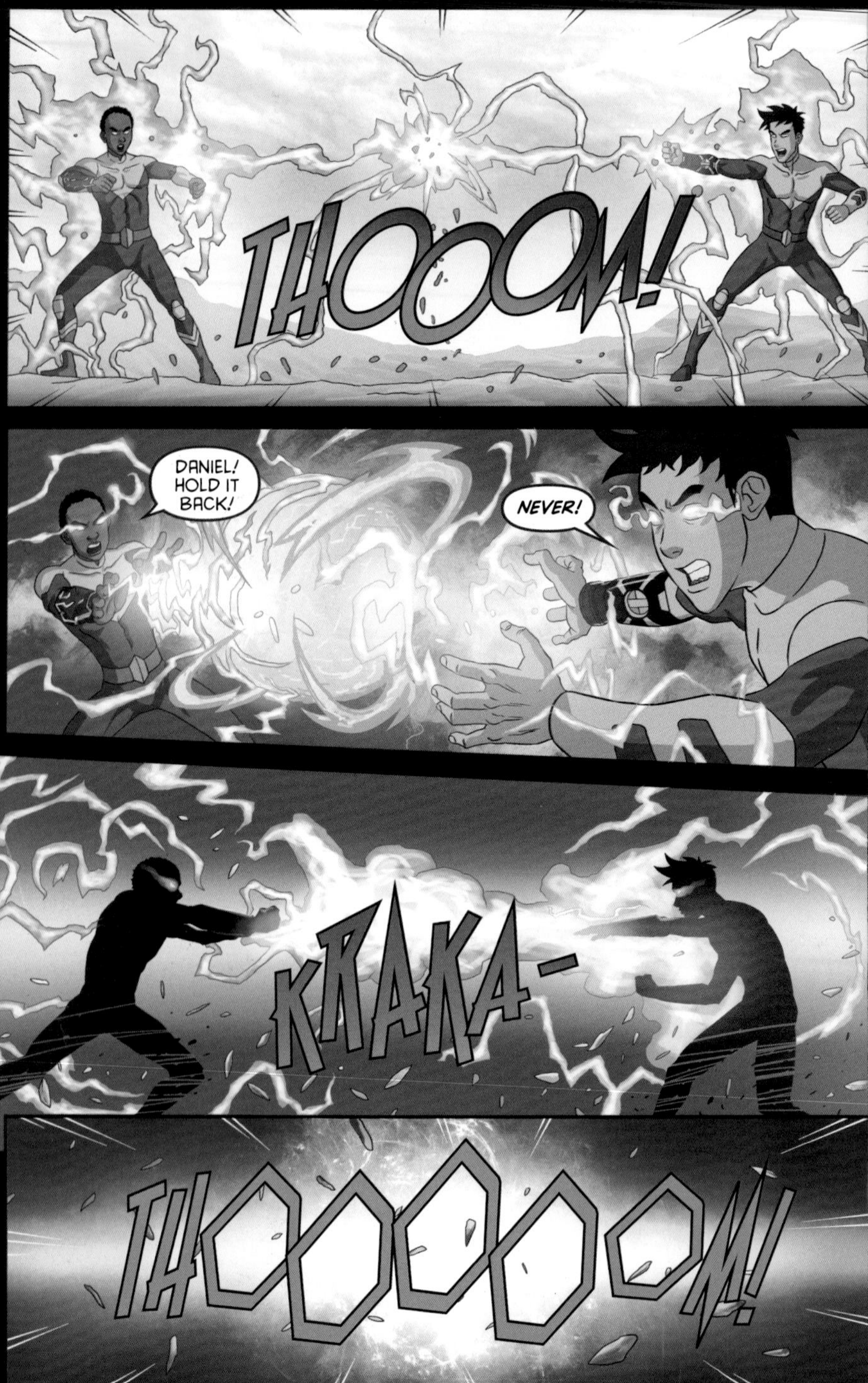
THOOOM!
DANIEL! HOLD IT BACK!
NEVER!
KRAKA-
THOOOOOM!

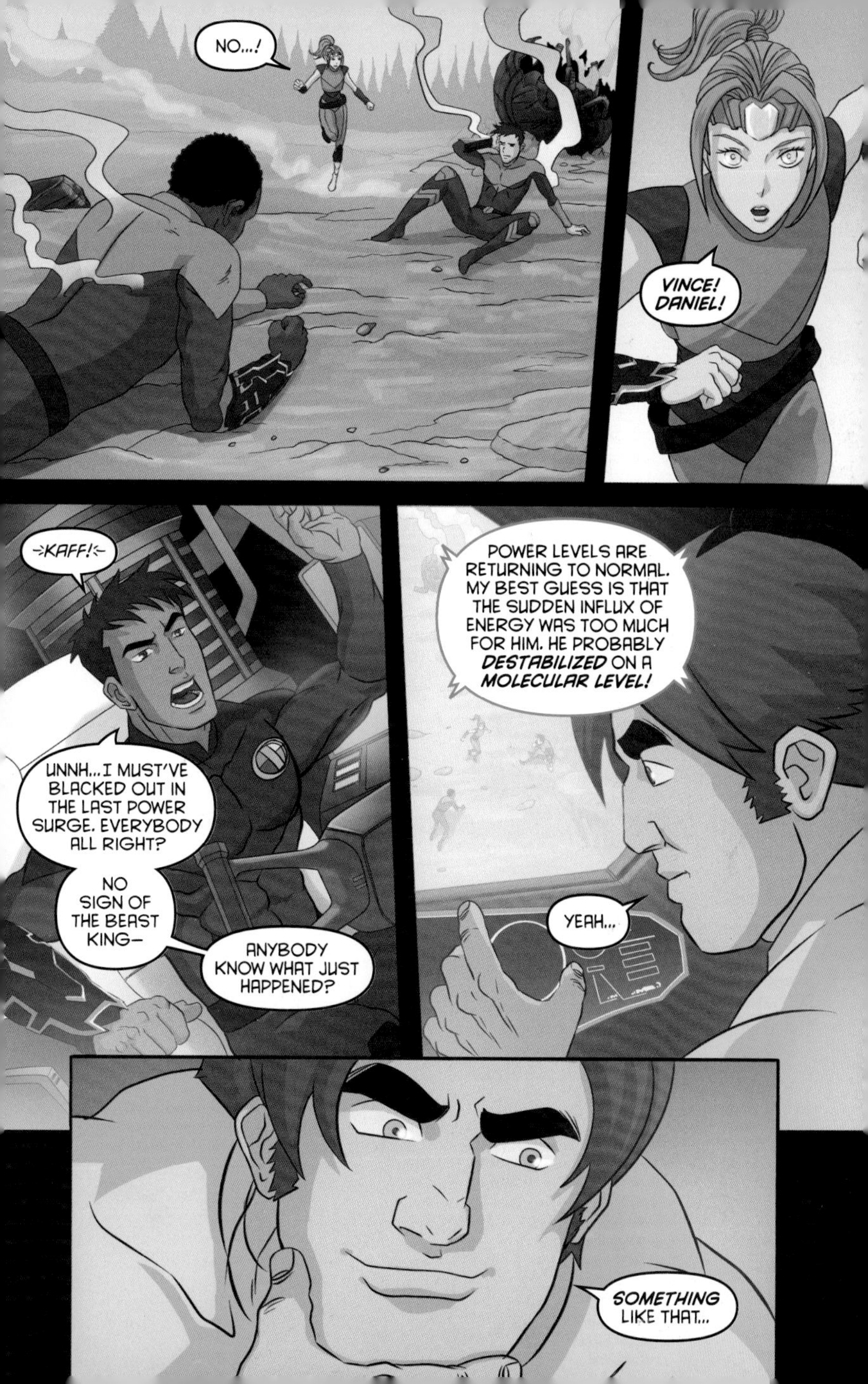
NO...!
VINCE! DANIEL!
-KAFF!-
POWER LEVELS ARE RETURNING TO NORMAL. MY BEST GUESS IS THAT THE SUDDEN INFLUX OF ENERGY WAS TOO MUCH FOR HIM. HE PROBABLY DESTABILIZED ON A MOLECULAR LEVEL!
UNNH...I MUST'VE BLACKED OUT IN THE LAST POWER SURGE. EVERYBODY ALL RIGHT?
NO SIGN OF THE BEAST KING—
ANYBODY KNOW WHAT JUST HAPPENED?
YEAH...
SOMETHING LIKE THAT...

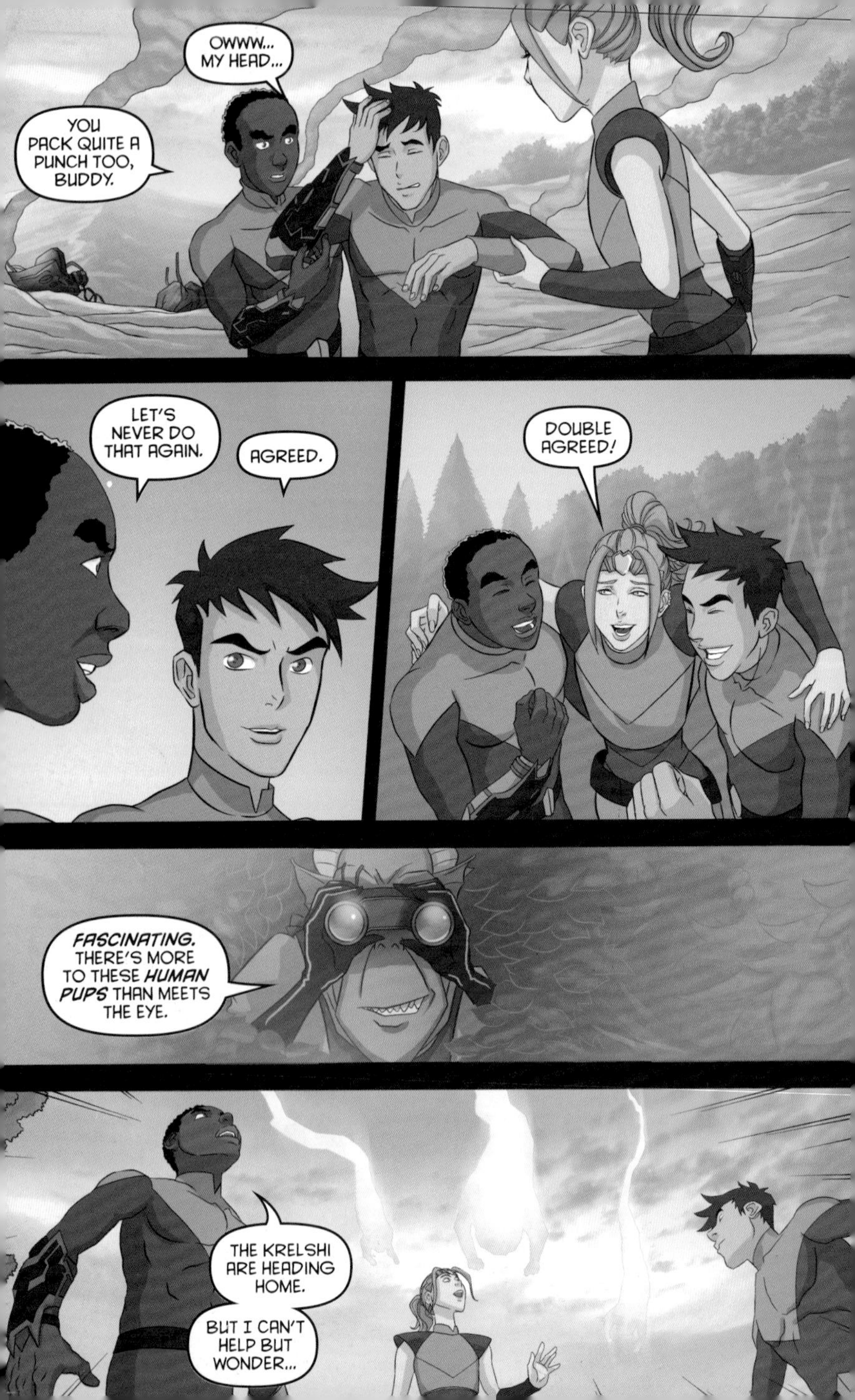
OWWW... MY HEAD...
YOU PACK QUITE A PUNCH TOO, BUDDY.
LET'S NEVER DO THAT AGAIN.
AGREED.
DOUBLE AGREED!
FASCINATING. THERE'S MORE TO THESE HUMAN PUPS THAN MEETS THE EYE.
THE KRELSHI ARE HEADING HOME.
BUT I CAN'T HELP BUT WONDER...

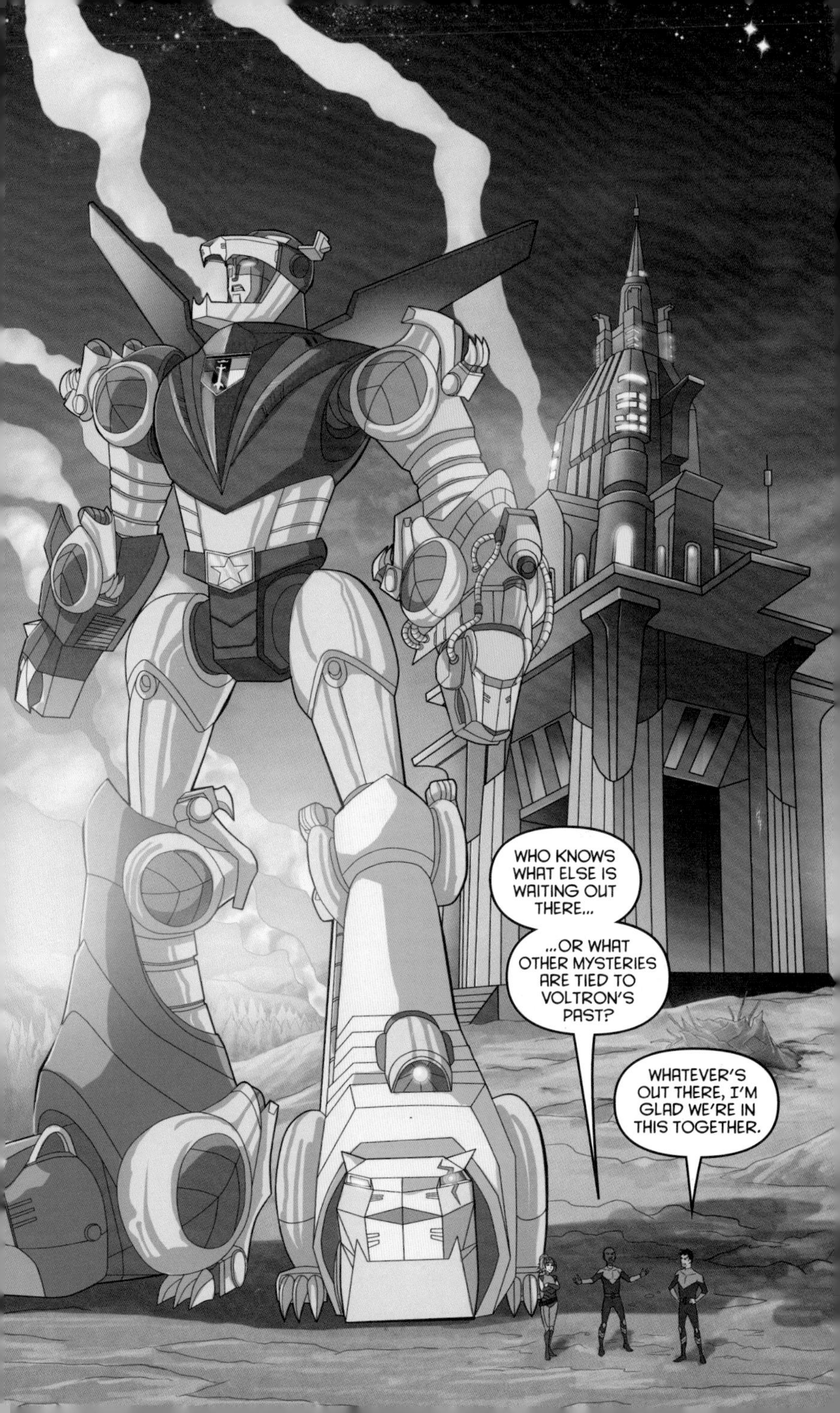
WHO KNOWS WHAT ELSE IS WAITING OUT THERE...
...OR WHAT OTHER MYSTERIES ARE TIED TO VOLTRON'S PAST?
WHATEVER'S OUT THERE, I'M GLAD WE'RE IN THIS TOGETHER.

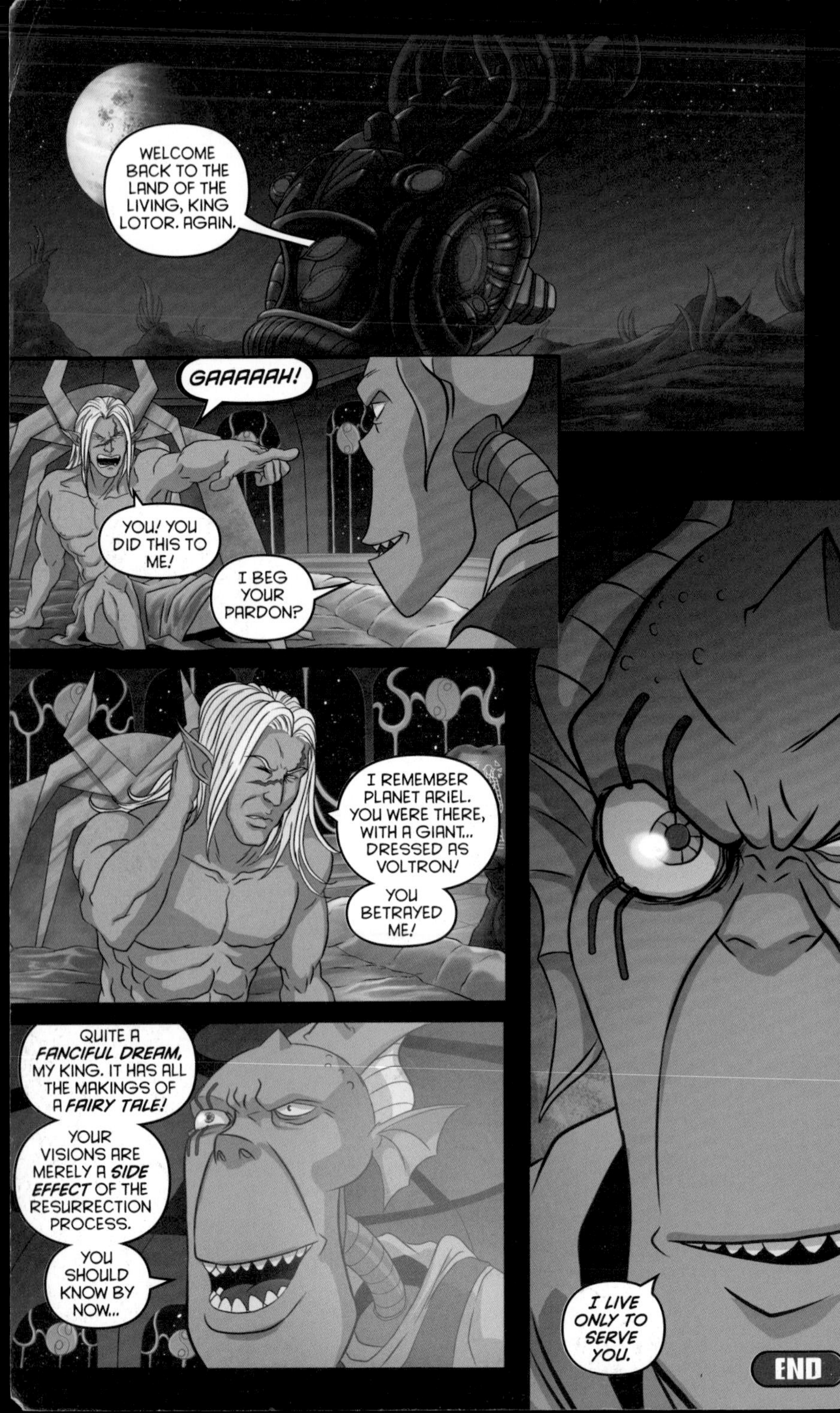
WELCOME BACK TO THE LAND OF THE LIVING, KING LOTOR. AGAIN.
GAAAAAH!
YOU! YOU DID THIS TO ME!
I BEG YOUR PARDON?
I REMEMBER PLANET ARIEL. YOU WERE THERE, WITH A GIANT... DRESSED AS VOLTRON!
YOU BETRAYED ME!
QUITE A FANCIFUL DREAM, MY KING. IT HAS ALL THE MAKINGS OF A FAIRY TALE!
YOUR VISIONS ARE MERELY A SIDE EFFECT OF THE RESURRECTION PROCESS.
YOU SHOULD KNOW BY NOW...
I LIVE ONLY TO SERVE YOU.
END

BRIAN SMITH Brian Smith is a former Marvel Comics editor. His credits include *The Ultimates*, *Ultimate Spider-Man*, *Iron Man*, *Captain America*, *The Incredible Hulk*, and dozens of other comics. Smith is the co-creator/writer behind the *New York Times* best-selling graphic novel *The Stuff of Legend*, and the writer/artist of the all-ages comic *The Intrepid EscapeGoat*. His writing credits include *Finding Nemo: Losing Dory* from BOOM! Studios and *SpongeBob Comics* from Bongo.

Smith is also the illustrator of *The Adventures of Daniel Boom AKA LOUDBOY!*, named one of The Top 10 Graphic Novels for Youths 2009 by Booklist Online. His illustration clients include *Time Out New York Magazine*, *Nickelodeon*, *MAD Kids Magazine*, Harper Collins, Bongo Comics, Grosset & Dunlap, and American Greetings.

ALFA ROBBI Alfa Robbi was born and raised in Semarang City, Central Java, Indonesia. His published works include *Boneka Kematian* (Elex Media Komputindo), *Go-Go F5* (Dahara Comic), *Planetary Brigade* (Boom Studios) and *Ev* (TokyoPop). In addition, he creates as many pinups and illustrations for comics, t-shirts and small projects as he can. Robbi's current focus is Papillon, a comic studio founded in 2002 that he runs with his good friends.

In his spare time, Robbi likes to sleep, eat, play video games, spend quality time with his beloved family, and work on his own clothing label.

BURHAN ARIF Burhan Arif was born in Semarang City, Central Java, Indonesia, and has worked as an illustrator and colorist with the Papillon Studio since 2002. His published works include *Ev* (TokyoPop), *Super Kaiju Hero Force*, (Crispy Comics), *The Ocktonia* (Demios Comic) and *Little Kori in Komaland*#2 (ECV Press).

Being a comic book artist has been an amazing, challenging adventure for Arif, and he loves working with different people and different styles of line art.

COMING SOON!

VOLTRON FORCE®
DRAGON DAWN

On Planet Doom, there's a horrible species of dragon that hatches every hundred years. Thousands of eggs are just about to hatch, and Maahox orders the Drule army to ship them off to Planet Arus! Will the dragon dawn be too much for the Voltron Force?